MAPMAKER

LISA MOORE RAMÉE

BALZER + BRAY
An Imprint of HarperCollins*Publishers*

MapMaker
Copyright © 2022 by Lisa Moore Ramée
Map and interior illustrations © 2022 by Francesca Baerald
All rights reserved. Printed in the United States of America.
No part of this book may be used or reproduced in any manner
whatsoever without written permission except in the case of brief
quotations embodied in critical articles and reviews. For information
address HarperCollins Children's Books, a division of HarperCollins
Publishers, 195 Broadway, New York, NY 10007.
www.harpercollinschildrens.com

Library of Congress Cataloging-in-Publication Data
Names: Ramée, Lisa Moore, author.
Title: Mapmaker / by Lisa Moore Ramée.
Description: First edition. | New York : Balzer + Bray, [2022] |
    Audience: Ages 8-12. | Audience: Grades 4-6. | Summary: Walt's
    magical ability to bring maps to life puts him, his twin sister, Van,
    and new friend Dylan in danger when an enchanted heirloom
    strands them in the fantastical world of Djaruba and they discover
    a malevolent rival to the kingdom, a fellow mapmaker, has
    nefarious plans for Walt.
Identifiers: LCCN 2022000163 | ISBN 978-0-06-303942-1
(hardcover)
Subjects: CYAC: Magic—Fiction. | Maps—Fiction. | Twins—Fiction.
    | Brothers and sisters—Fiction. | African Americans—Fiction. |
    Fantasy. | LCGFT: Fantasy fiction. | Novels.
Classification: LCC PZ7.1.R358 Map 2022 | DDC [Fic]—dc23
LC record available at https://lccn.loc.gov/2022000163

Typography by Molly Fehr
22 23 24 25 26   PC/LSCH   10 9 8 7 6 5 4 3 2 1

First Edition

For Jordan, who has long needed a book of his own, and has taught me a lot more than I've ever taught him

BARBER OCEAN

USTAZ FOREST

GULF OF DJARUBA

MOUNT YOKAY

BADLANDS

FOREST BIRDS

THE DULLEST PLACE
ON THE PLANET

Walt was hiding. The scraggly apple tree wasn't great cover, and it sure wasn't comfortable, but now he was stuck. At least until Dad left for work.

Dad heading into the office was something Walt still wasn't used to. In Los Angeles—back *home*—his father had telecommuted, spending all day in online meetings or wrestling with spreadsheets at the dining-room table. Walt had hoped that with Dad working at an office, at least one good thing might come out of the move. Dad would no longer be able to note how much time Walt spent—or, rather, *didn't* spend—practicing football drills.

But no dice. If anything, Dad was more intense about constantly checking in to see if Walt was keeping up with sprints and ladders and weight lifting.

"He needs to toughen up!" Dad had told Mom when he'd heard Walt had slacked off one day.

Walt knew what Dad saw when he looked at him. A scrawny weakling. And yeah, sure, Walt had gotten a little . . . sad when Dad announced they were moving (maybe, *maybe* there had been tears), but that didn't mean Walt was overly sensitive like Dad thought. He was just unhappy.

Blackbird Bay was the dullest place on the planet. And all Walt's friends were back home in LA. Who *wouldn't* be bummed about that?

And now Dad wanted to make it worse. Hiding wasn't the best plan, but that's all Walt could think to do. At least until Dad left for work. Then maybe Walt could convince Mom that Dad's plan was an awful one. There had to be *some* way of getting out of the pain and agony Dad wanted to put in his future.

The yard sprawled out below him, and Walt surveyed it as if it were a map. Large beige house (that looked exactly like all the other beige houses in the development). Four wide concrete steps leading down from the back-porch door. Big square of yellowing grass with a lopsided, sparse apple tree in the middle. Large wooden box overfull with flowering plants and intricately twin-ing vines. Next to that, a path of sand-colored pavers leading to Ms. Wilhope's small house. His family's landlord.

When he had first met Ms. Wilhope, she had taken a step toward him and peered into his face like he was a piece of art hanging in a museum. It had totally creeped him out, but Mom said she was just a little "eccentric." Walt didn't know why adults always got a pass when they acted weird. If you were a kid, you were told to stop messing around and to act right.

Just then, Ms. Wilhope's door swung open, and she stepped outside. Walt jerked back to make sure she didn't see him and smacked his head right into the tree trunk.

"Good morning," Ms. Wilhope said, and Walt almost answered, thinking she was talking to him, but when she bent over her plants, he realized she was talking to *them*.

She brushed her hand over the top of the flowers and leaves like she was petting a dog and then pulled some small clippers out of her pocket. "Pruning is good for you. It will help you grow." She started snipping pieces of vines and leaves and flowers and tossing the clipped bits into a basket hanging on her arm. Her pink hair glistened in the sun. And that wasn't all that was glistening. She wore typical old-lady clothes of stretchy slacks and a flowery top, but all the material had silver thread woven through, making it super shiny. Walt almost had to shield his eyes just to look at her.

Ms. Wilhope gazed up at the sky and squinted against the sun's glare. "Looks like a storm is brewing," she said. Walt looked up too, and didn't see a single cloud. "You're coming along nicely. Shouldn't be long now." Then she dusted her hands together and went back inside, her basket swinging perkily.

Walt was almost certain that *that* time, she had been talking to him. And that seemed awfully *eccentric*.

His stomach rumbled. He'd skipped breakfast, but he couldn't risk going back in the house and running into Dad. He stretched to pick an apple, but it was just out of reach and his other hand slipped from the branch and *wham!* He was on the ground.

A second later, the back door slammed and Walt's shoulders went to his ears. Busted.

But it was only Van. His sister sauntered over, reached up, and easily pulled the apple off the tree. "Want it?" She held the apple out to him.

"Nope," Walt said angrily.

"Whatcha doin'?" she asked, and took a big bite. When Walt didn't answer, she looked up at the tree, back to Walt on the ground, and then over at Ms.

Wilhope's house. "Oooh, were you up there spying on the witch?" Van held out her hand to Walt, to help him up, but he brushed it away. "You think she's got a cauldron in there?" Van grinned mischievously as she backed away from Walt, toward Ms. Wilhope's house. "Let's peek in a window."

"No way!" Walt said. "I'm not looking in her windows! What if she's changing or something?" He shuddered.

Van continued to move backward. "You mean changing her *skin,* or changing into a big spider?"

"Quit it, Van," Walt said. "You play too much."

"And you're no fun," Van pouted. "Come to the skate park with me, at least. I'm going to meet up with the guys."

"No thanks," Walt said. Van talked about "the guys" like they were so great and as if she didn't even miss her friends from home. For the hundredth time, Walt wondered if his friends in LA missed *him.* Without a cell phone, he was having a hard time keeping up with them. Maybe they'd already forgotten all about him. Or the Walt-sized hole in their universe had been filled by someone else.

"I suppose you're going to shut yourself up in your room and play with your maps?" Van pronounced *maps* like she was saying *turd.*

Walt didn't bother answering. No one but Mom got it. Dad sure didn't. Anyone would think, with Dad working in the video-gaming industry, that he'd appreciate creativity. But anyone would be wrong. Dad worked in finance. His world was all spreadsheets and budgets. And football. Walt didn't want any part of that world.

"Walt!" a voice shouted. A deep angry, Dad voice.

THIS ISN'T HOME

Walt hadn't even heard the back door open. For a big guy, Dad could be awfully sneaky. He was standing on the steps, clutching his bright red travel coffee cup. His large hands completely covered the *S* emblazoned on the side. It had been fifteen years since he'd played football at Stanford, but he still looked every inch a linebacker. The sleeves of his polo shirt strained to contain his biceps.

"Where've you been?" Dad called out. "I've been looking all over for you."

"Just around," Walt answered, avoiding looking at his father. He'd never been good at lying. That was more Van's area.

Van glanced at Walt and then at the apple tree. Her eyes widened in realization.

When he was younger, Walt had liked that he and his twin sister shared a sort of mental connection and could guess what the other was feeling. Now it was just a pain.

"I need to get to work. Hustle over." Dad flicked a hand forward in one brisk movement.

Walt jogged to his father, knowing that moving slowly would be a mistake.

"Don't forget, football camp starts next week," Dad said, sounding excited. "Boys who do this camp *always* make varsity when they start high school. This will be the beginning of the ride, son." He sounded like he wished *he* was going to camp.

"But I'm only going into seventh grade." Walt spoke to his shoes, knowing it was no use arguing. "And I'm not even big enough for football." His hands twisted nervously together.

"Yeah, Dad, he's a squirt," Van teased.

Walt's head jerked up to glare at her. He might not want to play football, but he definitely wanted to tackle his sister.

"You're not big enough *now*," Dad said. "Life is about being prepared for where you're going, not where you are."

Walt tried again. "But the other guys will—"

"It's not about the other guys. It's about *you*. Do you understand?"

"Yeah," Walt mumbled, still not meeting Dad's eyes. Then he cleared his throat and tried to say, louder, "Yes, sir." But it seemed to Walt that Dad was the one who didn't understand.

"What about me, Dad?" Van asked. "Can I go to the camp this time?"

Dad chuckled, for a moment all trace of his sternness gone. "Nope. This is only for Walt. It's a man thing, right, Walt?"

"But that's not fair," Van said. "Gender bias is *real*, Dad, and—"

"Giovanni," Dad said, cutting her off. "We'll have long, deep conversations about that when I force you to wear dresses." He held out a hand as if he was saying *case in point*, about her outfit.

Van was dressed in her normal garb of long shorts, big skater shoes, and one of Dad's old T-shirts. And now she was also wearing a huge frown. "Totally not the point," she muttered.

Dad didn't act as if he had heard. "This is *football*, and it's for Walt. Right, Walt?"

Walt hated that Dad made it seem like football was some special club Walt was being invited to. Or like Walt was being handed a precious gift, when really it was like a gift from Great-Aunt Ruth. A too-small, itchy sweater. Or a kit to grow lima beans. Not a thing precious about that.

"I guess," Walt answered, his eyes on Dad's polished loafers.

"All right then." Dad turned to go back inside, and just before heading in, he threw over his shoulder, "Do those drills I showed you. I don't want to hear you spent all day in your room."

It's not my room, Walt thought angrily, and for one horrible second, he thought he'd actually said it out loud when Dad paused, his hand tightening on the doorknob. But then Dad went into the house, letting the back door slam behind him. Walt let out a loud sigh.

"Walt, we moved," Van said. "It *happens.* Get over it."

Even though Walt knew she was more annoyed with Dad than with him, it still didn't make it cool for her to act like a jerk. "Maybe I'm not ready to get over it."

"What're you going to do?" Van demanded. "Hang out at home all day, *every* day, all summer long, pouting?"

"This is *not* home!" Walt shouted, and before Van could argue with him, he stormed into the house and marched up the stairs, thumping each step. He went into the room that would never be his and slammed the door, leaning against it as if he was trying to keep out a horde of zombies. He felt tears brimming, but he wiped his face hard before any could spill.

Mom kept saying Walt wasn't giving Blackbird Bay a chance, which was unfair since she hadn't wanted to move here either. His parents had had a huge fight about it. Her life was in LA, Mom had said. Her family was in LA. To land good jobs, she needed to be in LA. But Dad said that Mom could work remotely like he had done for years. He also said that her family was pretty peculiar anyway, with all their talk of swamp witches and magic. Mom *really* hadn't liked *that*. But still, she had agreed to the move.

And Walt *had* tried. The evidence was all around him. He'd plastered every inch of the walls with maps—as if he could somehow trick himself into believing that this room was just the same as his room back home. His favorite books were arranged on the bookshelf, and a half-finished Lego landscape was on the awkward built-in desk.

It wasn't a map-drawing desk. The one in his room back home had been just right. Big enough to spread out his largest maps. Only a piece of plywood on cinder blocks, but perfect. Dad said it made no sense to pack pieces of junk like that—especially when there was a perfectly serviceable desk built into this room.

Serviceable. What a dud of a word.

But then Walt noticed something on the desk that hadn't been there before. An envelope. More precisely, a piece of mail with his name written on it. *Finally* one of his friends from home had gotten in touch. Walt ripped open the envelope, but instead of a letter, it was just a coupon. BUY ONE SLURPEE, GET TWO FREE, the coupon said, in large, bold letters. And sure, maybe it was a really good deal, but Walt was furious that a coupon had the nerve to get his hopes up. He tore it into pieces, enjoying every last rip.

And suddenly the maps covering the walls seemed too bright and colorful. Too jolly. Like they were laughing at him. He approached a map that was pinned between Africa and Middle Earth.

Djaruba. A world Walt had been creating for years.

The map was dotted with landmarks and little notations. A large mountain stood in the east, near three pyramids. After seeing a documentary about Pompeii, Walt had erased the top of the mountain, turning it instantly into a volcano. He'd imagined the eruptions that might have happened over the centuries and the regrowth that would've followed, so using colored pencils, he'd created a lush green-and-blue jungle full of brilliant butterflies and birds.

On the other side of the volcano, blackened lava crusted into a reef-filled sea. In the west, he'd made a deep green rushing waterfall. Vast deserts were in shades of brown pastels and dotted with tent settlements. Oceans and lakes and rivers were different shades of purple and green marker, and futuristic cities were in stark thin black Sharpie. Different areas just called for different tools, and Walt didn't know exactly why he picked up a pencil or a Sharpie, he just knew what felt right.

Except now . . . everything felt wrong.

Walt yanked the map of Djaruba off the wall and gripped the edges, ready to tear the whole thing to pieces like he had the coupon.

But then he froze, his breath catching in his throat as if it was stuck in glue.

Had he just seen what he thought he had? Was something *moving* on the map?

CDRAGON WINGS

Walt's eyes strained wider, staring at the flapping wings. As if the dragon were *literally* flying. A dragon he'd drawn. He heard a soft *whoosh whoosh* as the wings pumped up and down.

Walt watched the dragon fly, not even feeling his mouth drop open. "What the—" He looked over both shoulders, and when he looked back at the map, the dragon's wings had stilled.

A slow, shaky breath squeezed out of him. That was . . . well, impossible was what it was. It had to have been a trick of light or something. He hadn't actually seen a drawing move like it was *alive*. Living here was making him bonkers.

Like the strange dreams he'd started having ever since they'd moved. Not exactly nightmares, but they still freaked him out. Always the same intense-looking man with long black hair streaked with gray. The man's eyes were so dark they seemed like coal or bottomless pits. Sometimes he seemed fifty feet tall. Sometimes he was riding hairy creatures that had too many legs. Sometimes he was just standing with an arm reached out as if he was beckoning to Walt. Nothing the man did was menacing, exactly, but it always seemed like he was watching Walt, and he sure didn't look friendly.

Walt shook off the uneasy feeling and carried his map over to the desk, pulled out the uncomfortable metal chair, plopped down, and gathered his drawing stuff. Pens, erasers, a ruler, and a string he liked to use to figure out bends in rivers.

Mom was the one who had first gotten him going on maps. They'd just finished reading *The Phantom Tollbooth*, and after examining the map in the book, they decided to draw more detailed maps of each individual land. Walt could completely see himself driving along with Milo, visiting each land and meeting strange creatures. Dad blamed Walt's (too) vivid imagination on Mom's grandmother, Mother Dear. She would tell Walt and Van stories about her travels, and sometimes she'd talk about places she'd been that they had never heard of and that Dad said didn't exist. Walt wanted to go everywhere she talked about, and started adding to his Tollbooth maps, drawing maps of places Mother Dear described. But Djaruba he'd come up with all on his own. And usually whenever he was upset or worried, spending time adding more details would calm him down.

Walt's eyes kept going back to the dragon in the sky. Knowing it wasn't possible, but still hoping it would move.

Dragons were by definition cool, but Walt had made them even better by imagining dragon races. He could see dragons zipping through canyons and over oceans, maybe bumping into each other to get the lead or breathing fire at another dragon's wings. Riders would be holding on tight, urging their dragon to go faster and faster. It would be exhilarating and scary and Walt so wished he could be there instead of here. No one would think drawing maps was pointless in a world like that. He'd be hired to map out new courses for the races. And there definitely wouldn't be any football.

Walt glanced at the closed window blinds. If only when he raised them he could see sparkling burgundy rivers and the colorful flags of the various dragon houses. As much as he loved drawing maps, the part no one could see was how much time he spent imagining himself going to those places. Getting away from football-obsessed dads and too-tall sisters. Djaruba was a world where he'd fit in perfectly.

He hunkered closer to the page. He drew a bunch of palm trees in the middle of the Badlands. "The wanderer had been lost for days, and was growing weak, but then, like magic, an oasis appeared," he whispered. Creating little stories while he worked on a map was part of his process. He imagined all sorts of histories and futures and *interesting* things happening.

He tapped his pencil on the small cluster of trees. Too bad there wasn't an oasis for him here in Blackbird Bay.

The neighborhood was as boring as tomato soup. A bunch of clone houses on row after row of dead-end cul-de-sacs.

Walt stared at his map. The oasis seemed wrong. Even the *word* was annoying. Walt scribbled over the trees until there was no trace of them, turning the oasis into an ugly splotch.

He reached for a white block eraser, planning to erase the mess he'd made, but instead he annihilated a whole town. It only took three seconds. He rubbed until all that was left were very faint lines of buildings. He'd spent hours creating it, and now it was gone. Walt felt good and horrible at the same time. Then he got an idea.

Instead of messing with a world that was basically perfect, he'd fix the boring one he was stuck in.

He pulled a crumpled page from a desk drawer and smoothed it out. He'd printed the map off the internet once he knew there was no getting out of the move. A satellite image so he could really see what he would be dealing with. Blackbird Bay was supposed to be "a great place to raise families" and to have "fantastic schools," but the map showed a different story. Just a flat piece of nothing.

Well, Walt could fix that.

He grabbed a pen and started to draw.

A hill that looked sort of like a butt. Some trees that had blue leaves and twisty branches. A windy creek and some tall rock formations. Grinning, he filled a blank area with the remnants of a stone wall. "Eons ago," he whispered, "the townsfolk of Blackbird Bay built a stone wall to keep out the monsters." Walt grabbed a light brown pencil and covered the stones and then drew over the whole area, making a large sandpit. "But as time passed and people forgot the old stories, the wall fell and was eventually covered over in sand." Walt surrounded the area with a fence. That made sense. People always want you to keep away from the interesting stuff.

Walt tapped the map with his pen and smiled. To live someplace that was filled with secrets and magic? How awesome would that be? But then his smile faded. *As if.*

SHORT END OF THE STICK

Walt's hand cramped, and he set the pen down and tried to shake the pain away. Must've been drawing too long. He smoothed the wrinkles of the map, folded it, then folded it again, pressing hard on the crease. The house trembled slightly, but Walt barely registered it. You get pretty used to small tremors when you live in California. He shoved the map into the drawer, stood up, and swayed on weak legs. That was when he realized how hungry he was. His stomach grumbled loudly as if adding an exclamation point. "Yeah, time for a break," Walt mumbled as he left the room.

In the kitchen, Mom sipped a bright green smoothie while she paged through a book of medieval clothing.

A pad of paper lay on the table, and small sketches of odd-shaped creatures filled the top page.

She was a costume designer. Not for Halloween costumes, for the movies. That was why she hadn't been excited about the move away from Los Angeles. Being close to the studios gave her an edge—at least that's what she'd said.

Her hair was up in a bun, and she had four different colored pencils stuck in there. Over the course of the day, she'd haphazardly stick in at least five more. By dinnertime, with all the pencils sticking out like quills, it would look like a porcupine had attached itself to the back of her head.

Dad was darker than Mom because Mom was "a light-skinned Creole girl," according to Grandma Elaine, and Walt and Van had ended up somewhere in the middle of them. Dark enough that people knew they were Black, but light enough to get called names like Light Bright by their cousins on Dad's side. Van had gotten Mom's wild mass of curls and, apparently, Dad's height, and what had Walt gotten? The short end of the stick.

"Hey," Mom said. "Do you think people would still be using leather in the future? Or would it be like fur and totally not cool anymore?"

Walt almost answered her. Almost. He used to enjoy talking with Mom about her work stuff. If she was working on a futuristic movie, they'd wonder about what the weather would be like in the future, and what cars might look like, or if there even would be cars, and if a second ice age might've happened. She had to think about stuff like that to figure out how people would dress. It was interesting. But that was before the move. Before she had agreed that another year of football camp sounded "great." Now he wasn't going to give her the satisfaction, so he just shrugged and poured a bowl of cereal.

"There's more smoothie in the fridge," Mom said, tapping her glass. "This one's delicious. Spinach, dandelion greens, a bit of banana, and some herbs from Ms. Wilhope's garden." She smacked her lips to prove the point.

Mom was always making concoctions, and it had gotten worse since the move. The one she had forced on him yesterday, saying it would promote growth, caused him to make huge explosive farts.

"I'll stick with cereal," Walt said, and ate standing up, staring out the window while he shoveled corn crispies into his mouth.

"Ms. Wilhope seems to have developed a shine for you," Mom said. "She was over here yesterday asking about your maps and saying what a wonderful hobby you had. She was positively glowing, talking about it. Although maybe that was the silver sequins. That woman sure does love to sparkle."

"How does she know I like maps?" Walt asked accusingly.

"Oh, I don't know, boo. I must've told her when we were moving in," Mom said dismissively.

He didn't like Mom talking about his private business. And she knew that. "I'm going for a ride," he said, not asking.

"To where?"

"Just a ride." Walt waved his hand vaguely toward the nothingness of the neighborhood.

Mom turned the page in her book. "Remember your dad wants you to get some conditioning in today so you're ready for camp."

"Mom, can't you talk him out of it? I don't want to go. It wasn't . . . fun last year." He hadn't told anyone just how awful it had been. A whole week of humiliation and torture. What else could you call getting pounded on all day, having your bed doused with water, getting random noogies anytime your guard was down, and wearing heavy stinky pads in the heat? Oh, and getting yelled at constantly. Torture was maybe not a strong *enough* word. Dad would've said Walt needed to "man up" and be able to take some good-natured ribbing. And Mom would've freaked and started calling parents and blowing the whole thing into an even bigger nightmare. No thanks to any of that.

"You know I can't change that man's mind once he's set on something." Mom shook her head. "Football camp will get you outside. It's only a week and you've been so . . ." Her voice trailed off, but then she added briskly, "It'll be good for you."

Mom was wrong. It would absolutely not be good for him. And it would be worse this year. The other campers were sure to have grown a few inches and even though he was almost twelve, Walt had only grown 0.24 of an inch. He'd be the smallest again for sure. One of the only good things about moving was getting away from those lines on the laundry-room door back home that showed exactly how much Van had grown, and exactly how much Walt hadn't.

Walt swallowed a groan. "Does Dad know the average NFL player is over six feet four inches? I'm never going to be that tall."

"You don't know how tall you're going to be. Dad's tall and Van's already—"

"Then Van should play football," Walt said, and immediately regretted it. Mom stared at him like he'd let loose a curse word.

"I know you're not up here in my kitchen trying to get smart," she said. "I am not one of your friends, young man. You hear me?"

Mom's favorite song was some lady spelling out respect, and she was *serious* about it. Walt knew if he wasn't careful, he'd be right back in his room, but not by choice this time. "I'm *sorry*," he said, hoping that would be good enough.

Mom didn't say anything for a second, but then she started tapping a pencil fast on her pad of paper. "Walt," Mom said. *Tap, tap, tap.* "I recognize the move has been hard on you." *Tap. Tap.* "It was hard on me too." That was followed by a whole flurry of tapping. "But this was an important opportunity for your father. And you know what? I'm making the best of it. I suggest you do the same."

"I . . ." Walt didn't know what to say. Moving away from where he fit in was terrible. And adding the punishment of football camp on top of that wasn't fair. But no one wanted to hear about it. He was supposed to suck it all up like he was a vacuum. "So can I go for a ride?" he asked, trying to keep the frustration out of his voice.

Mom went back to work without saying anything. She pulled out a blue pencil from her hair, marked something on a page, then stuck the pencil back in her bun. After a moment, she added the lime-green one too. Walt waited.

"Don't forget to wear your helmet," she finally said.

Walt left the kitchen scowling so hard it hurt. He grabbed his helmet off the hook in the service porch, noting that Van's was dangling next to it. He always wore his helmet. Van was the one who didn't. Mom knew that, so why did she have to remind him like he was the irresponsible one?

As he pushed through the door to the garage, he snapped the strap of his helmet and the clasp caught the tender skin under his chin. He unclipped and refastened, making sure to keep his chin up this time, tiny angry tears settling in the corners of his eyes. Walt took a deep breath and then another. He wasn't going to start blubbering all over the place.

The garage was dark and cool and felt like a cave and Walt imagined that it was the lair of his dragon. *That* would be cool. Walt got his bike down from its hook, then pushed the button to open the garage. As the door slowly lifted, Walt blinked rapidly. The brightness outside was making it too hard to see. And for a second it seemed like the air was actually glistening. Walt thought about something Mother Dear used to say: "Every day can be magical. If you've got a head on your shoulders, all you have to do is go out and *see* it." True, Mother Dear never had to live in Blackbird Bay, where there wasn't a smidge of magic. But he did have a head on his shoulders.

Walt hopped on his bike and tore off down the street. He imagined he was on the back of a dragon, racing to the finish line. He bent low over the handlebars, pedaling as fast as he could. Maybe if he really tried, he could take off into the air and sail far away from here.

But when he rounded a corner, Walt had to squeeze his brakes so hard, his butt raised in the air and his bike skidded. He jerked his handlebars to the left, but he still plowed into the boy who'd been walking down the sidewalk.

NO BLOOD, NO FOUL

"Jeez! Sorry, sorry," Walt said, getting off his bike. He went over and tried to help the boy up.

The boy waved Walt's hand away. "What's wrong with you? What are you doing riding on the sidewalk?"

"I . . ." Walt rubbed his chin with the back of his hand. "I said sorry."

The boy climbed to his feet and brushed himself off.

Walt took mental stats. The boy was taller than him—of course—but skinny, so Walt figured if they were about to fight, Walt had a shot at taking him. Sandy-brown hair flopped over his forehead, and his face was completely covered in freckles. A huge Golden

State Warriors basketball jersey barely managed to stay on his narrow shoulders, and basketball shorts grazed his knees. Walt didn't see any blood. "Basketball fan, huh?" he asked.

The boy hesitated for a minute and then nodded. He took a pretend shot, then wiped his hands on his shorts, leaving a dark streak. "You?"

"Yeah, but the Lakers are the one," Walt said. The Lakers were a Los Angeles team. No way was he going to switch allegiance to any Northern California team. "I'm from LA."

"The Lakers used to be cool," the boy said. "But the Warriors are the best." He put a hand over his eyes, shielding out the sun. "I'm Dylan."

"Walt." Walt got busy with straightening his bike back up. Filling the awkward moment with action. He started twisting the black rubber handlebar grips. He didn't know how to meet new people. He didn't *like* meeting new people. There didn't seem to be any rules of how it all worked. "I . . . I didn't mean to slam into you." Van would think of something funny to say. It was so easy for her. "So, uh, no harm, no foul, right?" he asked, noticing how anxious he sounded.

Dylan held out his arms and twisted them back and forth, as if checking for damage. Walt held his breath. "No *blood*, no foul," Dylan said. Then he smiled, making Walt smile back. "When did you move here?"

"Month ago." Walt didn't add that it had been the longest, worst month of his life.

"What street?" Dylan asked. Then, acting like he was in the middle of a basketball game, he pump-faked, took a shot, and left an arm dangling in the air. "Nothing but net."

"Hill," Walt said, ignoring the oddity of playing with an invisible basketball. "How much sense does that make when the street is as flat as—"

"Gum poop," Dylan interjected, starting to pass his imaginary ball from hand to hand.

"What?" Walt asked. That was definitely not what he was going to say.

"Gum poop. You know those dried-out flat pieces of gum that are always all over the playground?"

Walt nodded, knowing exactly what Dylan meant. And he had to admit, it was maybe a perfect name for those nasty flat blobs. "Yeah, exactly. Flat as gum poop. It's like . . . the next street over is *Bay*," Walt said. "And, like, where's the water?"

Dylan rested his hands on his hips and appraised Walt. "Is there a law street names have to be literal?"

Walt thought Dylan was maybe being a bit of a jerk, but he also appreciated the correct use of the word *literal*. "I guess not," he mumbled. He pulled the front wheel of his bike up and let it fall back down. He hated trying to think of things to say. "Uh, you into *Arch Angels*?"

"Dude, is your pee yellow?"

Walt laughed. It felt pretty good.

Dylan said, "I'm already doing chores and stuff for my mom to save money for when Uriel comes out."

"Uh, yeah," Walt said. "I have it already." He couldn't help showing off.

"No way!" Dylan cried. "It doesn't come out for another month!"

"I swear," Walt insisted. "My dad works for Imagitainment, so he gets review copies. Uriel is the best AA so far. Trust."

It often amazed Walt that his dad worked for the company that made the best video games in the universe. Up until they had transferred his dad to the corporate office in the Bay Area, Walt had thought they were the best company in the world. Now he low-grade hated Imagitainment. But he sure hadn't given up his review copies of AA games.

"Cool," Dylan said, a hint of awe in his voice.

Walt grinned, then looked down at the sidewalk as if there might be an arrow on the ground pointing a way to get from this moment to maybe them playing AA.

"Hey, you wanna get a Slurpee?" Dylan asked, and he didn't sound nervous or worried that Walt might say no thanks. He just stood there with an open hopeful expression, and Walt nodded.

"Come on, then," Dylan said.

It was tricky, trying to ride a bike when the other person was walking. Walt had to pedal really slowly. It was hard to do that and try to think of something to say. Dylan didn't seem uncomfortable about the silence, but Walt noticed that Dylan seemed unable to stop dribbling his imaginary ball.

They turned the corner, and for the second time, Walt hit his brakes hard. This time, since he'd been going so slow, there was no skidding or thumping or butt raising, just a sudden stop. "What the—"

"What?" Dylan asked.

Walt didn't answer. He was staring at a chain-link fence that had no business being there. He slowly climbed from his bike and took off his helmet while he eyed the fence suspiciously. The long expanse of chain-link was draped with sagging caution tape, and a few sections bowed forward. Behind the fence was a large plot of sand and a big hole.

He stuck out his hand, letting his fingertips glance the metal. No shocks or other strange sensations sizzled through his body. All he felt was just plain old metal. *Real* metal.

"What's wrong?" Dylan asked. "You look like you're going to barf."

Walt's fingers snaked through the steel loops and

pulled a section of fence toward him. He took a deep breath and got an enticing whiff of clay and heat and maybe salt. This was really here. Just like he'd drawn it.

Dylan dug a sneaker into an opening in the fence, climbed up, over, and dropped down on the other side.

"Hey!" Walt hollered. "What are you doing?" It's not as if there wasn't a Do Not Enter sign right there.

Dylan didn't seem bothered. "You coming?"

Walt gnawed on his bottom lip for a second but then climbed over the fence too, landing next to Dylan with a soft thump.

Dylan grinned at him, and Walt couldn't help grinning back. Clearly, Dylan was a bit impulsive. Walt was more cautious. He liked to wait and see what was up before diving in. You could stay out of a whole lot of trouble that way, but—as Van liked to point out—sometimes you missed out on stuff too. "What is this place?" he asked Dylan.

"There was supposed to be some big building or shopping mall here," Dylan answered. "But when they started excavating, they found *bones*." He showed all his teeth in a scary smile.

"Of people? Or like dinosaurs?" Walt asked excitedly.

"Dude, there weren't dinosaurs in California!" Dylan said. "It'd be like woolly mammoths or—"

"Sabertooths," Walt cut in. "Yeah, I *know*. We have

the La Brea Tar Pits in LA. I was just . . ." Walt knew if they wanted to be literal, there had been a couple of dinosaurs found in California. But he didn't want to start an argument. "So, um . . . which was it?"

Dylan's smile faltered and his cheeks flushed. "Okay, *maybe* it was just pottery. But it was really old, so they had to stop building." He grinned at Walt. "But it would have been a lot cooler if they *had* found bones."

"Way cooler," Walt agreed. He liked how Dylan seemed smart but also not too cool to pretend about things. "You think we might find something?" he asked hopefully.

"Let's look!" Dylan shouted.

They both charged down the side of the large hole, sliding toward the bottom. Once they stopped, they both started sifting through handfuls of sand, checking each clump for something. Not finding anything right away, they both got up and moved to a different spot, the whole time discussing Arch Angels.

"Seriously? You think Gabriel is better than Raguel?" Dylan asked. "But Gabriel is sneaky. Raguel fights *honorably*."

"The secrets are what makes Gabriel so cool, though," Walt argued, letting sand drift through his fingers.

"Man, it's hot," Dylan said, lying back on the sand.

"Too bad with all this sand there's not a beach close by."

Walt looked off in the distance. What if he had drawn that? He almost laughed out loud at the ridiculousness. "You think this is hot? There was this time we got to go on location with my mom for a movie getting filmed in Death Valley. Talk about hot!"

"Wait. Video games *and* movies? Do you have like the best parents or what?" Dylan asked.

Walt snickered. "Not even close. It's just my mom designs costumes for movies. I've only gone to a set that once. And sometimes a premiere." At Dylan's wide-eyed look of amazement, Walt quickly added, "But seriously, that *barely* happens. And she's majorly strict. Like I can't get away with *anything*. And yeah, my dad works for Imagitainment, but he's, like, an *accountant*." Walt said the word with the disgust it deserved. "He doesn't design games or anything. Trust me when I say they aren't going to win any best parent awards."

"I got you," Dylan said. "My mom is okay." He picked up a scoop of sand and shifted it from one hand to the other. "And my stepdad isn't awful but . . ." Dylan's shifting got faster and faster until all the sand had leaked away. He rubbed his hands together and then swiped them on his shirt.

Dylan's fingernails were chewed way down. Suddenly, Walt felt kind of guilty for talking badly about his own parents. "Let's get those Slurpees," he said, but then his hand hit something. A stone. Walt scooped sand away. The stone was connected to another one, and another. Like it could be the remnants of a . . . wall.

"Whoa," Dylan said. "That's probably ancient!"

Or maybe, Walt thought, *it's just a few hours old.* He wiped his hands on his shorts and hopped to his feet. He was being silly. "Ancient rocks. *Very* cool."

"We must alert the media." Dylan joked.

"What we must do is get something cold to drink before we burst into flames," Walt said.

The boys dusted themselves off and climbed back over the fence.

Walt grabbed his bike, pushing it between him and Dylan, his bike helmet dangling from the handlebars. They hadn't gotten far before Walt heard the distinctive sound of a skateboard behind them.

"Walter Anderson!" a voice called out. "Did I just see you breaking the law?"

SOME TROUBLE
TO GET INTO

Scowling, Walt turned around.

Van came at them fast, like she was going to barrel right into them, but then she tilted the back of her board down to the sidewalk and came to a stop. She rested one foot on the board, pushing it back and forth as if she was ready to take off again.

"Why aren't you at the skate park, *Giovanni*?" Walt asked her. If she was going to be a jerk about using his full name, he was sure going to use hers.

Van blew her curls out of her eyes and pointed to her knee. "Minor injury."

Walt hadn't noticed the rip in Van's shorts or the

splotch of blood. "Mom's going to kill you for not wear-ing pads."

"And look like a dork? No thanks," Van said. "And Mom doesn't need to know. It's *minor*." She tilted her head to the side and looked at Dylan as if she didn't know what to make of him. "And you are?"

"Dylan?" Dylan answered as if he wasn't sure.

Walt noticed Dylan's voice was suddenly too high and tight, and it made Walt want to whack him with a lightsaber. He didn't get what guys saw when they looked at his sister. What *he* saw was a messy mass of curly brown hair, wide mouth, funky greenish-gold eyes, and long legs—like a spider's. But guys thought she was pretty. Gross.

"Nice to meet you, Dylan?" Van said, keeping the question mark on the end. "Odd name," she teased.

"Gio-*vanni*?" Dylan joked back. He took an imagi-nary shot right above her head.

Walt immediately felt better. So Dylan wasn't going to be totally under Van's spell.

"*Van*," she corrected, with a quick nod. "So, Dylan, why were you risking arrest with my twin bro?"

Walt's shoulders slumped and his eyebrows pinched together. Every time. Every *single* time she had to tell people they were twins.

Dylan looked back and forth between them. His

eyes wide. "Twins?"

"Not identical, obviously," Walt said. The obviousness was what heated Walt. Van was easily three inches taller than him, and she just seemed larger somehow, all around. Like she was drowning in nutrients and health, while he was just . . . drowning. For years they'd looked exactly the same, except his eyes were brown. Then about two years ago, Van's legs had kept growing, while Walt's hadn't, and he had started demanding a buzz cut to keep his curls out of sight. It was still obvious they were siblings, but most people assumed he was Van's baby brother. Talk about messed up.

"Don't you have something better to do?" Walt asked her. "Some trouble to get into?"

Van pretended to be shocked by the suggestion. "*I* wasn't the one hopping over a fence right next to a Do Not Enter sign." She pulled her hair together and wrapped it into a big bun. "But as far as something better to do? As you like to point out an annoying number of times, there's not a whole lot to do here." She shrugged at Dylan. "No offense."

Dylan laughed. "None taken."

Van said, "I'm heading to 7-Eleven. I heard a Slurpee calling my name. Come with?"

"For sure," Dylan said, grinning wide at this new development.

Before Walt could argue, Van said, "Let's go then." And with that she kicked the back of her board, flipping it up and into her waiting hand. She started walking down the street with the confidence of someone used to being followed. Dylan trailed after her, so Walt had no choice except to follow behind with his bike.

Just his luck that his sister would come along and end up leading the way. Walt quickened his pace to catch up with Dylan, then nodded toward Van and made the classic finger twirl around his ear so Dylan would at least be warned, but Dylan just chuckled.

They went down the street, Van peppering Dylan with questions about kids they'd be going to school with, whether he liked Five Guys or In-N-Out, and if he thought women were taking over hip-hop. Van easily jumped from one subject to another and Walt listened jealously, wishing it came that easily to him. When Dylan took another of his imaginary shots, Van sprang up and slammed her hand down. "Block!" she shouted. "Hey, Walt! Did you see me knock that soft mess out of here?"

But Walt had stopped paying attention. "What is going on?" he whispered to himself.

"What's up?" Dylan asked. "The 7-Eleven is just one block over. I'm dying of thirst. Let's go."

Walt looked behind them and to either side. They

were halfway across a bridge that Walt knew shouldn't be there. Even though it *looked* like it had been there forever. The cement was faded and cracked, and the iron fencing along the sides showed rusty age spots, except . . . Walt had just drawn it on the Blackbird Bay map that morning. Just like the dig. And the wall. And now this bridge. He looked at Dylan and Van as if he suspected he was being pranked.

"*What?*" Van asked.

"I . . . I just . . ." Walt tapped the bridge with his foot as if he expected it to melt through the concrete. "How long has this bridge been here?"

"What do you mean?" Dylan asked. "It's always been here. How else would we get across Tamayo Creek?" Dylan walked to the railing and pointed down.

Walt took in the rocky embankment and the narrow, weed-choked water that was more stream than creek. He had thought he had made up the word *Tamayo*. He must've read it on a sign or something.

Van looked at her brother in exasperation. "It's a *creek*. You put them on your maps all the time."

"Maps?" Dylan asked.

Walt ignored them both. "But . . ." He felt like there was a rope wrapped around him, pulling tighter and tighter.

"But what?" Dylan asked.

When Walt didn't say anything, Van nudged him. "Earth to Walter."

"Huh? What?" Walt asked. Dad complained all the time that Walt always seemed to be only halfway in this world, and that his brain was too often elsewhere.

"What are you *doing*?" Van asked.

"Leave me alone, Giovanni." Walt started walking again, as if he wanted to get off the bridge as fast as possible, or as if something was chasing him.

A few minutes later, they were outside 7-Eleven.

Dylan and Van pushed through the glass doors while Walt placed his bike in the rack. By the time he got inside, he couldn't see Dylan or Van, but he could hear them bickering over what Slurpee flavor was better, Atomic Cherry or Blue Bombshell. Walt couldn't help being annoyed. Van already had friends here. Did she need to take the one person he had met?

He was about to rush over to claim his rightful place as Dylan's new friend when his attention was caught by a display rack that had every wire pocket stuffed with maps. He was shocked to see it. Who, other than him, actually used paper maps these days? Everybody had GPS now. Which wasn't very smart, in Walt's opinion. No GPS screen was big enough to see the whole place you wanted to look at. He thought of the things he'd seen today that hadn't been on the map of Blackbird

Bay. Maybe there would be a more accurate one here. Walt gave the rack a push, to check out the pockets on the other side, and the rack squeaked loudly, as if no one had touched it in ages.

He pulled a map out. It was sun faded, and Walt guessed it had been in the rack for years.

"Whatcha got there, boy?" A man glared down at him. His tan uniform had a California Highway Patrol patch on the sleeve. They'd seen lots of CHP officers on the drive from LA to the Bay, and Dad had gotten tense every time.

Walt carefully placed the map back, then let his hands drift open, showing they were empty. He tried to stand up straight like Dad had warned him to do if he ever had to deal with the police. The fact that it was a Black officer didn't matter. Walt still needed to "not give them a reason." The way this guy was staring at Walt so angrily, it seemed as if he was *looking* for a reason. His dark eyes were edged with deep wrinkles, and Walt was certain they weren't laugh lines.

The cop grabbed Walt's shoulder. He was big like Dad, with bulging arm muscles, and his grip was like a tightened pipe wrench. "You hear me talking to you?"

Walt tried to pull away. "It was j-j-just a map. I'm not doing anything wrong!" He was trying to sound strong, but his voice came out thin and shaky.

"Wrong is all ones like you do," the officer growled.

"Let him go, Canter," the clerk said, coming from behind the counter. Walt hadn't noticed him before. He was an elderly man. Skinny but with a bit of a belly, and not very tall. His tidy white-dusted afro made him look as if he'd been caught out in a snowstorm. One of his eyes was a dark black pit, while the other was a chip of brilliant blue sky.

Walt had a moment to think how the clerk's eyes were like those huskies with mixed colored eyes— freaky but cool—before Canter's grip tightened and Walt started to feel as if his shoulder was in serious jeopardy of being dislocated. "You're hurting me!" Walt cried out.

Hearing the commotion, Van rushed over but came to a quick stop when she saw a patrol officer holding on to her brother. "Walt?"

Dylan followed behind Van. "Hey!" he shouted. "You can't do that. Let him go!"

Walt's stomach clenched, waiting for things to go from bad to worse. Guess white kids didn't get the same lectures about how to talk to the police. Sure enough, the cop's grip tightened and Walt whimpered in pain.

"You were wrong," Canter said to the clerk. "He's just like Statica. He's already *changed* things."

"I didn't do anything," Walt asserted.

"That's not true and you know it," the clerk said.

Walt wasn't sure whether the clerk was challenging him or the officer.

"Better if I just take care of things." Canter glared down at Walt.

"Canter," the clerk said calmly. "I said, *let him go.*"

Walt was shocked when Canter *did* release him, but his shoulder ached as if it were still caught in the big man's grip.

Canter sucked his cheeks, and his eyes flicked away from the clerk's. "He broke the law."

"Not here. Not yet, anyway," the clerk countered. "Besides, I told you. He can *help.*"

Help do what? Walt wondered but was too rattled to speak up.

"That's what you keep saying," Canter said. "Doesn't mean it's true. Mapmakers can't be trusted."

"Mapmaker?" That time Walt had spoken aloud, and the clerk and Canter both turned to peer at him as if just remembering he was there.

"Look at him," Canter said. "How is he going to save—"

The door jingled and a young woman in workout attire jogged up to the counter. "Lotto tickets?"

The clerk moved behind the counter and helped her with her QuickPicks.

Van moved closer to Walt and whispered, "Is this about . . ." She made an up-and-over motion with her hand, and Walt shook his head. He was certain that whatever was going on, it had nothing to do with climbing over a fence.

Dylan pointed his head toward the door, and that seemed like a very good idea to Walt. But before they could make a move, the clerk gave the woman a cheery "Good luck!" and followed her to the door. Once she left, the clerk turned and faced them, his hands clasped together. It was clear to Walt that their way out was now blocked. Was this dude seriously going to trap them in this store?

"Now then." The clerk smiled, but Walt still felt uneasy. "This isn't going at all how it was supposed to. Let's take a step back. First, introductions." He dipped his head at Canter. "This tall angry man is Patrol Officer Canter, and I'm Orsten." He held out his hand, and for a moment there was no sound except the hum of the hot-dog oven. It was as if everyone was waiting for someone to feed them the next line, but then Van brushed by Canter to shake Orsten's hand.

"Van," she said. "That's Dylan over there and this is my twin brother, Walt, who you both seem to think is someone else."

Dylan gave a little salute, and Walt shuffled forward

and shook Orsten's hand. Their parents were really big about that kind of thing. "Don't leave someone hanging." "Have a firm grip." "Look people in the eye." Even if they were some total rando.

"Nice to meet you, Mr. Orsten," Walt mumbled before turning to his sister. "Not everyone needs to know we're twins, Van," he barked at her.

Van's eyes widened in surprise. "But—" she started to say, before Orsten cut her off.

"Goodness, anyone could see you are twins," he said. "Now no need for the mister. Orsten will do just fine."

Canter threw in, "And you're *exactly* who we think you are."

"In fact," Orsten said. "We've been waiting for you. I must admit, I thought the lure of snacks might bring you here sooner, but I guess you got the coupon?"

"*You* sent that to me?" Walt exclaimed.

"Who else?" Orsten said, as if it should've been obvious.

Walt thought of the pieces of coupon torn up in the trash. What if it had been some kind of golden ticket thing? "I . . . I didn't bring it with me."

"Oh, no matter. You're here. That's what's important. Now let's get to it, shall we?"

"Finally," Canter grumbled.

Orsten glanced behind him at the door. "Best if we're not disturbed." He moved over to the map rack and gave it a push. It slowly began to spin.

"You sure that's a good idea?" Canter asked.

"My store. My rules." Orsten gave the rack another push. It squealed a complaint but started turning a bit faster, and the store shelves rattled. "There's something it would be good for you to see, young mapmaker."

Scratching his head, Dylan asked, "What's a mapmaker?"

"Ask your friend," Canter growled.

Dylan turned to Walt curiously.

Walt was about to say, "I have no clue," but maybe that wasn't exactly true. Thoughts were swirling in his head. In sixth grade he had taken French, and at the end of the year he could conjugate a few verbs but definitely couldn't speak the language or anything. But every once in a while, Monsieur Privet would say a simple sentence in French, and Walt would understand it. He was feeling like that now. As if Orsten and Canter were speaking a foreign language, but tiny bits and pieces were beginning to make sense.

"Is it . . . ," he started. He watched the spinning rack. It seemed impossible that it kept spinning around and around. And it seemed like now the floor was creaking too. "I think that it's being able to draw things that . . ." His voice was quaking. He cleared his throat. He felt uncomfortably exposed, almost like his shorts had dropped to the floor—but he *had* drawn things on a map of Blackbird Bay that he was almost certain hadn't been there before, no matter what Dylan said. "That, um, appear for real?"

"Hah!" Dylan said. But then when he saw the look on Walt's face, he asked, "Wait, are you being serious?"

Instead of answering, Walt looked quickly at Orsten, who nodded at him.

"But you'll pay a price for it," the old man said, his dark eye somber. "That's the way it is with gifts. You get something, you got to give something."

Walt didn't know what Orsten meant. He looked over at Canter, who was watching him like Walt was a bug he wanted to squash.

Walt wasn't sure if this was such a great gift or what he was going to have to pay for it, but he gave an almost imperceptible nod. "I can do it."

"Do *what* exactly?" Van asked, her head swinging back and forth between her brother and Orsten.

"When I draw things on a map . . . ," Walt started. He sucked his lip for a second. "They actually appear in, like . . . the world."

"Well, in one world," Orsten corrected. "There's plenty of worlds out there. Many created by mapmakers."

"Walt! You're being ridiculous!" Van said. "Get real!"

"This is as real as it gets," Orsten said, his blue eye twinkling. "You might want to settle yourselves for this next part."

"Huh?" Dylan asked. *"What* next part?"

Orsten didn't answer. He just reached toward the map rack again and pushed it so hard Walt thought the whole thing would just topple over, but instead the squealing got louder and the rack spun faster.

VERY DISCONCERTING

The ground shook, and it sounded like stones were grinding together. Or maybe cannon fire.

"Earth . . . earthquake?" Van looked around for somewhere to take cover, but there wasn't anywhere to go.

Walt held out his arms to steady himself. He knew it couldn't be an earthquake. Earthquakes didn't make rooms spin. And that was definitely what was happening. It wasn't just the rack anymore; it was the entire store. The 7-Eleven turned faster and faster, matching the wild spinning of the map rack that was now shrieking so horribly, it sounded as if it were in pain. The walls melted into a blur.

It was like being on the Spin Out! ride at the county fair, except they weren't stuck to the wall like flies on flypaper. Instead it was as if they were all in a protective bubble. Orsten and Canter both looked calm, but Walt, Van, and Dylan were clearly freaked out. A thunderous explosion of noise blasted the air. The spinning got faster. And now the store *was* shaking.

"What's happening?" Walt cried.

"Make it stop!" Van said.

Dylan shut his eyes and shook his head hard, as if he was saying no thank you to the whole thing.

And then, with a bang, everything stopped.

Walt took a few steps forward and almost stumbled. He felt dizzy and a little sick. It was as if he'd just gotten off a ride that had ended in a totally different place than where he'd gotten on. He looked around in amazement. "Wow," he said in awe. He took a deep breath and got whiffs of juniper and eucalyptus and . . . smoke. The harsh fluorescent lights were gone, and instead candles burned all around the store.

Because even though everything was different, it still was clearly a store. A large metal cash register that had no hint of electric components was on the counter. And instead of candy, laundry detergent, and chips, there were shelves of dusty bottles, shimmering jars, and messy wrapped packages. The shelves themselves were now rough-hewn wood. The stone walls seemed really, really old. Strange, twisted plants climbed the walls, and the floor wasn't linoleum, but hard-packed earth. Walt's head was on a swivel as he tried to take everything in. Nothing was left from the original store except the rack of maps. But the maps were no longer old and faded.

Van gripped her head. "I think I might puke."

Orsten chuckled. "It can be a little disconcerting the first time."

"Disconcerting?" Dylan yelped. He started to back up slowly, like he was trying to sneak away from the whole place, but he banged into a low table stacked with rusted metal containers and wooden boxes. A box fell to the floor with a soft thump, and something hissed from inside.

"Before I forget," Canter said calmly, as if a store hadn't just magically transformed. "Something for your collection." He reached into his pocket and took out a triangular-shaped coin. It had a rough hole in the middle. "Found it in Hedgerow," he told Orsten. "Couldn't smell if anyone had used it." He tossed it to the clerk.

Orsten caught it with a sigh. "Did you really have to—"

"You know I did," Canter said.

Orsten moved over to the counter, and that was when Walt noticed that the clerk now had hooves. When he saw Walt staring, he winked at him. All things considered, Walt couldn't help but think the clerk not being fully human wasn't even that odd.

Orsten dropped the gold coinlike thing in a dish that was already full with other ones that looked just the same. All triangular, and all with the rough, jagged hole in the middle. "Every talisman." Orsten shook his head. "Shoots the magic right out," he explained, although as an explanation it wasn't much.

"Speaking of which," Canter said. "I need to reload." He went over to a case that had vials of brightly colored liquid intermingled with tiny jars, and dishes of what looked like sand in equally vivid colors.

Orsten barked, "That's not to be played with!" and Walt jumped. But Orsten was talking to Dylan, who had a glass orb he was tossing up and catching like it was a baseball.

"What is it?" Dylan asked, looking at the small orb suspiciously.

"Cying globe," Orsten said.

Dylan put the ball to his ear. "It *sighs?*"

Orsten held his hand out and reluctantly, Dylan handed it to him. "Cying globes can show the past, present, and possible futures," Orsten said, and Dylan's eyes brightened with interest. "And they are notoriously unreliable." Orsten put the cying globe on a high shelf. Out of reach.

Van wandered to luminescent wings, folded in a stack like fabric.

She'll be flying around the store in a minute, and we'll all be talking about how great she is. Walt pulled one of the maps out of the rack and distractedly unfolded it. It was awash with gold ink and watercolors. A large tree was drawn in the center, and its branches moved with an invisible breeze. Behind it, a small lagoon sparkled, and Walt's breath caught when a splash caused ripples to spread across the water.

"Stunning, isn't it?" Orsten said reverently, coming up behind him. "*This* is what I wanted you to see. See how much *beauty* there is to mapmaking. And what you said about being able to change things on a map?" Orsten said. "That's only part of it. The smallest part. Mapmakers create *worlds*, Walter."

Something bright and shiny fluttered in Walt's belly. It was a delicious feeling, and a little scary too.

Canter strode over and glowered down at Walt and Orsten. "Tell him the whole thing. Not just the good parts."

Orsten eyed Canter for a minute, his mouth a straight line, but then he nodded. "Making worlds? There are always consequences. And worlds, once born, take on a life of their own."

"Get *on* with it," Canter said, and clenched his teeth.

Orsten glared at him. "I *am*." He started scratching

one of his ears, and as he scratched the ear became furry and grew until it was wide and had a pointy tip.

Walt tried to keep his mouth from dropping open. It seemed like it might be rude.

Orsten closed his eyes for a moment, and when he opened them, his blue eye had faded to the color of smoke. "Walter, there will always be some who are pulled to ugliness. And a mapmaker like that is a danger to everyone."

Van and Dylan had drawn closer as Orsten talked, pulled in by his deep somber voice.

"Why?" Dylan asked, his voice just above a whisper.

"Well, you see," Orsten started, "mapmakers can destroy worlds too."

Walt's mouth dropped open. "What? I'm not . . . I can't . . ."

"Oh, but you can, Walter." Orsten spoke matter-of-factly, but his voice was tinged with sadness too, as if he was so very sorry to be delivering that unfortunate news.

"And you *will*," Canter said, just about spitting the words. "If you join forces with him."

"No!" Orsten shouted at Canter. "This boy isn't Statica."

"Who?" Walt asked, but Orsten acted as if he hadn't heard him.

"Walter will make a different choice." Orsten faced

Walt. "Your fate doesn't have to be tied to Statica's. You get to decide. It depends on what you got inside you." He reached over and laid a long skinny finger on Walt's chest.

Walt inhaled deeply and stepped back. All he had inside of him was a sweaty tangled ball of confusion. "Who are you *talking* about?" he asked again, feeling close to tears. A second ago he had felt important. Special. Now he felt awful.

"A mapmaker," Orsten said.

"Like *you*," Canter added accusingly. "And he needs to be stopped. You all do."

The store got completely quiet.

After chewing on his lip for a moment, Walt asked, "Why did you send me the coupon?" He was afraid with the way Canter was acting, that this was some kind of trap.

"We're worried, Walter," Orsten explained. "Statica wants something. And he's destroyed a world every year he doesn't get it. It's been eleven years since he made his demand, and we're getting close to the twelfth year."

"He's destroyed *eleven* worlds?" Van exclaimed. "What does that even mean?"

Walt couldn't comprehend the magnitude of that either. It seemed impossible. "Why doesn't whoever's in charge just give him what he wants, then?" he asked, imagining some enormous sum of money. But to save an entire world? Let alone *eleven* of them. Shouldn't they just pay it?

Orsten stared at him intently. "Because what he wants, Walter . . . is you."

Van gasped, and Walt took a step back. "Me? Why?" he asked.

"So he can cause twice as much chaos and destruction," Canter said gruffly. "Raise you up like a pup. I'm not about to let that happen. The time of mapmaking needs to be over."

At Walt's shocked expression, Orsten said, "There *are* those who believe there shouldn't be any more mapmaking, and have forbidden it—"

"It's a crime!" Canter broke in.

"Not *here* it isn't, as you very well know," Orsten told Canter. "And personally, I think you can change the tide, Walter. If you're given a chance."

"What chance?" Walt asked. He felt just the way he did when Dad talked to him about football. Like he was about to be asked to do something awful, and that he had no choice in the matter.

"Lead Canter to Statica," Orsten said. Two bumps appeared on his forehead, and Walt watched in amazement as the tips of horns sprouted. "If you're the one that helps stop Statica, everyone will see that you can do good."

"How am I supposed to lead anyone to Statica?"

Walt asked. "I don't know where he is. I don't even know *who* he is!"

"Mapmakers share a connection. Have you felt him, Walter?" Orsten asked.

Walt shook his head even though he wasn't sure. The man in his dreams. That couldn't be Statica, could it?

Orsten's eyes went to Canter, who looked like he wanted to punch something. "You have to try and open yourself up to him. You can find him for us. That's all you need to do. Canter will do the rest."

Canter stepped close to Walt. "That means you tell me if you get even a whiff." He pulled a card out of his pocket. It reminded Walt of the business cards his dad took with him when he went to conferences, except this one was solid black with just Canter's name on it, written in silver block letters. No phone number. No address. "You grip this tight when you feel him. And call me. That'll bring me to you. You understand?"

Walt couldn't get his mouth to work.

"I said, do you understand me?"

Walt nodded.

Canter tipped his hat. Then he strode quickly down an aisle, disappearing from view. The sound of an iron door slamming echoed throughout the store. There was an answering groan as the walls seemed to strain and bend. And then silence.

YOUR STRENGTH IS YOUR WEAKNESS–YEAH, RIGHT

"I know Officer Canter is a bit imposing, but he'll make sure that Statica doesn't get to you," Orsten said.

Walt let out a long, shaky breath. Canter seemed more like he wanted to smash Walt flat like a pancake. "He doesn't seem like he's on my side."

Orsten nodded. "It's true he is no friend of mapmakers. If you knew . . . well, that doesn't matter. His aim is simple. To stop Statica before anyone else is made to suffer."

"If mapmakers share some cosmic connection, then why can't this evil Statica person just swoop in and find Walt?" Van asked.

"Well . . ." Orsten looked like he had words swimming around in his mouth that he didn't want to let spill.

"What is it?" Walt asked, certain he didn't want to know.

"While it's true that mapmakers share a connection, your power isn't really . . . developed," Orsten told Walt. "You will be able to feel him because . . . well, because his power is strong enough to reverberate throughout all the worlds. While yours is . . ."

Orsten didn't have to finish. Walt knew exactly what he was saying. The thing that was saving Walt from some evil mapmaker was . . . being a *weakling*. Fantastic.

Dylan stumbled as the floor shifted.

"Gotta reopen the store. It's getting impatient," Orsten said. "This way." He ushered them to the back of the store and pulled a heavy velvet curtain aside, revealing a big iron door. It must have been the way Canter went out.

"Be careful, Walter. Statica may not be able to find exactly where you are, but changes like the ones you made tend to send ripples out into other worlds." His fingers waggled around like he was playing invisible piano keys. "I recommend you don't make any more alterations. There are all sorts of beings out there. There are those who would hunt you for what you could draw into a world."

The candle flames seemed to punctuate Orsten's words, flickering and then rising high for a moment before going back to normal size. The smell in the room changed to something rotten.

The store trembled again, and Walt heard something shatter. Orsten pushed the three of them out the door, and before they could ask questions or say anything, they found themselves in an alley.

They stood in stunned silence for a second. Then Dylan said, "Okay. What. Was. *That?*"

"Let's get out of here," Walt said, his words coming out shaky and breathless.

Nobody needed convincing. They walked quickly down the alley, and then Walt found himself heading down the block. Back to the 7-Eleven.

"What are you doing?" Van asked. "Haven't we had enough?"

"I have to get my bike," Walt said. But that wasn't the reason. He had to see what a big strange magic store right in the middle of Blackbird Bay was going to look like now. But when they turned the corner and got close, all they saw was a regular 7-Eleven. Not a whiff of magic in the air.

Peering in the window, Walt saw Orsten—with two very human-looking ears—behind the counter, slowly counting out change to a couple buying coffee.

Walt pulled his bike out of the rack without a word

and started pushing it down the street. He didn't trust himself to try and ride. He felt like he was sleepwalking. Van tossed her skateboard down and hopped on, but then she hopped right back off and picked up the board. It was if they were all stuck in molasses. They slowly made their way down the sidewalk.

Dylan muttered under his breath, "Roberts passes off to Harrington who fakes left . . . Harrington with the ball as the clock counts down to . . ." He wiped his nose with the back of his hand and stopped. Van and Walt stopped too.

They all stared at each other.

"Okay, can we talk about what happened back there?" Van asked.

Dylan ran his fingers through his hair. "A virtual reality thing? The store must have an advanced version or something. Like, there were screens and it reflected those images." He noticed the way Van and Walt were looking at him. "What?"

Van said, "Dude, the whole store changed." She spoke slowly, like Dylan was a small child. "That was no virtual projection."

Walt hated ganging up against Dylan, but he had to agree with his sister. "Yeah," he said. "That was real."

"But how could it be?" Dylan looked more angry than confused. "It's just not possible. Like, there's *physics!*"

"We walked around in there. We *touched* stuff," Van said. "Maybe there's a magical version of physics?"

For some reason that got Dylan to smile. And then nod. "Okay, sure. *Magic* physics."

Van turned to Walt. "But what is this whole"—she put up air quotes—"*mapmaker* business?"

Walt's shoulders lifted, and he took a deep breath and let it out in a big gush. "Like I said back there. I can change stuff . . ." They were never going to believe him. "I'll show you."

"Okay," Dylan said, and stood back as if he expected Walt to perform some type of magic trick.

"It's at ho—" Walt started but cut himself off. "It's at the house," he finished. It *wasn't* home.

"Come on," Van said, as if it was her idea.

Walt found himself trailing behind her and Dylan again, slowly pushing his bike.

Mom came out of the kitchen just as they walked through the front door. She was wearing one long leather glove and had it stretched out in front of her like she was about to summon someone. She also had on a purple top hat. Not surprisingly, the sight of that made Dylan stop dead in his tracks.

"Just going upstairs, Mom," Walt tried, but of course she came over and extended her non-gloved hand to Dylan.

"Hello there," Mom said. "I'm Mrs. Anderson, Walt and Van's mom."

"Hi," Dylan said, stepping forward. "I'm Dylan."

Walt was relieved to see Dylan shake her hand instead of giving a salute.

"Nice to meet you," Mom said. "I hadn't realized Walt had met anyone in the neighborhood." Walt wanted to crawl into a hole. Mom sounded way too excited. "Or are you a friend of Van's?"

"Walt's," Dylan said, and then he looked shyly at Van. "I mean, both, I guess."

"Great!" Mom said, grinning wide, and then maybe realizing she was coming on a little too strong, she gave a small nod. "Nice." She dialed her smile back a few watts. "And what are you three up to?"

"Up to?" Dylan looked at Walt for help.

"We're just gonna play some AA, Mom," Walt said, shocked at how easily the lie slipped out.

"I should've known. Arch Angels fo-evah," Mom said in a completely ridiculous way. But then she looked at Van. "*You're* playing?"

Van nodded. "Just doing my part to support Dad."

Walt rolled his eyes. Mom was never going to fall for that. Van couldn't sit still long enough to play video games, and her lie was going to get Mom all up in their business. But Mom just smiled even wider. Proof at how desperate she was for Walt to stop being so miserable.

Mom turned her gloved hand this way and that and asked Dylan, "What do you think? Would full gloves become the thing in a dystopian world, or those finger-less kinds?"

"Uh, maybe, the, uh, fingerless ones?" Dylan said.

"Right," Mom said. Her eyes lit on Dylan's basket-ball jersey. "What about sports teams? Do you think we'd figure out a way to have sports after the apoca-lypse, and would teams still wear jerseys like those?" She pointed to Dylan's Warriors jersey.

Dylan's face got bright red. "M-maybe?"

Walt had to get Dylan out of there before Mom got even more embarrassing. "Dylan isn't here to be part of a focus group, Mom. Come on, guys, let's go upstairs."

"*Very* nice to meet you, Dylan," Mom said. She waved at Dylan and then headed back into the kitchen.

"What was up with the glove?" Dylan whispered as soon as she was gone.

"I told you. She's a costume designer." Walt tried to make it clear with his tone how normal and not unusual it was. With what he planned to show him, he didn't want Dylan spooked by a *glove*. "Let's go."

They all hustled upstairs, but as soon as Walt opened the door, Dylan stopped as if he had hit a wall. "You, uh, like maps, huh?"

"Does he like maps?" Van snorted. "Is water wet? Is snow cold? Are donkeys stub—"

"Are *you*, like, super annoying?" Walt asked. Then he looked around, trying to see the room from Dylan's perspective. It *was* an awful lot of maps. "Yeah, I like maps," he said, a bit apologetically.

"No, you *really* like maps," Dylan said, slowly coming in. He walked around the room looking at the various maps and gliding his imaginary basketball through the air.

Walt considered saying that liking maps wasn't any stranger than constantly playing with a basketball that wasn't actually there.

"So are you going to show us this map-changing business, or what?" Van said.

Walt sucked in his lips. He felt nervous and a bit afraid. "Okay," he said, and walked over to the desk, pulled open a drawer, and took out the map of Blackbird Bay. "This morning, I drew some stuff because, you know, it's so boring here—"

"Hah!" Van said, and Walt had to agree. Blackbird Bay sure didn't seem to be boring anymore.

Walt pointed to what he had drawn on the map. "The dig, the creek, the bridge *over* the creek. None of that was here before today. I made it appear in real life by drawing it. Because I'm a . . . mapmaker."

Dylan just stared at him for a second and then laughed as if Walt had told a joke. "Good one. All that stuff was here already."

"You think so because . . ." Walt started pacing around the room. "Well, I don't understand why you think so, but I drew them and they weren't there before." He stopped in front of the bookcase. Took deep breaths to calm down so he would sound logical and not as if he was delusional. He straightened his books, then moved to the desk and lined up all his pens and pencils. He turned back to face Dylan and Van. "It's *magic*. Like a 7-Eleven completely transforming."

Neither Van nor Dylan looked convinced. "Really," Walt insisted.

Dylan pulled a cell phone out of his pocket, and Walt had the outlandish idea that Dylan was about to call Ghostbusters. Dylan started typing in something, and Van murmured, "Must be nice." Walt knew what she meant. No matter how often he and Van asked for cell phones, their parents wouldn't change their no-cell-phones-until-high-school rule. It was a pain.

Dylan found what he'd been looking for and read, "Tamayo Creek is home to blue egrets and other wildlife. Although a smallish waterway now, long ago it provided fresh water to the Muwekma Ohlone tribe . . ." He looked up at Walt and then over at Van. He held out his phone. "There's a phone number for a visitor center!"

"But . . . ," Walt said.

"How're you going to argue with a phone number?" Van said derisively.

"How are you going to argue with a 7-Eleven changing into a . . . a magic store? Run by a . . . well, I don't know what he was. I'm telling you, I drew it. And now it's part of the history. That's how it *works!*" Walt was breathing hard. He didn't know why he was so sure now, but he had to get Van and Dylan to believe him.

"Prove it," Dylan said. "Draw something now."

Walt smiled and nodded enthusiastically. He should've thought of that himself. A couple of blocks away, there was a park that was the duddiest park Walt had ever seen. A big square of grass. No play structure. No picnic tables or barbeques. *Typical Blackbird Bay,* Walt had thought when he first saw it. He grabbed a pencil.

"Wait!" Van cried. "Didn't Mr.—I mean, Orsten— didn't he say not to?"

"You don't even believe it's a thing, though, so . . ." Walt shrugged and tried to pretend he wasn't at all nervous that he was already doing exactly what Orsten had told him not to. But none of that warning stuff could be true. Nobody had destroyed eleven whole worlds just to get to him. That was ludicrous. Walt started drawing a T. rex right in the middle of the grass. "We all agree that there are no dinosaurs in Blackbird Bay, right?"

"Is that thing going to be *alive?*" Dylan asked.

"No," Walt said. Then he added, "I don't *think* it will be alive." But then he considered all the impossible things that had already happened. "Okay, wait." He erased what he'd started and began again.

Dylan sat down on the bed. "Ugh, I don't feel so good."

Walt felt a little shaky, like when he'd had a fully caffeinated drink. He started drawing faster. A dinosaur began to form, but this time it was made just of black lines. "A dinosaur-shaped jungle gym," Walt said, going over the lines a few times, thickening and darkening them. "It's one of the favorite places for little kids in Blackbird Bay to play," he murmured.

"Like at Centinela Park!" Van said, grinning.

When Grandma Nadine used to babysit them, she'd take them there most days after lunch. Letting them climb the dinosaur and the rocket ship next to it for hours. That was back when Walt and Van did everything together.

"Okay, let's see if it's there," Dylan said, standing up. He rubbed a knuckle between his eyebrows as if he had a headache.

"You okay?" Walt asked. He wasn't feeling great himself. He hoped there wasn't some bug going around.

Now that things were starting to get interesting, he didn't want to be laid up in bed. But he felt more than just a little shaky, and his legs hurt. Maybe it was growing pains.

"I'm fine," Dylan said.

Walt shook his legs to get rid of the ache and beckoned Van and Dylan to follow him. He couldn't wait to get to the park.

A REASONABLE
EXPLANATION

A few minutes later they were at the spot where Walt had drawn the dinosaur.

Van and Dylan both stood with their mouths gaping open.

After taking a moment to bask in the glory of being proven right, Walt started to feel anxious. Maybe he shouldn't have drawn anything else after being warned not to, especially not something so big. He looked around to see if there was any sign of a scary man in a tan uniform. But all he saw was young kids climbing all over the dinosaur, laughing and crying out in delight. Adults sat gossiping on benches, drinking coffees and smoothies. This was a good thing.

"I don't—" Dylan started, and then gripped his head with both hands like he was trying to keep it from exploding. "This is unbelievable. Like completely, absolutely *un*. I saw you draw this. I saw it, but I know my little brother loves this thing. How could that be possible? How can he love something that wasn't here an hour ago?"

Walt's mouth dried up like he had swallowed sand. The sun felt blazing hot, and sweat dampened his T-shirt. He stared at the dinosaur, then at all the people around. It didn't make sense, but he got it. Whatever he drew became part of the landscape. Part of the history. So poor Dylan not only saw Walt draw it and knew it hadn't been there before, but now it was part of Blackbird Bay and part of Dylan's memories too. That would hurt anyone's brain.

Van was still looking at the dinosaur in awe. "How did you do this?" she asked Walt, as if she hadn't seen him draw it. Then she threw her arms wide. "Whoo hoo!"

"Shh," Walt hushed her.

Van cupped her hands around her mouth and shouted, "Magic is real!" She gave another wild whoop and started spinning in circles with her arms spread wide.

"What are you? Two?" Walt complained. "Quit it! Everyone's staring!"

Only a few grown-ups frowned at them; other than that, no one seemed to care.

Van held up her hand to Dylan for a high five, but he just gave her hand a confused look.

"Come on, you guys, there must be a reasonable explanation for all of this," Dylan said, not sounding certain of that at all.

"There is!" Van crowed. "The reasonable explanation is magic."

Although he didn't want to, Walt couldn't help smiling at his sister. She was being her usual self: too loud, obnoxious, ridiculous. But right now it was sort of great. "Magic," he said. He nudged Dylan. He didn't know why it felt so important to get Dylan to cosign this wave of excitement. Walt barely even knew Dylan, but if Dylan could see it, could *believe*—well, then it was true.

It was slow coming, just a twitch at the corner of his mouth at first, but then Dylan had a smile on his face almost as big as Van's. "Magic," he agreed. "That's the only reasonable explanation."

"So what are you going to draw next?" Van asked. "A pile of cash? The tallest building in the world? A pyramid with zombie mummies inside?" Van's voice got higher and more excited with each outlandish idea.

It was as if Van had been waiting her whole life to come up with this list of nonsense. Walt sucked his teeth. Typical Van. He wouldn't draw any of *those* things. "I'll draw a Johnnie's Pastrami, and over there, Olvera Street where we get those tacos, and maybe I can draw Mychae's house right next—"

Dylan stopped him. "You can't do that," he said sternly.

"What do you mean?" Walt asked, and at the same time Van asked, "Why not?"

Dylan just stood there for a moment. Walt said, "Oh, you mean the whole thing about not doing it? I think that guy was just—"

"No!" Dylan said with such force Walt had to take a step back. "You can't just change Blackbird Bay any way you want. I mean, the dinosaur thing is cool. But you can't just make the whole place different. That's what Officer Canter meant. It's not your . . . your right to do it."

Walt rubbed his ear. "You don't want it to be . . . like, cooler here?"

"What, you're just going to change Blackbird Bay into Los Angeles?" Dylan asked, pronouncing *Los Angeles* like it was raw sewage. "And who's Mychae? You're going to draw someone's house here? And what, they would just live here now?"

"No, I . . ." Walt glanced at the dinosaur and then back at Dylan. "I guess that wouldn't be . . ." He *had* been thinking he could just bring a friend from Los Angeles here. And for half a second it hadn't even seemed like that big of a deal. But looking at Dylan's horrified face, he could see that it would've been. Lots of *consequences* came with doing something like that.

"Okay, you're right." Walt tried to smile, to show Dylan that he could trust him. "I wouldn't, uh . . . I mean, I'm sure I *can't* even do something like that. I just got excited for a second. But there must be stuff you'd think it would be fun to have."

Dylan frowned, but then his shoulders relaxed. "Yeah. Sure. But I wouldn't want it not to be home anymore. To not be *here*."

"Um . . . okay," Walt said. "Sorry?"

"No worries," Dylan said, and Walt could tell he meant it by the smile that stole over his face. "So your dad works with video games, your mom works on movies." He ticked both things off on his fingers. "And you're a . . . a mapmaker." He looked over at Van. He raised his arms and pretended to take a shot as if Van was the basket. "And you're what? You must have some *thing* too."

"Thing?" Van questioned.

Walt looked at his sister and saw . . . what was that look? Jealousy? Of *him*? Walt felt just a tiny bit of warm buzz in his stomach.

"Don't make our family sound like a bunch of freaks," Van warned.

Dylan mumbled, "I guess that's a nothing, then."

Walt smiled. Then he heard an odd chattering sound. "What's that?"

Dylan pulled out his cell phone. "My mom. I made her ringtone chattering teeth. She hardly ever texts, though." He read a text message and frowned. "Oh, figures," he said under his breath. "My mom needs me to watch Flip."

"Flip?" Van asked.

"My brother," Dylan answered. "His dad . . . my stepdad, Stanley, gave him that nickname. Stanley, uh, really likes nicknames." Dylan shrugged. "My brother's name is Phillip. And he likes tumbling and stuff. It makes sense, I guess."

"So what's your nickname?" Van asked.

"Wink." Dylan looked down.

"Wink?" Van prodded.

"When Stanley and my mom started, um, like, going out? I had some messed-up eye infection, and you know, it was like I was winking?" Dylan was trying to sound like it was no big deal, but it was obvious he found it embarrassing.

"That's messed up," Walt said.

"I don't mind," Dylan hurriedly said, but he avoided looking at them. "My mom says nicknames are a sign of affection." He typed a text and shoved his phone back into his pocket. "I gotta go." Dylan bit his lip.

He looked as if he wanted to say something else, but when he just swished his hands back and forth in a slow imitation of dribbling, Van put her hands on her hips and said, *"What?"*

"Just, um, are you worried? About the Sta . . . Sac . . . ta . . ."

"Statica," Walt filled in.

Dylan nodded. "Yeah, him. Do you think he maybe felt all the stuff you drew, like they were saying? Can you feel *him?*"

Walt shook his head but thought again about the odd dreams he'd been having. The confusing images and the stern eyes. But the way Orsten talked about it, and how powerful Statica was, wouldn't Walt know if that was who was stalking him while he slept? Walt pulled at his ear, thinking things over. Van eyed him suspiciously. "What? I *don't*," Walt claimed.

Van held up her hands. "Fine. I didn't even say anything."

Walt heard the chattering teeth again.

"I better jet," Dylan said.

"Okay, then," Walt said. "See you tomorrow?" he asked hopefully. "We can play AA?"

"Totally," Dylan said. He turned to go, then stopped. "Seriously, though, don't make any more changes to Blackbird?"

Walt shook his head even though he felt annoyed about being asked. He was a mapmaker. Shouldn't he get to do what mapmakers could do?

"Think fast!" Dylan said, pretending to toss Walt a ball, and Walt, without even thinking, raised his hands to catch it. Back home he and his friends would give each other dap when they said goodbye. Dylan was a different sort of a dude. Walt watched as he made his way down the street.

Once he was out of sight, Van launched an attack. "You know you totally don't have to listen to that. Wink won't even know you made the changes. And I'm dying for a pastrami sandwich."

"First off, don't call him that. He obviously doesn't like it. And second . . . really?" Walt demanded. "I should just write off what he wants so you can have a sandwich?"

"I thought the name Wink was kind of funny. You think he—" Van cut herself off. "Yeah, I guess you're right." She shrugged. "Not that it matters. You've probably seen the last of him anyway."

Walt thought of how often Mom tried to tell him that Van was just not always as focused on things. That she didn't realize she was being a jerk. (Mom didn't say *jerk*. She would say things like *insensitive*, but it was the same thing.) None of that really mattered when his sister was standing there with her typical smirk, saying exactly what Walt feared. He couldn't help asking, "You really don't think he'll come back?"

"Guess it depends on what his tolerance is for woo-woo stuff," Van said. *Woo-woo* was what Grandma Nadine called magic. "But you know, with you being a destroyer of worlds and people *hunting* you for your powers," Van said, turning her hands into claws and cackling, "I wouldn't count on it."

"Shut up!" Walt said.

"Jeesh, don't be so grim," Van said, letting her arms drop. "I'm just messing with you. There's lots of time left before streetlights. Let's go to the skate park. I'll show you how to do some easy tricks."

"No thanks," Walt said. "I like having two working wrists." He held his arms out and twisted his hands back and forth. The one and only time he'd let Van convince him to try skateboarding, he'd broken his wrist and hadn't been able to draw for weeks.

Van huffed. "You are the most *careful*, aggravating person on the planet." She spun on her heel and stomped off down the street.

Walt stood in the shadow of the T. rex play structure feeling torn and confused. He could do this amazing thing, and yet he wasn't supposed to. He looked behind him at the kids laughing and squealing as they climbed up on the steel structure. Wasn't Blackbird Bay better with this?

As he slowly walked down the street, he kept feeling as if someone was following him, and every time he looked over his shoulder, he expected to see Officer Canter glowering down at him. But no one was there.

When he got back to the house, he went to the backyard, plopped down on the concrete steps, and rested his chin in his hands. Magic. It was real and wonderful . . . so why did he feel twisted and confused? And here he was back in the boring yard with nothing to do and maybe he'd already lost the one friend he'd almost made. *Fantastic.*

He stared moodily at Ms. Wilhope's cottage. Mom loved Ms. Wilhope. Saying how wonderful it was to find an affordable rental in the Bay Area. And if the sweet landlady wanted to live in the back cottage, that was just fine. In Walt's opinion, *fine* seemed to be a synonym for *strange.*

Almost as if she heard him thinking of her, Ms. Wilhope opened her door.

"Walter!" she said, clearly pleased to see him. She smiled at him kindly, but then her smile faded and she asked, "Are you all right? You seem a bit glum. I know how hard this move has been."

Walt bristled. Obviously Mom and Ms. Wilhope had had *quite* a chatty talk about him. "I'm okay," he claimed.

"But of *course* you are," Ms. Wilhope said, taking a few steps forward. "Things may seem a bit lopsided right now, but, Walter, you have such a gift," she said. "Your skill with maps is simply remarkable." She clasped her hands. "Such a *strong* talent."

Walt startled. How did Ms. Wilhope know about the mapmaking thing?

"Mothers can't help showing off a bit when they have such a gifted child," Ms. Wilhope said, beaming at him.

Oh, that's what she meant, Walt thought, relaxing. Of course. Mom had shown her his maps. Which was annoying . . . except it was kind of hard to be mad when he was getting a bunch of compliments. "Uh, thanks."

Ms. Wilhope came closer. "It's nice you have an outlet. I wish I had something. I miss my home too."

"Isn't this your home?" Walt asked.

Ms. Wilhope gave a sad smile. "Oh no. Home for me is *very* far away. I miss it terribly. I guess you and I are sitting in the same pot."

"You mean the same *boat*," Walt corrected.

"Ah, yes. It's so easy to get things wrong."

"Couldn't you just go back?" Walt asked. Not to be mean, but he wouldn't mind if she moved back to wherever she came from. Maybe he could turn her cottage into a mapmaking office. But Ms. Wilhope shook her head.

"I'm afraid not," she said. "Not anymore." Her eyes drooped with sadness.

Walt thought of all the various places he'd heard about in school. Places where people had to flee from their homes. He guessed that's what she meant, and he felt ashamed that he'd been so quick to wish her away.

"Still, even if I can't go home, it would be fun to go somewhere new and exciting. A fantastic world. Perhaps one day you can draw my little house in a place like that. Wouldn't that be something?"

Walt opened his mouth and then closed it quick. Had he really been about to tell Ms. Wilhope he'd try to give her what she wanted? She would run screaming if he started talking about mapmaking. His shoulders sank down and he felt the frown that he'd been wearing for a month steal back on his face. "Yeah, I guess that would be something, all right," he muttered.

Ms. Wilhope's face grew concerned, but then she clapped her hands together, startling Walt. "I know just what you need." She walked back to her house and pushed the door open wide. "Come in! Come in!"

Walt didn't move for a second. But then he got up and took a hesitant step forward. He thought about Van saying Ms. Wilhope was a witch, and the story of Hansel and Gretel crossed his mind, but he followed Ms. Wilhope anyway. At least it was something to do.

There wasn't anything witchy inside Ms. Wilhope's little home, which was sort of disappointing. But it felt welcoming and comfortable.

There was a tidily made bed, a tiny kitchenette that held a small round table with two chairs, and a door that must lead to a bathroom. One wall was full of decorative mirrors, and Walt looked into one to see if perhaps they were portals to other worlds, but all he saw was his own small, worried face. What was he doing in here?

There was a bureau tucked in a corner, with multicolored fabric draped over it, and Ms. Wilhope had opened one of its drawers and was pushing things around. Walt thought he heard something squeak, and he worried a mouse was about to jump out at her. And there was an odd smell starting to fill the room. Something sort of musty and *thick*.

"Ah!" Ms. Wilhope said. "Here it is. A compass is what you need."

Walt had a deep appreciation for compasses, but what Ms. Wilhope held out wasn't what he expected. It wasn't for directions. Instead it was one of those things they had used last year to do geometry problems, with one side ending in a point and the other with a piece of graphite.

"Do you know how these work?" Ms. Wilhope asked.

"You put the pointy end on a piece of paper and use the other side to draw a circle," Walt answered with a shrug. He might know how it worked, but he had no clue why she was handing him something he'd normally use for homework.

"Yes, but this is a very special compass. I got it from a little shop that is quite remarkable. Sometimes we can feel very vulnerable, and in eye of fact, we *are*. You must be careful, Walter, that in helping others you don't expose yourself. If you need to hide, draw a circle and then get yourself inside it."

Walt's mouth dropped open. Was she talking about Orsten's shop? And did she know about Statica? The hair on his neck felt frozen. "Do you . . ." He looked over at the door. Maybe it hadn't been such a good idea to come inside. It suddenly felt creepy, and the smell was getting stronger. Walt could just about taste it. Like licking a dirty fish tank. "What do you mean?"

"Oh, come now, Walter. You're supposed to be clever. And your instinct not to be too trusting is a good one. Follow it. Not everyone has the best intentions, you know. And sometimes hiding *is* the best strategy."

Walt was very confused. Ms. Wilhope wasn't making any sense. "Hide?"

She nodded like a parent watching her baby take its first step.

Walt wanted to be clever. He didn't want to ask obvious questions, but . . . he looked at the floor and slowly turned to look around him, trying to figure out what Ms. Wilhope meant. "Draw a circle?" He looked at her. "Around myself?"

"On a map!" Now Ms. Wilhope sounded impatient. But then she clucked at him. "Dear me, I sometimes get a bit whipped up." She smoothed her perfectly tidy pink hair. "You'll find your perch." She winked at him and asked, "Should I make us a cup of tea?" She walked briskly to the miniature stove and turned on the burner under a shiny copper teapot as if nothing unusual had happened.

Walt looked at the compass, over at Ms. Wilhope . . . started to ask a question and then thought better of it. He shoved the compass in his pocket. Having a great-grandmother like Mother Dear had made him used to old people being a bit wacky sometimes. He noticed the salt-and-pepper shakers on the table. Case in point. Two lizards with sparkly ruby shoes. "Lizards of Oz. That's funny."

Ms. Wilhope followed his gaze. "Quite," she said. She busied herself with cups and a jar of honey and spoons and a tin of tea bags.

Walt watched as Ms. Wilhope set everything down on the table. "Chamomile?"

Walt shrugged. He didn't know anything about tea.

Ms. Wilhope put fragrant tea bags into the two cups and then poured in steaming hot water. She motioned to one chair and Walt took a seat and then she sat down. She dunked her tea bag up and down in the hot water and stared dreamily off, her mind clearly elsewhere.

Walt was transfixed by the tea bag going up and down, but then Ms. Wilhope snapped back and smiled at him. Her smile was a bit crooked, and Walt noticed a bit of lipstick stained a tooth. Were you supposed to mention stuff like that? He took a sip of tea and made a face. It was very bitter. Ms. Wilhope pushed the bear-shaped container of honey forward, and Walt squeezed quite a bit into his cup.

He took another sip of tea, and this time it was much better.

"I think I was wrong before," Ms. Wilhope said. "I don't think I'd much want my lovely little home being whisked off, but the thought of bringing a bit of fantasy here? Now *that* would be quite marvelous."

Walt couldn't help but nod happily.

Ms. Wilhope set her cup down and leaned forward with her elbows on the table. She flexed her fingers back and forth as if they ached. "You know I wasn't just blowing steam. Your talent is quite brilliant. Your parents must be so proud."

At first Walt was too stuck on Ms. Wilhope's mix-up to register the rest of what she'd said. "Hot air, you mean." Then his brain caught up with his ears . . . or the other way around . . . and he added, "Thanks. Well, my mom is."

Ms. Wilhope smiled. "Hot air. I'll remember." Then she placed her hand gently on one of Walt's. "Don't worry, Walter. Everything will be right as soup."

Her hand felt damp and it shook a bit and Walt didn't have the heart to fix her mistake. *It must suck getting old.*

That night at dinner, Van shoved a big chunk of meat in her mouth, chewed, swallowed, and then asked, "Dad, what do you think about fantasy stuff? Magic." She picked up her knife and waved it around as if it was a wand.

"I'd love a bit of magic," Mom said. "Bibbidi bob-bidi boo and Michael Levine would give Kelsey and me the contract for his new sci-fi movie. The costumes are going to be *sliced.*"

"Mom, please don't try to sound current," Van complained. "It makes you sound ridiculous." She turned back to Dad. "But what about you, Dad?" She looked around, pretending to be thinking. "Um, like if you could magically make Walt an awesome football player . . ." She winked at Walt as if he was in on her joke, which he definitely was not. "Would you do it?"

"Van," Mom warned, no longer smiling.

"What?" Van asked innocently.

"That's the trouble with kids today," Dad said. "Magic," he grunted. "Afraid of hard work?" he asked Walt.

"Me?" Walt squeaked. "I didn't even—"

"Nothing good is worth having without working for it," Dad interrupted. "You can't always look for the easy way. There are no magical solutions to life."

Walt stared down at his plate. His pork chop and greens heavy with bacon didn't seem so great anymore. Leave it to Van to ruin his favorite meal.

"Dad," Van said. "I was messing around. You don't have to go all Darth Vader."

Dad's face hardened for a moment, but then he relented, and smiled. "That cat wasn't about working hard. Wasn't he all . . ." He put his hand out like he was grasping someone by the throat. Then he squeezed the air and in a raspy voice said, "Luke, you must do what your father says."

Van giggled and smiled at Walt. He did not smile back.

Dad put his arm down and cleared his throat. "Your dinner isn't going to get finished by you staring at it," he said, frowning at Walt. "That's why you're small. You don't eat enough." He reached over and dumped some more mashed potatoes on Walt's plate.

Walt bit back a sigh and went back to eating.

Van held up her empty plate. "Pile on some more of those potatoes, Daddy," she said.

Dad put a small dab of potatoes on her plate.

"Seriously?" Van asked, but Dad ignored her.

"How's your chop?" Mom asked Walt.

"It's great. It's—"

"Whatever it is, he'll eat it," Dad threatened.

Walt sniffed.

"Richard," Mom said to Dad.

"I'm fine," Walt said, wiping his nose with the back of his hand. He must be getting sick. Yeah, that was it. His whole body ached.

As Walt was getting ready for bed, he heard the soft rise and fall of his parents' voices. He crept out to the top of the stairs where he could hear them better.

"You know what happens to a boy like that? Especially a Black one? He can't be sniveling about stuff, Wanda. There's no crying on the field."

"I'm just saying maybe throwing him at football isn't the best strategy," Mom said. "I don't think camp was an easy time for him last year, and—"

"It's not *supposed* to be easy. Kids don't know what's good for them."

Slowly Walt went back to the bedroom. He wasn't going to cry. He wasn't. He just wanted to be someplace, *any* place that wasn't here. He went over to his map of Djaruba and stared at it. If only he could be there.

He carefully took the map down. Then Walt took out a soft pencil. Where could he go? An answer sprang into his head right away. A windmill. *Up on a bluff, in the middle of the field, there was a windmill.* He'd seen a windmill on the drive from Los Angeles to Blackbird Bay. His family had eaten at the restaurant inside it. It had been one moment on that miserable drive that had jolted him out of his bad mood. Even though it was a restaurant, the huge sails actually really spun around. Walt had been fascinated by it.

A powerful mapmaker lives inside, spending his days creating the most incredible maps ever seen. Walt smiled down at the drawing, then added a small window at the top. "Let there be light," he whispered, and giggled. Real windmills probably didn't even have windows. He'd look online tomorrow. The windmill seemed right at home in Djaruba, as if it should've been there all along. Walt sighed.

Why *couldn't* he live someplace where people thought mapmaking was cool? Much better than Blackbird Bay. Walt drew and drew. Getting lost in miles and miles of trees. The soft scent of pine filled the room, and Walt kept drawing.

Walt's eyes popped open. He couldn't even remember getting into bed and had been having a curious dream where a circle had lifted from the ground and chased him. Now that he was awake, it was sort of funny. But the idea of a magical circle of protection was ridiculous and—

A swooshing noise in the corner broke into his thoughts. It was as if a strong wind had blown through the room. Walt looked around but couldn't see anything in the dark. Was that what had woken him up? Then the sound of the wind was replaced with a *creeeak* . . . *creeeeeeak* . . . *creeeak* . . . It was too dark to see anything, and the desk lamp was all the way across the room. Slowly he shoved off his covers and slid his legs out of bed.

Creeeak . . . *creeeeeeak* . . . *creeeak* . . .

Walt tiptoed across the carpet, reached a hand to the lamp, and clicked on the light.

"Gotchu," Walt whispered. But the noise stopped as soon as the light came on, and nobody was there. He peered around the room. Nope. Nothing.

Wait.

His scalp started to itch, and prickly fingers poked

at his neck. He stepped close to the map lying on the desk.

The small sails of the windmill were spinning. Walt heard the creaking noise with every turn. The sails started spinning faster and faster, and for a moment Walt worried they would spin right off the page.

A voice entered his head.

Come to the windmill.

Walt looked around the room in a panic, but no one was there. After taking a few steadying breaths, he asked out loud, "What?" His voice sounded wispy and frail.

Come to the windmill, Mapmaker.

Somewhere in the house Walt thought he heard a window slam shut.

His mouth dried to cotton and he couldn't swallow. He needed to get some water. But when he opened the door, he heard soft shuffling. Were those footsteps on the stairs? Walt felt his stomach flop and twist. He was going to barf. What if Canter had somehow found out about the dinosaur? He definitely seemed like the type of dude who would sneak into someone's house. Walt wondered if he threw up on him, would Canter run off screaming? Vomit wasn't much of a weapon, but what else did he have? He peered out into the dark hallway, straining to see.

Oh no. There was definitely something there. It wasn't Canter. It was something *worse*. A flowy thing in white, making its way up the stairs. A spirit?

Walt bit his fist and wondered if screaming would help. He thought about shutting the door and moving the dresser or something in front of it, but the door opened out, so that wouldn't work. Where could he hide? Should he grab the compass?

ANYWHERE YOU
WANT TO GO

The shape on the steps paused.

"Walt?" it called.

"*Mom?*" Walt called back.

"What are you doing up, boo?" his mother said, finishing her way up the stairs, her white nightgown billowing around her. She came up to Walt and rested a hand on his forehead. "*Are* you sick?"

Walt shook his head. "Just couldn't sleep."

Mom stared at him for a few seconds, then she said, "I'll be right back. Get into bed."

Walt did as he was told, but the bed was uncomfortable and hot. He wondered what Mom was doing.

Whatever it was, it seemed to take a long time. Finally she reappeared at the door.

One hand was behind her back. She came over and sat on the edge of his bed. "When I was a young girl, Mother Dear would tell me stories about her travels. Just like she told them to you. I loved hearing about them. And I told her one day how much I wished I could go to some of the places she talked about, and she gave me this." Slowly she pulled her hand out, revealing what appeared to be a wad of aluminum foil.

"What *is* that?"

"A traveling machine," Mom said with a bemused smile. "Sometimes where we are doesn't seem like the best place. And we just want a way to get . . . somewhere else. And maybe it doesn't matter if we really go or not, but feeling like we *could* go. That's what's important." She patted Walt's arm. "Your father loves you very much, and sometimes that love can feel like expectation and pressure, but it's just that he knows how hard things can be. And he doesn't have a whole lot of imagination." She laughed softly. "He's not a big fan of my family's . . . beliefs." She untwisted the shiny mass a bit, then set it on Walt's lap. "You have a wonderful imagination, son. And you can go anywhere you want to. Just close your eyes and see it."

Walt looked down at his lap. Three helmets that

actually weren't foil but maybe that material they made emergency blankets out of? He touched one of them and was surprised that it felt like buttery soft leather. With shiny goggles attached, the helmets made Walt think of those old-timey aviator hats. A tangle of vividly colored cords connected the three helmets together. He had a ton of questions. He started with, "Why *three* helmets?"

Mom touched one of the helmets softly. "I think Mother Dear wanted to make sure I had friends. I didn't . . . well, that was hard for me. Making friends. Keeping friends. I think she wanted me to know I wasn't going anywhere alone."

Walt didn't know what to make of what Mom was saying. First off, it seemed to him she had like a million friends, and he couldn't imagine a time when she would've felt . . . well, like him. And was she really implying he could magically go someplace? Away from here and football camp? That seemed highly unlikely. Although with all the impossible things that had happened today, who knew? "Why didn't you give it to me before?"

"I guess before we moved, you didn't seem to need it, and after . . . well, the whole three helmets thing. But now you've met Dylan. He seems nice. And of course you have your sister."

Her voice was too full of hope for Walt to tell her that he'd probably seen the last of Dylan and that his sister was an annoying jerk, so all he said was, "Thanks, Mom."

Mom leaned over and pressed her cheek against his. "Boys get their growth spurt later than girls," she whispered.

Walt wanted to ask her if she could swear that would be the case for him, but he didn't want to sound pathetic. "Cool," he said.

With a sigh, Mom stood up and rubbed his head. "Try to get some sleep. It's awfully late. Maybe tomorrow you can go somewhere with your new friend and Van." She looked significantly at the pile of helmets and tangled cords on the bed.

"Yeah," Walt said. An image of Ms. Wilhope flashed through his head, and he almost laughed out loud. Mom sure hadn't been talking about a little old lady when she said *new friend*.

Walt lay back on his pillow and closed his eyes, one hand on the traveling machine as if it was a favorite stuffed animal.

When sleep overtook him again, he dreamed he was outside a windmill. Wind blew around so hard he thought he'd be lifted right off the ground. He struggled to get the door open, and when he finally did, waiting inside for him was the man. This time, he was almost tall enough for his head to hit the ceiling, and his long black hair was blowing in a breeze. His murky brown eyes stared at Walt hungrily. "Can you see me, Mapmaker?" he asked. "Because I see *you*!"

Walt trembled in his sleep.

ROUGH TERRAIN

When he woke up the next morning, Walt just lay in bed, staring at the bumpy ceiling. His mom called it popcorn and Dad called it tacky. Walt liked it. It was like the rough terrain of a faraway planet.

He rubbed a hand over his head, trying to smooth out his thoughts. Grandma Nadine always said to pay attention to your dreams because they meant something. He'd had so many odd dreams lately. And it couldn't be a coincidence that the dreams had started after they moved here. Lots of strange places and scary creatures chasing him. And the man. Walt thought it was just missing home, but the man with the brown eyes worried him. He was always watching Walt so intensely, as if waiting for Walt to do something. Last night, though, was the first time the man had seemed to be talking directly to him. What if it *was* Statica?

Walt stumbled out of bed and tripped over the thing Mom had brought him in the middle of the night. So *that* hadn't been a dream. He picked up the machine, twisting it around and around in his hands. When he was really little, Mom used to read him a story about a bear who went to space in a box. Walt would make her read it over and over.

This was like the box, and it seemed like Mom had put it together. He wondered how long it had taken her. Maybe she should've taken a little more time. It was sort of wacky looking. But maybe she'd made it that way on purpose, so it would *seem* like something really old that used to be Mother Dear's? Being a costume designer, Mom could make almost anything. His last birthday party, she'd made apocalypse outfits for everyone and separated them into survivors and zombies. Everyone said it was the best party they'd ever been to. Because she knew how much Walt would appreciate it, she had even made a map for the survivors to follow and escape to safety.

As a joke, he put on a helmet and said, "Take me back to Los Angeles." He thought he felt a buzzing sensation in his head, but after waiting an embarrassingly long while, of course he didn't actually go anywhere. He slid the helmet off and inhaled deeply, trying to catch a whiff of . . . he didn't know exactly. What did *weird* smell like?

After he was cleaned up and dressed, Walt traveled the only way he knew how. He bent over the map of Djaruba and imagined himself swimming in the ocean and climbing mountains. He could almost feel the wind blowing in his face as he sailed away on the back of a dragon.

It was nice getting his brain off whether Dylan would come back or not. He could still hear how pathetic he had sounded trying to dangle Arch Angels like a bribe.

There was a knock on the door.

"Come in," he called, not even trying to disguise the total relief and joy in his voice.

Van poked her head into the room. Her hair was a wild mass of tangles, and her eyes were still sleep crusted. "What are you doing?"

Walt's disappointment bit him like a tick. He looked at Van, then down at the map, then back at her as if to say, *It's pretty obvious, isn't it?*

"Did you *want* something?" he asked.

Ignoring him, Van sauntered over to the desk. "Are you adding stuff to Blackbird Bay?" she asked excitedly, but then she jabbed her finger at the map. "You know, maps don't have stuff like every little tree and rock and . . . what is that? A big mushroom? Maps don't have stuff like that on them."

Walt pushed Van's hand away. "What do you know about it?" He pointed to his Middle Earth map, tacked on the wall. "I guess Tolkien didn't know how to draw maps either?" he asked.

"So, you're Tolkien now? All that mapmaking business really went to *some*one's head," Van teased.

"I'm just saying *fantasy* maps are different. I didn't—" Walt cut himself off. Van was just trying to bait him into an argument. "Seriously, Van, what do you want?"

"I don't want to just wait around for Dylan. Can we at least draw a fun box at the skate park? Or something even smaller? A trampoline in the backyard? Come on, let's draw that!"

Walt didn't like the way Van was trying to take ownership of *his* stuff. "I told Dylan *I'm* not drawing anything else here. You saw how he got freaked out about it."

"I did. That's why he's probably staying as far away as possible," Van said. She looked around the room as if it was all strange and unfamiliar. "What's the real issue?" Van said. "You scared because of the cop?"

Walt didn't appreciate at all the way Van made it seem like he shouldn't be worried about getting arrested, or something worse. "No one said I was scared," he mumbled.

"You know that whole thing was probably not even true. An evil mapmaker? I mean, come on. Didn't that sound over-the-top?"

"*You're* over-the-top," Walt said.

"Wow, thanks," Van said, sounding as if her feelings were hurt.

Walt *almost* felt guilty but really, couldn't she just leave him alone?

"Okay, well . . . ," Van started. She gave one last look at Walt as she left the room. "In the unlikely event of Dylan showing up, come find me?"

"I'll do that," Walt mumbled. Suddenly working on his map of Djaruba didn't seem nearly as comforting as usual. He felt achy and his hand hurt. With a sigh he got up and stretched, and then grabbed the traveling machine off the bed. If only he could feel a tiny bit of magic. But all he felt was sore. He needed some fuel.

Walt hurried downstairs, but just his luck, Dad was in the kitchen. Walt wished he could make himself invisible.

Dad stared at him over a steaming cup of coffee. "What's that?"

"Uh, just a . . . thing Mom gave me. It's sort of a . . ." Walt didn't know what to say, or how to explain why he had the odd contraption wrapped around his neck like a scarf. It had been an impulse that he was now very much regretting. "Toy?"

Dad took a sip of coffee, wincing over the heat. "Son."

Walt inhaled deeply, but he could already feel his throat tightening. "Yes?" He tried to lift his head to look at Dad in the eyes the way Dad always wanted, but it was like his head weighed a hundred pounds.

"Look, your mom told me I should try and appreciate your . . ." He glanced at the traveling machine. "Uh, your imagination. And I do, I guess. But you need to toughen up. You can bet you need to work a lot harder than other guys."

Because I'm Black. Walt knew it by heart. "I know, Dad," he said softly.

Dad nodded to a piece of paper stuck to the refrigerator with a magnet. "There's a list of drills for you to practice. Camp starts next week and you'll be prepared," he warned. "You might want to put that, uh, *thing* away before you get started."

Walt chewed his lower lip painfully. The list of drills was very long. "Okay," he mumbled, feeling as if he had agreed to let himself get punched in the face.

"Good man," Dad said, and left the kitchen, whistling a little to himself as if they had had a really nice talk.

It was as if Dad didn't see him at all.

Walt put bread in the toaster, stared moodily out the window while he waited, jumped like a bomb had exploded when the toast popped up, grabbed butter out the fridge, and messily buttered his toast, all while twisting and untwisting the cords of the traveling machine. Why had Mom given it to him? He took an angry bite of toast, butter dribbling down his chin. It was almost mean. A tease. As if he could get away from any of this. And Dylan wasn't coming back and Walt was stuck.

He gobbled the rest of his toast in two big bites, the half-chewed clumps scratching his throat when he swallowed. A coming storm of tears brewed in the back of his nose, and that wasn't *fair*. Dad was right. It was ridiculous to walk around with some *toy* draped around your neck like a chump. Walt pushed away from the counter and trudged out of the kitchen, feeling smaller with every step. He could feel magic leaking from the air as if it knew it wasn't wanted. *Fine. Let it go.* What was it good for anyway? He wasn't supposed to do mapmaking. His big *protection* from harm was a school supply. And if magic was real, why hadn't it made football camp disappear? The machine was going straight in the trash.

Then there was a knock on the front door. Walt stopped and stared at it. He felt the smallest glimmer of hope. He'd do the painful football drills after a few hours of Arch Angels. He'd even let Dylan pick what angel he wanted to be. But when he yanked open the door, he was shocked by the anger in Dylan's face.

"What did you do?" Dylan demanded.

"Huh?" Walt said, taking a step back. "What are you talking about?"

"You drew stuff. I know you did. Walking over here I saw—I didn't see you do it, but you must've."

"Dylan, slow down," Walt said, trying to keep his voice calm although he wanted to shout right back at Dylan. What kind of person comes at someone like that? Walt's hands clenched into fists. He tried to keep his words even but could hear the heat as he said, "I have no clue what you're talking about. I didn't draw anything."

"Where's Van?" Dylan asked, pushing his way into the house.

Okay, this dude was seriously about to get popped. "Van? What does she have to do with this?"

"Because she'll know."

"Know what?" Van asked, appearing at the top of the stairs. She'd washed her face, but her hair was still a mess. "What's all the shouting about?" she asked.

"Did you see him do it?" Dylan called up to her.

Walt felt as if they were stuck on some endless loop, so he jumped in. "I don't know why, but he thinks I changed more things in Blackbird Bay," he told Van. "I don't even know what things he's *talking* about."

Van surprised both of the boys by exploding in laughter as she came down the stairs. "Seriously, Dylan? Do you know how hard I tried to make Walt change something? He wouldn't even give me a teensy-tiny trampoline in the backyard." She went back to laughing, but when she saw Dylan's face, she stopped. "You *are* serious, aren't you? Okay, but wait. Exactly what changes?"

"Things!" Dylan said. "A lake. It's purple and, like . . . okay, there are boats, but they're not . . . Trees that looked like they were *walking*. Well, maybe that was just . . . A cave! And I heard a scary noise from inside, like something is *in* there. Stuff is . . . *different!*"

"Well, I didn't do any of that!" Walt claimed.

"Then what's going on?" Dylan asked, sounding worried and frustrated, but not, Walt noted, angry anymore.

Van shut the front door, then put her hands on her hips. "Okay, first things first." She jabbed her thumb at her brother. "Walt, you have butter on your chin." She waited for Walt to rub his chin with the back of his hand. "Second, let's go up to my room to talk about this. Mom will be getting back from Zumba soon and we don't want her joining this convo, right?" Without waiting for the boys to answer, Van turned and headed back upstairs.

Dylan looked suspiciously at Walt, and Walt glared back until Dylan dropped his gaze. "Not cool, man," Walt muttered, then added, "Come on."

They trailed after Van, keeping distance between them.

The sun shone perkily through the window in Van's room, making it clear just what a slob Van was. Even Walt was surprised that her room had reached this level of grossness. Dirty dishes were scattered around and her trash can was brimming over with garbage. A basketball net was attached to the back of the door and small balled-up pieces of paper were littered underneath it.

Dylan plopped down on the beanbag chair that was spilling its guts onto the carpet while Walt shoved a pile of clothes out of his way so he could sit on the bed. Walt looked at the posters on the walls, some of them hanging on by a single loose staple. Instead of maps, Van's walls were covered with pictures of skateboarders doing amazing tricks.

"Hey," Dylan said, pointing at an image of a skateboarder. "That's—"

"Me," Van said, with more than a touch of pride. Then, as if she hadn't ever stopped her list, she went on, "*Third*, like I said, I tried to get Walt to make changes, and he wouldn't, because he told you he wouldn't. No way would he put any of those things here. Even though it sounds sort of amazing. Well, maybe not the scary cave thing."

Dylan looked confused and a little embarrassed. "But—"

Before he could argue, Van held up a finger to cut him off. "Fourth, *if* there's been changes, then another mapmaker made them." She delivered the information as if it was completely logical.

Walt sat straight up. *But that meant . . .* "You think Statica is here?"

"Does he have to be?" Van asked. She picked some of the crumpled paper balls off the floor and Walt thought for a second she was actually going to try and clean up a little, but instead she lobbed them at the basket. Only one went through, and Dylan snickered. Ignoring him, Van asked Walt, "He just has to have a map of this place, right? Just like you?"

Walt felt as if a heavy storm cloud was pressing down on him. "Yeah." He hoped Van was right, but what if Statica was here? What if he had found him?

Dylan picked up one of the paper balls that had missed its target and took a shot, his hand staying raised in the air until the ball banked against the door and dropped in. "I'm voting he's not here. I mean, if he was, wouldn't he just grab you up?"

Walt didn't like the logic of that. "What do we *do*?"

"Should you use the card?" Van asked. "Call Canter?"

Walt had forgotten about the card. He was wearing the same shorts from yesterday, so it must still be in his pocket. "I don't want that dude anywhere near me," Walt said. "What's he going to do when he finds out about the dinosaur?"

"Truth," Van said pensively. Then she looked back at Walt. "Uh, *fifth*, what is that thing?" She pointed at the traveling machine.

"I had the same question," Dylan said.

Walt untwisted it from around his neck. The helmets glistened brightly in the sun. "Something Mom gave me," he said, his voice heavy with embarrassment. "She said it was a traveling machine."

"For real?" Dylan asked excitedly.

Van scowled at Walt. "Must be nice," she said.

"What? What do you mean?" Walt asked.

"*I* didn't get anything." Van crossed her arms over her chest. "Guess I should've gone around pouting for weeks."

"You want it?" Walt asked, holding the machine out. "It doesn't *do* anything."

Van scoffed and said, "Keep it," at the same time as Dylan asked, "How do you know?"

Walt and Van both turned to him. "What?" they

said, looking and sounding at that moment very much like twins.

"You're a mapmaker," Dylan said, as if this explained it all. "We saw a 7-Eleven become like a . . . a *magic* store. And I saw . . . all that wild stuff. Doesn't seem that outlandish for your mother to have given you a traveling machine that actually works." His eyes twinkled.

Walt was surprised at how quickly Dylan had moved from not believing any of this stuff could be possible, to furious, to excited. Wasn't his brain getting whiplash?

Walt twisted the machine around and around in his hands. "Doesn't seem possible, does it?" he whispered. But he was already thinking of all the places he would go.

Van came over and ripped the machine out of his hands. She put a helmet on. "Let's test it," she said. She adjusted the goggles over her eyes. When neither boy moved, she put her hands on her hips. "Come on!"

Walt grabbed one of the dangling helmets and put it on, feeling a bit ridiculous, but also annoyed. "You act like it's yours," he muttered. The third helmet dangled, with the cords hanging between him and Van.

Van said, "Come on, Dylan."

Without hesitation, Dylan pulled on a helmet. "Oh, that feels strange!"

Walt knew what Dylan meant. As soon as Dylan had put the helmet on, it was like the machine woke up or something. The cords started to glow, and it seemed to Walt as if his helmet had sort of melted onto his head. Could this thing actually take them somewhere?

"Someplace easy?" Van said. "Just to see, right?"

Walt wasn't sure how the machine was supposed to take them somewhere. Could it read his mind? He thought hard, and nothing happened. "Uh, take us . . . downstairs to the kitchen." The cords started to heat up and glow with neon colors and then, with a big snap, the room disappeared. *Everything* disappeared, except for Walt, Van, and Dylan. And then, as if they had been dumped from a big bucket, they were tossed onto the kitchen floor.

Walt jumped to his feet, which yanked Van's and Dylan's heads to uncomfortable angles.

"Jeesh, bro. A little consideration." Van stood and offered a hand to Dylan to help him up.

"Sorry," Walt said, but his voice was filled with wonder.

All three of them looked like they had just gotten off the best ride.

"It *worked*?" Dylan whispered. "*Amazing*."

"This is like the greatest thing ever!" Van said. "Tell it to take us to Disneyland. To the front of the line of the Star Wars ride!" She pulled her goggles back down.

Walt grinned excitedly. That wasn't a bad idea at all.

"Do you have to get back home right away?" he asked Dylan.

"Naw," Dylan said. "My mom and Stanley took Flip to Legoland." He fiddled with the cords that were no longer glowing.

Van and Walt exchanged glances. "You didn't want to go?" Walt asked.

"It's for *little* kids," Dylan said, sounding like he was repeating what he'd been told. "They'll be back in the morning."

"Wait," Van said, holding her hands up. "They left you over*night*? By your*self*?" She sounded extremely jealous.

"That doesn't seem okay," Walt said.

Dylan flushed. "What's the big deal? I'm twelve," he said, as if that explained things. "Our neighbor is cool. She always tells me I can come over if I need anything."

"But is it even legal?" Walt asked.

"Sometimes my stepfather is better when I'm not around." Dylan looked at the floor, twisting one of the colorful cords in his hands. "It's no big deal, you guys. Let's go to wherever we're going."

Walt rubbed his chin. It was obvious that Dylan didn't have the same type of family Walt and Van did. And as much as it could be a pain the way Mom always seemed to be checking up on them, and making them get home before the streetlights came on, it would be worse if she didn't care.

"When we get back, you can stay here if you want," Walt said.

Dylan didn't raise his head. "Cool. Thanks." Then he peered up through his shaggy hair. "Uh, sorry about . . . before."

Walt held out his fist, and Dylan met it with a fist of his own. "No blood, no foul," Walt said, happy to have their argument behind them.

"Okay, that's settled," Van said, her voice tinged with impatience. "So where are we going for *real*?"

A slow smile lit up Walt's eyes. Disneyland had sounded cool, but if he could go anywhere he wanted, there was really only one choice. "Djaruba," he announced, and the cords started to glow.

"What?" Van cried, before the kitchen disappeared.

A WORLD YOU CREATED

Hot steamy wind hurtled them through the air like they had become comets streaking across the sky.

Walt's cheeks pushed back from his face as the wind slammed him forward. Even wearing the goggles, he could barely keep his eyes open. Van's hair had become untethered and whipped around, getting in their faces. They were being blown like rag dolls, with the cords still keeping them close together. As they shot through the air, Walt started to panic. What if he had just sentenced them to die? This contraption couldn't actually take them someplace that didn't even—

Before Walt could finish the thought, he found himself entangled with Dylan and Van on spongy soft grass.

The air shimmered and felt electric, and smelled like oranges and laundry dryer sheets. Walt took his helmet off and gripped his knees. It seemed as if his heart had traveled to his throat, making it hard to swallow. He felt like if he didn't hold himself together, he was going to explode like a supernova.

Color abounded everywhere, as if a toddler had dumped a whole carton of crayons. Blue and orange and green and yellow.

"Whoa," Van said, panting a little.

Dylan slid up the goggles, wiped his nose with the back of his hand, and sniffed loudly.

Walt thought if he pushed off from the ground, he could start flying. As his heart moved from a thundering gallop to more of a trot, he slowly got to his feet. He took a few steps away from Van and Dylan, getting his bearings.

They had landed on a high bluff, giving him an excellent view of the wide expanse of a chartreuse field, and trees that seemed to touch the sky, and huge boulders that looked as if they'd been sprinkled around like confetti. Below them was a rippling periwinkle river, sparkling like it was filled with diamonds.

Where should they go first? The caves? The whispering forest? Obviously not the Badlands. *The windmill?* Walt got an odd sensation, like someone was whispering in his ear. He brushed it away. A lazy breeze ruffled his shirt. Behind them stood a thick bank of mustard-colored trees.

First Van and then Dylan took off their helmets and set them down.

"You have got to be kidding me," Van whispered, standing up and joining her brother.

"George . . . oomba em . . . m-moomba?" Dylan asked. "What's . . . where's ja um, rumba?"

"Jah-roo-bah," Walt corrected. "There's a D, but it's silent." He grinned at Dylan, but Dylan didn't smile back.

"But *where* is it?" Dylan asked. "I've never even heard of it before." His hair stuck out in all directions.

"Djaruba," Van said, "is my brother's world. *His* world. He created this." She fluttered her hand around. "All this. On a piece of paper." She pronounced *paper* like it was dangerous. "It's just a map." She gripped her shoulders as if holding herself together. "This can't be happening. No *way* can this be happening." Her voice was just above a whisper and sounded very un-Van-like.

Walt was surprised. He couldn't remember Van ever sounding afraid like she did now. That was more often his part to play, but he didn't feel a bit scared. He put his hands on his hips, leaned back on his heels, and let out a loud whoop. He spun around a few times, and the air seemed to spin around him. "It *is* happening, though. We're in my world!"

The sky was pink and flecked with gold, and the sun peeked through puffy marshmallow-looking clouds. Far in the distance, a large mountain, shrouded in gray mist, loomed against the pale sky.

"Mount Yoray," Walt whispered. It had been the highest peak in Djaruba before he erased the top.

It was like the first day of summer vacation, when it seemed like time stretched out endlessly in front of you. He breathed in deep and turned to face the forest. Crowded with trees that twinkled as if tiny lights had been strung through the swirling branches. The forest itself seemed alive and breathing.

"I can't believe we're really here," Walt said. "I can't believe it. I never thought . . ." The river streamed melodically below them as if it was laughing along with Walt. This was better than anything he had imagined or hoped for, and he wanted to see every single thing. His world. *His* world. "Come on, let's explore."

"Wait!" Dylan cried. "We're in a *world* you *created*? One that only exists on a map you made? Like, we're not on planet *Earth* anymore?" Dylan scratched his head. "Even with everything that's happened, this is . . . this is *impossible*."

"Yeah, but . . . ," Van started, and then looked up at the sky, then behind them at the trees. "*Is* it, though?" she asked. "Walt drew things on a map that suddenly

118

appeared. That you remembered always being there. We walked across that bridge, remember? That should've been impossible too."

The breeze picked up, ruffling Walt's T-shirt, and he heard a loud *creeeaaak*. Followed by another. Then another.

"What is *that*?" Van asked.

Walt knew exactly what it was. His dream came back to him, and he rubbed his ear thoughtfully. It wouldn't be an awful place to start. "Come on, follow me." He started to walk toward the noise.

Van said, "Hey, *I* have a good idea," and Walt turned back.

Van rolled her eyes and picked the traveling machine off the ground. "Let's take care of this thing." She held the soft helmets and cords out to Walt and he grabbed it from her.

"Not like I was going to leave it," Walt muttered. He tucked the helmets into each other and wrapped the cords around them. Then he slid it all under his arm like a football.

Dylan elbowed him in the ribs. "You totally were," he teased.

"Let's *go*!" Walt said.

In a few minutes, the three of them stood in front of a tall windmill. Its slowly moving sails were the source of the loud creaking and moaning.

"Whoa, this looks ancient," Dylan said.

The building was stone and squat and wide at the base but narrowed as it went up. Walt felt a crick developing in his neck as he stared up at the small window near the top. The windmill was nothing like those skinny silver ones planted next to the freeway between Los Angeles and the Bay Area. This was way better. Just like he'd drawn it.

Van clamped her hands to her hips and asked, "A windmill? And this is fascinating because . . . why?"

"Let's look inside," Walt said. Why had he been told to come here? Was someone inside waiting for him? Goose bumps erupted on his arms. The voice had been strong and rumbly, but more inviting than scary. Still. Walt felt anxious. He swallowed a few times and then approached the windmill as if it was no big deal.

He pushed open the heavy wooden door. It felt like he was about to walk into a stranger's house without their permission, and he hoped alarm bells didn't start ringing.

"This is pretty sweet," Dylan said as soon as he entered, and whistled. His hands, usually in perpetual motion, stilled by his sides.

"*Very* cool, bro," Van said.

That was the truth. The inside was fascinating. It

was as if the mill existed in two different time periods. Two enormous wooden gears fit into smaller gears made of a shiny gold metal. Stainless steel rods glistened as if they had just been polished, but right next to the modern rods were ancient-looking wooden beams. Three different-sized millstones slowly turned. Two were pitted and worn down with age, and one looked as if it had been delivered from the stonecutters the day before. Gas lanterns blazed on the walls, and bright electrical lights were strung across the room. It was all very cool, but it also felt eerie. Walt breathed in deep. The room smelled like moss and old trees and something acrid.

"You drew all this?" Van asked.

Walt didn't know how to explain. He'd drawn a windmill. But he hadn't really even considered what it might look like inside. And he'd felt odd when he was drawing it. Angry, sad, and almost like his hand drew with a mind of its own. But all he said was, "Sort of?"

Dylan was standing by a wide shaft in the center of the room that cut through a hole in the ceiling. And emitting from the hole was a soft glow. "What's up there?" he asked.

Walt looked around for a way up and saw a narrow spiral staircase off to the side.

"Let's take a quick peek," he whispered.

"Why are you whispering?" Dylan asked. "Are we not supposed to be in here?" He looked over at the door.

"Yeah, Walt, you're acting . . . strange, even for you," Van said.

Walt cleared his throat and made himself speak in a normal tone of voice. "Fine. Stay down here. *I'm* going up. For a *second*." Walt marched over to the stairs, not caring if they followed. Van really got on his nerves. *Too bad the traveling machine didn't just have two helmets.*

Walt twisted around and around as he went up the spirals. Dylan followed him, but Van was standing with her arms crossed. *Would've left your sorry butt back home if I could've.* Walt bit his lip so hard he could taste the tang of blood. Had he really thought of Blackbird Bay as *home*?

At the top, the stairs twisted right through a hole in the floor, just like the shaft. As soon as Walt made it onto the second floor, he stopped short, and Dylan banged right into him.

The windmill's walls had narrowed going up, so the second floor was a little smaller than the first, but it was still a pretty big room, cluttered with tables haphazardly arranged. Boxes and tools and glass containers full of pens and pencils dotted the tables. And tools littered the floor. The room was like an old garage with a bunch of junk strewn everywhere.

And it smelled like an old garage too.

Noise pounded Walt's ears. Loud machinery that probably controlled the sails was spinning and thumping.

Right in the middle of the floor was the source of the glow Walt had seen from downstairs. Walt had no clue what it could be. It reminded him of a nest . . . if a nest could be built of shards of crystal. The crystal glowed softly. The pillar was in the middle of it and continued straight up, right through the roof.

A stream of dust-filled light trailed in through the small window cut high in the wall.

And he could see the sails as they made their slow turn. Walt remembered drawing that window just yesterday. But that wasn't what was twisting his brain. . . .

It was maybe the coolest thing he'd ever seen.

SO MANY STRANGE WORLDS

Everywhere, *everywhere*, there were maps. Tons of them. Covering the curved walls and the small tables. Tossed on the floor in dusty piles. Hanging from the side of the bookcase wall. More maps than Walt had ever imagined.

The sight filled Walt with awe. He took a few steps forward, but it was like walking through sand. The room felt heavy, as if there wasn't quite enough air. He clasped his hands behind his head in a futile effort to get some space in his lungs.

"Whoa," Dylan said, then started sneezing.

Each wispy breath Walt took brought in a mouthful of dust, making him feel like he was eating dirt, and he sneezed a few times too. Which for some reason made both boys laugh, and as they laughed, Walt felt like a hundred pounds of tension flittered out the window.

He didn't know why the voice had told him to come here . . . unless it was just because the voice knew how much he'd appreciate seeing all this. But whose voice was it? And where were they now?

Movement danced right outside his peripheral vision. As hot as it was upstairs, a chill whipped down Walt's neck. He snapped his head to catch whatever was moving. *Oh!* Something was moving on one of the maps.

It was a map a few over from where he stood. Walt watched as a wide river flowed smoothly and soundlessly under a bridge. Walt stepped closer to the map, his legs shaking a little. He studied the river in awe.

"So many strange worlds," Dylan said.

"Strange worlds?" Walt echoed, thinking Dylan was talking about the map Walt had been staring at. "It's not strange, it's—" *Oh.* Dylan was looking at a different map. One that had trees growing upside down and rainbows under the dirt. That *was* strange.

But the one in front of Walt wasn't. He had recognized the location as soon as he'd seen it, even though the map didn't have any writing on it. He and Van had spent last spring break with their auntie Dom. He reached out and let his finger hang in front of the map, almost but not quite touching it. The water that had moved was clearly the East River. The Brooklyn Bridge crossed over it. "New York," Walt said, his voice coming out croaky.

Something glittered on the floor. He bent down to look. Water. He glanced up at the ceiling, expecting to see a leaky hole, but right above them was solid. Had water leaked out of the map?

It was no longer all that odd to Walt for something to move on a map, but stuff coming out of one? That he wasn't prepared for. But was he supposed to see something here? Or do something? If it was Statica's voice . . .

He glanced over his shoulder. There was a row of bookcases on the other side of the crystal nest thing, creating a wall that separated the room in two. What was on the other side? More maps? Better maps? Maybe the source of the voice? He wanted to go see.

Before he could cross the room, Van's head popped through the opening. When she saw all the maps, she said, "Oh, great, I guess we're going to be here all day. So far this world of yours is a big yawnfest."

Walt scowled at her. "It is *not*."

"Yeah?" she asked. "Prove it."

"Fine," Walt said. Whatever was on the other side of the bookcases would have to wait.

Dylan hurried back down the stairs behind Van,

while Walt went down more slowly. Each step felt wrong, but Walt didn't turn back. He definitely wasn't about to let Van make fun of Djaruba.

As the windmill door slammed behind them, Walt warned his sister, "I'm going to make you eat those words. Come on."

He led them back the way they'd come, up a small hill and into tight-fitted trees. Van didn't know what she was talking about, and he *would* prove it. She'd be sorry she'd teased him about his "mushrooms."

It was dark in the trees, and the trunks were covered with odd-colored moss. Dylan laid a hand on a tree trunk and then quickly pulled his hand away. "It feels like it has a heartbeat!" Walt just laughed. After a few more yards, a wall of vines blocked their path, but Walt didn't even hesitate. He just pushed right through, and Van and Dylan followed.

Past the vines, the trees thinned a little, and after a few more minutes they reached a large, tree-encircled field, full of big circular mounds in all different colors. Some were as much as twelve feet across.

"They're like trampolines," Walt said, setting the machine down and hauling himself up on the closest mushroom thing. "I put this in a super long time ago, after I went to a birthday party at Jump Around." He bounced from one top to another, and then on to another.

127

No way could Van resist, and she climbed up, with Dylan close behind.

They jumped from top to top, doing flips, bouncing on their butts and hands, and making each other stumble and fall.

After a while everyone's legs gave out, and they each laid down on a top, catching their breath.

"Okay, bro," Van said. "*This* is actually pretty great."

Walt smiled. Yeah, it was. He stretched his arms wide. Thinking about all those maps. In some other cosmic universe, did he somehow create them? That seemed unlikely. He could see the man in his head. If Statica had created those, then he couldn't be bad like Canter said.

Walt wished he could just meet Statica. Talk to someone else who could do what he could. Who would understand. Another mapmaker. He couldn't just deliver Statica to Canter. Canter was the one who seemed like a bad guy. Maybe that whole destroying-worlds thing was just a trick to get Walt to do what Canter wanted.

All of a sudden, Dylan sat straight up. "Did you guys see that? Something in the trees over there?"

Walt sat up too. "I didn't see anything. Van?"

"Nope," Van said, not bothering to sit up.

"It was right out of the corner of my eye," Dylan said. "When I turned to try and see it, it was gone."

"Probably a bird," Walt said. "Can't have a forest without birds."

"No, it was bigger than that."

"I thought you didn't really see it?" Walt said.

Dylan stared at the trees for a minute and then shrugged.

Walt was glad Dylan wasn't going to mess this up for him. He wanted to see as much of Djaruba as possible and maybe return to the windmill later. "Hey," he said. "There's even better stuff than the mushrooms. I thought a lot about Africa when I was drawing, you know? How it's such a big continent, so there's all sorts of terrains. There are cities, but it was more fun drawing less modern places. Like ancient stuff . . ." He could see he was losing his audience. "But there's a city with flying *skateboards*."

That got Van's attention. "Let's go *there!*" she said, already sliding off her mushroom trampoline. "Is it close? We can have the machine—"

Something moved through the woods, rustling leaves. From the sound of it, it was something big.

"What is that?" Van's head whipped back and forth as she tried to find the source of the noise.

The rustling got louder and was coming toward them. Van yelled at Walt, "What exactly is *in* this world?"

"N-nothing. I mean, I don't know. Nothing," Walt said, sounding scared.

Whatever the sound was, it was getting closer. And then trees seemed to be crashing down. And then suddenly there was silence, and that was somehow worse. What was out there? Was it gone?

Dylan climbed off a springy mushroom and joined Van. He picked up the travel machine. "Time to go back, right?"

Walt slowly joined his sister and Dylan. He couldn't believe they already had to leave. Just because of a *noise*? They had so much to explore.

"Come on, Walt," Van said. "Let's go."

It felt like tears were gathering right behind Walt's nose. "But—"

There was a loud snort somewhere close by.

"Walt!"

"Fine!" Walt said. He grabbed the machine and put on a helmet. Dylan and Van followed suit. "Take us back to Blackbird Bay," Walt said angrily. Nothing happened.

After waiting a minute, Dylan slid his helmet off. "What's wrong with it? Is it broken?"

A smile tugged at Walt's mouth. He didn't have to leave. "Maybe?"

Van held out her hands for the boys' helmets and then started turning the whole contraption around as if she could find a broken piece. "I wonder if—"

A loud squeal cut her off.

"We need to bail!" Dylan cried, and they all started to run.

When they pushed through the hanging vines, they came face-to-face with a large gray creature.

"Ahhhh!" Dylan screamed, and the thing raised its head, roared, and pawed the ground. Two thick horns protruded from its broad head. It seemed like a mis-shapen bull, or maybe a triceratops missing a horn.

Van jumped back and stumbled over an exposed root, and the machine flew from her hands.

Another one of the strange creatures broke through the heavy brush and almost stepped right on a helmet. Its large body stood right over the shiny bundle.

Then the beast lowered its head with a grunt.

"It's gonna charge!" Dylan called out, and turned to flee.

Van and Walt took off after him.

They hadn't gone far when trumpeting roars blasted through the trees and a dozen or more of the beasts came crashing after them.

"Faster!" Van hollered.

They broke through the trees and didn't stop. The sound of pounding hooves was getting closer.

But then they were at the bluff's edge, with no place to go.

IF YOU KNEW ANYTHING ABOUT MAPS

"What now?" Dylan cried.

"Can you swim?" Walt asked him.

"Are you serious?" Van asked, looking down at her long shorts and scuffed-up shoes that were great for skateboarding but probably not so good for swimming.

"Are *you* serious?" Walt retorted, and pointed at the tree line. The scarily misshapen animals emerged from the trees and were heading straight toward them. They looked like a wall of muscle. Of *massive* muscle, with horns.

Dylan asked, "How deep is it?"

"Deep enough!" Walt called out. "On three. One,

two . . ." And as he said, "Three," they all leaped into the air.

They broke the water as one and then all popped back up like corks.

Van shouted, "I have always wanted to do that!"

"Get chased by angry monsters?" Dylan asked, and Van laughed.

Walt treaded in the bracingly cold water and checked to see whether the things that had been chasing them would jump in too, but he could see them up there, stamping their hooves at the edge and blaring angry grunts.

Van dog-paddled over to Dylan and raised her hand for a high five, which wasn't that easy while trying to keep her head above water, but Dylan gave her a half-hearted slap.

"So yeah, that was pretty, um, exhilarating," Dylan said. "Didn't know I'd be taking a swim today. Now what?" He peered down at the water. "Is it safe in *here*?"

The water was crystal clear. Vivid ribbons of red and orange plants twirled and waved, and far below, mossy green stones nestled in the sandy bottom.

"It's deep, but it's just a gentle river here. Let's swim to the other side and figure out what to do next," Walt said, trying to sound like everything was fine.

"Exactly how do you make a river *gentle* on a map?

Isn't it only a squiggly line? Do you write the word *gentle* over it?" Van asked.

"No," Walt said, giving a little snort. "If you knew anything about maps—" He dove under for a second. The water was cold, but it felt great. *If Van would just stop being so irritating* . . . He popped back up. "It's all about the terrain and the slope," he tried to explain.

As they swam, the water was getting even colder, which Walt knew meant it was getting deeper, which could be bad. A lot of things could live in deep water, but he kept his voice calm. "You can add things to slow the current." It was all so obvious to him. "Now, if we were by the falls . . . ," he said, and he seemed to be talking more to the water than to Van or Dylan, "it would be different, that's a pretty big drop. I have to make a lot of white patches to show the rapids, and then the river goes straight—"

"Tell us *all* about it," Van said, cutting him off. She laughed in that teasing, obnoxious way of hers.

Walt scowled at her. Excuse him for trying to *explain.* "Yeah, so, *anyway,* we're not there, we're here."

"Great," Van said, her voice dripping with sarcasm.

"When we get back on firm ground, you can tell me," Dylan said.

Walt smiled at him appreciatively. It was nice having someone on his side. For a moment, Walt stopped worrying about all the bad things that could happen, but then at the halfway point, he saw the tail. *No way.*

"Come on, we gotta go faster," he said, little gulps of air peppering each word.

Dylan groaned as he splashed next to Walt. "Please tell me I didn't see a fin in the water. Tell me you didn't put sharks in here."

"No. No sharks in the river. Come *on.*"

"What's that shadow?" Van asked, and then she made a sound like a dog being stepped on. She stopped swimming and went under water for a second, some of her curls floating on the surface like tiny tentacles. Gulping and splashing frantically, she came back up. "I felt something," she said, breathing hard. "Walt, what is it?"

"Nothing," Walt lied. The shore now seemed miles away. And the current bit and tugged at him.

We got this, Walt repeated in his head over and over. Then, right behind him, a large snakelike head rose out of the water, its mouth wide open, baring a set of gnarly—and sharp—gray teeth. Before Walt could even yell, the monster sank back underwater and then came up again. Right beneath them. Sending Van in one direction, while Walt and Dylan were tossed the other way.

Walt flailed his arms in a fruitless attempt to reach Van, but she got pulled downstream. The creature opened its mouth wide. Walt kicked furiously, and

Dylan followed. A mouthful of sharp teeth bit down, missing them by inches.

The water frothed from the creature's movements, making it harder to swim. Walt's muscles were on fire.

A roar, and snapping teeth were right next to Walt's head. Trying to escape, Walt sank under the water.

Water pulsed in his ears. He opened his eyes and was met with a murky brown blur from all the silt being stirred up. He swam frantically, not sure if he was going up or down or in the right direction. Then his feet scraped the ground. With extreme effort, Walt propelled himself forward. His chest heaved as he pulled at the long grassy weeds on the river's edge. But he couldn't get a good grip. He kept slipping. Panic made his hands useless. He almost screamed when something touched his arm, but it was only Dylan grabbing for him, trying to pull Walt up. Walt scrambled out of the water.

He turned around and was met with a splash that seemed large enough to drain the river. Then the creature's head came up out of the water, and Walt felt like it almost winked a dark empty eye at him as it started to move downstream.

"Van!" Walt stumbled away from the muddy shore. He ran along the river's edge, his T-shirt plastered to his body and his cargo shorts sticking uncomfortably to his legs. "Van!" Water sloshed out of his shoes and all the pockets of his shorts. Dylan ran right behind him, his shoes making loud squelching noises.

For a few seconds, the shadow of the creature moved swiftly under the water next to them, but then it was gone, riding the current much faster than they could run. Walt kept checking the water for signs of Van. It felt like a rope was being tied around his heart, tangling into knots, trying to stop him, but he couldn't stop. He wouldn't stop.

Suddenly, he was facedown on the ground. Dylan tripped right over him. Their wet clothes stuck to them. Walt sat up, spitting dirt from his mouth. He looked back at the rock that had tripped him and wanted to kick it. Shakily he stood, ready to take off again, when he heard her.

"Walt! Walt!" Van's voice was like a hundred fingers struggling at the knots around his heart. He could breathe again.

"Van?" he called out, and then she came around a bend just up ahead, running toward him with a big smile on her face. Her hair was plastered to her head, and her T-shirt and shorts were dark with river water.

"Jeez, am I glad to see you," she said. "I thought that thing had gotten you!"

"I thought the same thing about you," Walt said, wanting to give his sister a hug and also not wanting to make a big deal. She was safe. They were all safe.

Dylan brushed mud and leaves out of his hair. "That

was . . ." He tilted his head one way and then the other. "Uh, *not* fun."

Van put her hands on her hips. "So?" she asked, looking at Walt.

"What?" he said.

"We've had two things trying to kill us so far. Care to explain, *Mapmaker*?"

Walt swallowed a hot lump of guilt. "I drew . . . a . . . a kind of . . . sea serpent?" At the last two words, Walt's voice dropped to an almost inaudible level.

"A what?" Dylan asked.

"A sea serpent," Walt said again. "More like a swimming dinosaur? Like from the Land Before Time movies." It was pretty embarrassing to have something here from a kids' cartoon. "I didn't imagine it quite so . . ."

"Deadly?" Dylan finished for him, and Walt gave him a sheepish smile.

"Fantastic," Van said, and shook her head. "And those things that were chasing us? What are they?"

Walt looked at the ground. "I heard about all the rhinos that were going extinct, so I . . . um . . . added some here?" His voice rose.

"Sorry to tell you, bro, but those were like rabid rhinos," Van said.

"Rhinos on steroids," Dylan added. "They looked

funky. Like, not put together right or something."

"I was eight when I drew them, okay?" Walt said, his face heating with embarrassment. This was not at all how he'd hoped a visit to Djaruba would go.

"And the traveling machine is over there." Van pointed across the river.

"It's broken anyway," Dylan said. "How are we supposed to get home?"

"I'm sorry!" Walt shouted. "I don't know why the machine didn't work. It *should've*. I told it to take us back!"

"I was about to say, back there before those creatures came after us," Van started. "I may know why it didn't work." She faced her brother. "You said Mom called it a machine that would take someone wherever they *wanted* to go, right?"

Walt nodded slowly, seeing right away where she was going.

"Did you actually want to leave?" Van asked suspiciously.

Walt scratched his nose.

Van nodded rapidly, as if he had answered. "The machine knew you didn't want to go. *That's* why it didn't work."

"Wow. Thanks for *that*," Dylan said.

Walt couldn't look at his sister or Dylan. No matter

which way you sliced it, it came down to everything being his fault.

"No big deal," Dylan said, clearly noticing Walt's discomfort. "So you're saying we just have to get back to the other side, grab the machine, and when we . . . I mean *you*"—he bent his head toward Walt—"tell it to take us back, as long as you really want it to, it will." He smiled at Walt.

"How about *I* tell it where to take us?" Van said.

"It's *mine*," Walt argued. "I get to say."

Van frowned at him. "Fine. *If* you actually *want* to get back," she said accusingly.

"I *do* now," Walt said. "Honest." It was mostly true. He didn't want to be *stuck* here. He did want to go back eventually.

They all stared across the water. "Well," Walt said. "We're much farther downstream now. We could swim back over to that side. And climb—"

"Sorry, man," Dylan said. "I'm going to have to take a hard pass on getting back in that water."

Van nodded. "Even if there wasn't a sea *serpent*, we'd have to deal with zombie rhinos."

"They're not zombies!" Walt said, not sure what he was defending.

Dylan held up his hands. "Wait. Are you saying we're trapped here? As in, *forever*?"

"Guess you're happy," Van told Walt, her eyes narrowing.

"What is that supposed to mean?" Walt's jaw clenched. "How am I happy about this?"

"You didn't want to live in Blackbird Bay. I've had to listen to you complain all month." Van ticked Walt's crimes off on her fingers. "You bring us to your world, and now we're *stuck!*" She gave Walt a shove.

"I didn't do this on purpose." Walt shoved Van back, harder than she had shoved him.

Of course she shoved him even harder, and they pushed and shoved each other like that until Dylan stopped them with, "Come on. That doesn't make sense, Van. Walt didn't do this on purpose, and you know it. If we hadn't left the machine over there, we'd already be back home."

Walt was glad Dylan was on his side, even if it meant his sister was now giving them both dagger looks.

Then she tossed her hands up, surrendering. "Fine. But what do we *do?*"

"If only I had brought the map with me," Walt said. "I could just draw a bridge over the water. And erase the rhinos or, like, put them somewhere else." He didn't add that the map would also be safe from a mapmaker getting his hands on it. It was something he had worried about. How easily he had changed things in Blackbird Bay.

Canter and Orsten hadn't said if there were more mapmakers than just Walt and Statica. Someone had made more changes to Blackbird Bay. Had it been Statica? Maybe he had finally figured out where Walt was. Would he go to Walt's house? Find the map of Djaruba? Change things here too? Walt rubbed a hand over his face. None of that made sense. Why would another mapmaker want to change things here?

"Convenient you forgot it," Van mumbled, breaking into his thoughts.

"I don't know, don't you think getting it all wet would've messed this place up?" Dylan asked, slowly threading his invisible basketball ball through his legs. "Could you imagine if it just became a big smear? Maybe that would've killed us!"

As awful as the image was, Walt couldn't help but admire the way Dylan's mind worked. "Exactly! You should be *thanking* me for not bringing the map."

"*Thanks,*" Van said, not sounding a bit grateful.

The twins glared at each other and Dylan shuffled away, still dribbling, looking around as if a magic Exit sign might appear. After a moment, something caught his attention. "Hey!" he exclaimed. "Check these out." He pointed to the ground.

Walt glanced where Dylan was pointing and saw them. Tracks. They were big and made by some type of three-toed (three-*sharp*-toed) creature.

"What would make tracks like that?" Van asked her brother suspiciously.

Dylan knelt down. "Not many animals have three toes. Some birds. But even an emu wouldn't leave tracks this big." He looked up at Van and Walt, who were both looking at him like he was speaking a foreign language. "What? I like knowing about stuff."

"An *emu*?" Van asked.

"I said, *not* an emu," Dylan said. He set his hand next to one of the prints. It was easily more than three times the size of his hand. "Maybe the biggest armadillo in the world? But it seems more bird. . . ." Dylan stood up and stepped away from the print to see it at a better angle. His head tilted in confusion. "I just don't know anything that would leave tracks like these." He looked over at Walt. "What else did you draw?"

Walt knew exactly what had left the tracks, and an idea began to form in his head. "Look, I think I know a way to get back to the machine," he said, slowly, carefully, knowing that he couldn't possibly say what his plan was.

"How?" Van asked.

"If I said, just trust me . . . would you?" Walt asked his sister, and tried to plead with her with his eyes. Remind her of all the times she had asked him to follow where she wanted to go without asking questions.

"And it has something to do with what made these tracks?" Dylan asked.

Walt gave a quick nod but avoided making eye contact.

Van raised her eyebrows, then wiped her hands on her shorts. "Guess we don't have anything to lose."

Walt started following the tracks, hoping Van and Dylan would come with him.

Dylan leaned close to Van. "I don't have a great feeling."

"You and me both, Dylan," Van said, but she followed her brother anyway.

As they walked along, Van picked up a fallen vine and wrapped it around her neck.

"What are you doing?" Dylan asked her.

"When my brother's idea is a bust, we're going to need to build a raft," she said. She tugged on the vine. "This is our rope."

Even Walt had to laugh.

A low buzz of insects filled the air, and every once in a while, Walt got a mouthful of gnat. *Nice.* His T-shirt was starting to dry, but his shorts were still wet. Making it worse was how sticky and thick the air felt.

"Remember when Dad's friend installed a sauna in his house?" Van asked Walt. "It feels just like that here. Hot and steamy."

"I was just thinking the same thing," Walt said.

"Why anyone would waste good money!" he and Van said at the same time in a pretty good imitation of Dad, which made them both laugh. For a minute it felt like old times.

Sometimes it was hard for Walt to believe that this was how it had been between him and Van just a couple of years ago. Kidding around. Hanging out together. Getting along. Before she got taller than him and started ditching him for her skater friends. Well, to be fair, she always asked him to join them, but that wasn't his thing and she knew it. Asking him to join her doing something he didn't want to do was the same as ditching him.

The path took a sharp turn, and then Walt had to stop in amazement because even after seeing those tracks he didn't know if he could believe it, but there it was.

A dragon.

CDRAGONS DON'T EAT PEOPLE

The dragon's scales were a mixture of green, brown, and gold and glistened as if they were wet. Amber eyes appraised them with curiosity, but not, Walt was relieved to see, with any meanness. Its head was large but slender and held proudly on a long neck. Large three-toed talons ended with what looked like *very* sharp claws. Wings dusted the ground, and through them, Walt could see the shadow of armlike bones. It was, Walt noted, exactly as he had drawn it.

Standing next to the dragon was a boy. He looked like he was their age, and tall like Van. Walt noticed *that* right away. His hair was really out there. Some of the Black guys Walt knew tried out some interesting hairstyles, but this guy's hair? It stuck up in five distinct points, with the point in the middle a little taller than the two on either side. Walt couldn't tell if it was supposed to be the beginning of locks or twists or something else. An ornate, too-large tunic brushed the boy's knees, and he looked as shocked to see the threesome as they were to see him.

Walt's eyes went back and forth between the boy and the dragon. He was terrified and excited. A real dragon! Was this the one he'd seen flying on his map?

"Hi," Walt said hesitantly. He hadn't expected a *person* and didn't know how to handle this development. He figured trying to act normally was the best option. Except normal for him meant awkward and shy.

"Where did *you* come from?" the boy asked.

"We are, um, travelers?" Walt said, or more like asked, and seeing the boy's disbelieving expression, he added, "From the other side of the Badlands."

"Walt?" Van nudged her brother, ignoring the boy. "What *exactly* was your plan?"

"We can, um, ride the dragon over the river." Walt tried to whisper, but his voice came out a little too loud.

Dylan grabbed Walt's arm. "*Ride* it? No way! That thing's gonna eat us!"

The boy's laughter echoed around the clearing. "Eat

you? Only if she wanted to get sick. Dragons don't eat people." The way he said it made it sound as if everybody knew that.

"Hah!" Dylan said, but not like he was laughing.

The dragon's wings shuddered, making Walt jump. And then—he probably imagined it— but it seemed as if the dragon smiled at him.

"Afraid?" the boy teased.

"So what?" Van crossed her arms and scowled. "It's a *dragon*."

"Speak for yourself, Van. I'm not afraid," Walt said. He wasn't exactly sure if that was true.

"You want us to take you over the river?" the boy asked. "Why?"

Walt said, "We, uh, left something over there."

And at the same time Dylan said, "It's our way home," and Van said, "What business is it of yours?"

Walt frowned at his sister.

"And home is on the other side of the Badlands?" The boy smirked. "It's *my* business because you want *my* help," he told Van. Then he turned to Walt. "*What did you leave?*"

Walt could tell this boy wasn't going to help them unless Walt told him some of their business. It seemed a little unfair. The dragon seemed like it really should belong to Walt. He had drawn it, after all. But how could he explain that?

Dad always said that telling the truth was easier because you never forgot the truth. "Look," Walt said. "We're from . . . farther away than the Badlands. Like, super far. And there's a device that will get us back to our families." At the word *families,* the boy's expression changed.

He went from proud to sad, his eyes becoming downcast and solemn. "Sounds like you might be just telling stories. A *device* that can take you back to family? Seems incredible . . . as in, not *believable.*"

"But it's true," Walt said. "It's a special thing I . . . made." He didn't know what he would say if the boy started asking hard questions.

"*You* made?" the boy asked. "You some type of magician?"

Walt laughed uncomfortably. "No. That's not what—" He didn't know how to save this. Would it be better if he did say it was magic?

"You believe in that kind of stuff?" Dylan asked, making it sound ridiculous.

The boy stared at them for a long minute. "Okay, I'll take you," he finally said. "Jump on."

Walt inched slowly toward the boy and the dragon. When he was about five feet away, he stopped and cocked his head. "Who are you?"

"The person who just agreed to help some strangers," the boy said at first, but then gave a small smile.

"I'm Fenn, and Heckett is my dragon," he said, sounding defensive. "Who are *you?*"

Walt ignored the question. "And he'll really let us ride him?"

"*She,*" Fenn said and nodded. "They're bred for it. Well, not rides so much as for racing. Heckett's super fast, aren't you, big girl?" Fenn reached up and rubbed right where the dragon's neck met her massive chest. Heckett lowered her head, twisting her neck so Fenn could reach under what Walt figured was a spiky ear. It wouldn't surprise Walt if Heckett dropped to the ground and rolled over so Fenn could rub her belly.

"*You* race?" Van asked, unimpressed with Heckett's doglike antics.

Fenn jammed his hands on his hips. "I said they were bred for racing, didn't I?"

"But do *you* race?" Van prodded.

"Chill out, Van," Walt told his sister. Why was she acting so distrustful? Usually she was ready to make friends with any guy that came along. Fenn hadn't answered, probably because she was annoying him. In a way it was funny. It made sense that a boy that lived in a world Walt had drawn would find Van as annoying as Walt did. But whether that made sense or not, they needed Fenn's help and Van's attitude was getting in the way. "I bet the races are fantastic to see," Walt told Fenn.

"Well . . . ," Fenn started. "Heckett's kind of young for racing, but she'll be a champion one day."

"I bet she's not the only one who's too young to race," Van said quietly, but loud enough to be heard.

"*Van*," Walt said.

Fenn scowled and faced Walt. "Are you coming or not?"

"Not," Van said.

"No one was asking you," Fenn said, not even bothering to turn his head toward Van. "I mean, if you don't *really* need to get across the river, that's fine," he told Walt.

Walt turned to his sister. "Do you have a better idea?"

With an annoyed grunt, Van pushed past Walt and approached Heckett. She put one hand on the side of the dragon and looked up. "How do you get on?"

Fenn smirked at her. "Most people just jump on. But I guess I could give you a boost." He clasped his hands together, holding them as a step.

Van looked at his hands like she might spit on them. "I got it," she said. She took a few steps back, then ran forward and vaulted right onto Heckett's back like the dragon was a pommel horse. Van slipped and almost slid right off the other side. "Whoa!" She righted herself and settled in the middle of Heckett's broad back. The dragon didn't even seem to notice. Van smiled proudly.

"I did it!" Then her eyes caught Fenn's, and her smile slipped. "I mean, it wasn't all that hard. Come on, Walt."

Dylan said, "Surprised you're not the first one up, Walt. It's your world and everything."

Fenn stepped back like he'd been poked. "His what?"

Dylan kicked at the dirt. "Uh, nothing. Forget it."

Walt didn't know how it had happened. Here he was standing on the ground looking up at his sister, who had bested him again. And it was *his* plan. Dylan was right, Walt should've been the first one to get on the dragon. *His* dragon.

Walt chewed on his bottom lip for a second, then stepped closer in order to touch Heckett. Her skin was bumpy and rough. "How . . . how do you stay on? I mean, once she starts flying?"

"Grip her spikes," Fenn said. "They're like handles. It'll be the most fun you've ever had."

Walt looked up at Van.

She met her brother's eyes. "You can't let me die alone. It'd be horrible being a single twin."

"Twins?" Fenn said. "But there's three of you."

Dylan made a sound that sounded like a duck. "Not me! *They're* twins."

"Yep," Walt said, rolling his eyes.

"Got it," Fenn said. Then he bent down a little and laced his hands back together. Walt put one foot squarely in Fenn's hands and hoisted himself up onto Heckett's back, right in front of Van.

Just below the surface of Heckett's scales, Walt could feel a steady pulse, like a rush of pounding water. It was like the dragon's massive muscles were in continuous motion.

Van patted him on the back. "Cool, right?"

Cool didn't even come close to describing it. Walt's eyes caught Dylan's. "Come on, Dylan," he said.

Dylan said, "Never thought asking someone to get a Slurpee would lead to dragon riding." He took a deep breath and, with a hoist from Fenn, scrambled up behind Van. "Oh, wow," he said as he settled himself on the dragon's back.

Fenn looked up at them and said, "Walt, Van, Dylan. Got it." He hitched up his tunic and bounded on easily, sitting in front of Walt, right behind Heckett's head, and grinned back at them. Then he gave Heckett a slight rub on her neck, and she responded by immediately spreading her wings. With a big push against the ground, she began to rise into the air. "Hold on, everyone!" Fenn shouted.

Heckett rose slowly, straight up from the ground like a large curtain rising from a stage floor. Walt didn't see how it could be possible for her to move like that, but since he had never actually seen a real, live (and for all he knew, fire-breathing) dragon, he didn't know how they would fly or anything else about them. She was making small adjustments in her wings—they spread out at least twelve feet on both sides—which seemed to control how quickly she rose up into the air. When they had cleared the trees, she tilted her wings and, with a movement that looked almost like a matador shedding their cape, she drew back her shoulders, lifted her head, and took off.

Van's arms tightened around Walt's waist, and she exhaled sharply. Walt wasn't comfortable gripping Fenn like that—he had just met the guy—but he did grip Heckett's spikes more firmly and squeezed his legs in as best as he could. He turned around to get a glimpse of Dylan. Dylan looked like he was trying to decide which would be worse, grabbing on to Van or risk falling off the dragon. Walt smiled and turned back around.

The view from the dragon was thrilling. They could see so much. The glistening purple water of Inca Bay, the massive Galaia Falls, and far in the distance were the snow-tipped peaks of the Nato Range.

Then something below him caught his eye. "Hey," Walt said, prodding Fenn. "What is that?"

Fenn turned Heckett and had her hover over what seemed to be the remnants of a small town. It was odd. It looked almost like a collapsed movie set. Or rather the *ghost* of a collapsed movie set. "That used to be Harwood," Fenn said. "No one knows what happened to it."

Walt's stomach felt like it had squeezed up into his throat, and he momentarily lost his grip on Heckett. Walt knew what had happened to the town. It had only taken him three seconds. He felt like he might throw up and, without thinking, let go of Heckett. He immediately started to slide sideways.

"Walt!" Van cried, grabbing the back of his shirt to try and stop his slide. But instead she slipped right after him.

"Hold on!" Fenn called out.

Walt was trying, but he couldn't grip anything.

Dylan shouted in panic, but then Walt felt Heckett shift underneath him, tilting enough that he and Van stopped their dangerous slide. Both managed to right themselves.

Fenn glanced over his shoulder and grinned at them. "Heckett's not about to lose a passenger."

"Thanks," Walt said breathlessly, patting the dragon's back. She quivered in appreciation. He looked back down at the remnants of Harwood.

"Did people live there?" Walt asked in a raspy voice. He couldn't help thinking about Canter saying how awful mapmakers were.

Fenn shook his head, and the relief that washed

over Walt almost made him lose his grip again. Erasing the town had felt good. It had made him feel strong. He remembered being annoyed that he could still see the faint lines on the map. He had wanted it completely gone. And he had gotten close to what he'd wanted. But what if *people* had lived there?

"It was deserted," Fenn said.

Maybe it was just being so high up, but what was left of the town looked like a mirage to Walt, as if what was left of the buildings was a shimmering illusion. "I didn't . . ."

"Didn't what?" Fenn asked.

Walt couldn't answer. He wondered if he redrew it when they got back, if people would be there. Maybe if he thought hard enough. "Nothing," he said softly.

Fenn looked at Walt over his shoulder. Examined him like he was something strange and a bit frightening before he shrugged and faced forward again. "All right, across the river we go."

The thought of the machine didn't make Walt feel any better. What if Van was wrong? What if it didn't work? Walt was torn. Even with sea serpents and poorly drawn rhinos, Djaruba was fantastic. So much better than anywhere else. And going back meant football camp and feeling small and lousy. So it was almost too soon when he saw the familiar bends of the Sentry

River below them. As they started to lower, he could see the glint of the shiny helmets. It was a relief that the machine was still there.

"Uh-oh," Fenn said.

"What?" Walt asked, but then he saw it too. What had at first seemed like just a shadow, spread mangy wings and flew to the machine. Then several more of the odd-looking creatures flew down from trees and tried to get the machine from the first one. And then more came.

"Bazzards," Fenn said. "Looks like a whole volt of them. They'll go after anything shiny. That's the device you made? What *is* it?"

Walt's forehead was covered in sweat and he felt a little dizzy. Volt? Bazzards? He'd never heard of either of those things and certainly hadn't drawn them. Something Orsten had said came back to him. Worlds couldn't be controlled once life was breathed into them. Just their luck Djaruba had brought *this* funky life into being.

They were close enough now for him to see that they looked like a cross between bats and turkey vultures. Except uglier. They had slick white feathers over their shoulders, but their heads were dark gray, hairless, and covered with loose wrinkly skin. And at the tips of their wings they had a couple of . . . *fingers?* There were now so many of them he could barely see the traveling machine.

"Get away from that!" Van shouted at them, but the bazzards ignored her.

Heckett landed with a loud thump, and even that didn't distract the creatures. They just made a racket of screeching at each other until one of them clamped its long beak on some of the cords of the machine and started to rise up into the air.

"No!" Walt cried, sliding off Heckett.

"Walt, wait! Let us help!" Van called out, but Walt raced toward the bazzards, and suddenly he was surrounded by beating wings and grabbing fingers.

"Ack!" He swung his arms around, trying to get the things off him. But it was useless. He couldn't escape. They pulled at his hair and clothes. Walt couldn't even see. Suddenly he felt a strong wind, and an arm grabbed him, pulling him free.

"Gotchu!" Dylan said.

Heckett stopped beating her mighty wings, and Walt had just a second of relief before watching in horror as the bazzards took off, flying away . . . with the machine.

SWALLOWED BY A VOLCANO

"We have to get it from them!" Walt yelled, running after the bazzards and waving his hands like they were seagulls stealing his lunch.

"Come back!" Fenn shouted. "We'll go after them."

Walt ran back to Heckett, and he, Van, and Dylan all jumped onto the dragon's back. She made little yippy noises like she was excited to start the chase, and once everyone was settled, Heckett lifted straight up from the ground.

Fenn hollered over his shoulder, "Hold on!"

Heckett turned sharply and they streaked across the sky.

In the distance was a large gray shape that looked like a dirty cloud, and it took Walt a moment to realize it was the swarm—no, what had Fenn called it? It was the *volt* of bazzards.

"There!" Walt cried, pointing over Fenn's shoulder and almost sliding right off Heckett. He quickly regained his grip.

"We see them," Fenn said, and bent low again on Heckett, but Heckett had seen the volt too and was already adjusting in order to follow the bazzards.

Looming in front of them was the massive Mount Yoray. Walt got a bad feeling, and just as he feared, the volt dove right into the mouth of the volcano.

Fenn looked back at Walt, and Walt gave a nervous quick nod.

"Okay, then," Fenn said and turned around, urging Heckett on.

At the lip of the volcano, Heckett didn't even pause. She whipped right down into the darkness.

The smell was overwhelming. Rotten eggs and something acidic like vinegar. It was dark except for a faint glow of rocks embedded in the walls. The sound of the bazzards' wings and squawks echoed and grew, surrounding them in a thick cloud of noise.

And as they went lower and lower, Walt started to think his decision to have a volcano in Djaruba might have been a big mistake. Especially since he didn't actually know all that much about volcanos. How often did they erupt? And just how far down could they go?

He got his answer almost immediately, when Heckett landed hard on a narrow shelf. She dug her talons into the edge, and Walt's breath sank to his ankles as rocks crumbled off the side and plummeted down into darkness. His hands were sweaty, and it didn't seem like there was anything keeping him from sliding right off Heckett's back.

"It's gotten too narrow for her wings," Fenn shouted over the noise of the bazzards. "I mean, I could have her dive, but we might never get back up again."

"Definitely don't have her dive," Walt said.

Bazzards flew up and down and around them, almost like they were teasing them. They called out to each other in shrieks and whistles.

"Can anyone see the one that got the traveling machine?" Dylan yelled.

"There! There!" Van shouted, pointing up.

Walt scanned the air, thick with the large white creatures, and finally found the bazzard Van was pointing at. It was settled on a small outcrop and tossing the machine up in the air and opening its mouth, as if it was food it wanted to swallow.

"I think I can climb up there," Van said, already

sliding from Heckett's back to the rocky wall. "I've seen people bouldering and stuff."

"No way!" Walt yelled. "You'll fall!" He looked below them and then back up.

"I can do it!" Van was already a few feet up. Walt was torn between wanting to yank his sister back down and hoping she could actually climb high enough to grab the machine.

"You'll never get it," Fenn said. "I better do it." He moved off Heckett and started climbing. The way he maneuvered up the wall, it was apparent he had done stuff like that before.

Dylan leaned close to Walt. "How is this a good idea?"

"It's not," Walt said. It was hurting his neck looking up at Van and Fenn. If only he could get Heckett to fly back up somehow. "Hey, girl," he said. "Go get the shiny machine." He squeezed his legs in, as if he was riding a horse, but Heckett just gave Walt a narrow look. She wasn't going anywhere. Walt went back to anxiously watching Van and Fenn.

The bazzard biting at the machine lost it to another one, and Van tried to shift to go after the new target. It was like the bazzards were playing keep-away.

Van's face was covered in sweat. "Walt, this thing isn't going to erupt or anything, right?" she shouted down to him.

"Why are you asking me? I'm not psychic!" Walt yelled.

Van was just about close enough to touch the bazzard that now had the machine. "Okay, ugly birdy," she said in a singsong voice. "Just stay right there." She reached out and the bazzard croaked, letting the machine drop from its mouth. But before it fell far, another of the pale creatures caught it, spread its wings, and flew up past them and into a yawning crevice. Dozens of bazzards followed right behind, screaming and squawking.

"No!" Walt cried out.

"Don't worry," Van hollered back, and climbed up and disappeared into the opening. Fenn followed right behind her.

The sound of the bazzards got more and more distant until there was only silence. Walt stared up, waiting for his sister and Fenn to reappear.

"So, uh, we just wait here?" Dylan asked.

Walt didn't see what choice they had, but then Dylan climbed off Heckett's back. "They might need our help."

Walt knew Dylan was right, but the idea of trying to scale the inside of the volcano made his teeth hurt. Slowly he got off Heckett and dug his fingers into tiny nooks in the wall.

A few minutes later, Walt was high enough to realize

this had probably been a *very* bad idea. Heckett was far below, still clinging to the edge of the jutting-out ridge of rock. And the shaft was getting hot. Like *way* hot.

Walt's hands were slick with sweat and one slipped off his hold, making him wheeze with the effort of trying not to fall. Dylan was struggling too.

Walt found another place to grab. His legs were starting to burn and shake and his eyes felt like they were dried-up cotton balls. Somehow he managed to force himself to keep climbing. Dylan seemed frozen. "Come on," Walt told him. "Just one grip at a time." Dylan gave a quick nod and started up again.

With relief, Walt managed to climb the last several feet and reach the hole in the wall. It was pitch-black inside and he could hear echoing squawks. He offered his hand to Dylan and pulled him up into the large crack in the wall. Then he turned and squeezed along the tight tunnel. After a few feet, it was too dark to see anything. Walt could hear Dylan close behind him, but he couldn't hear Fenn or Van. The hole narrowed, and Walt dropped to his hands and knees and started to crawl. It seemed like the ground was going down. And it was getting really hot.

"I made a volcano for my third-grade science project," Dylan said, his voice coming out in breathless huffs.

"Yeah?" Walt asked.

"This might be a branch pipe," Dylan said.

"Thanks for that information," Walt said.

"Anytime," Dylan said.

Walt heard something in front of them. "Van?" he called. "Is that you?" But nothing answered back. "Van!" he called again. Still she didn't answer. Walt went another few feet, and then placed a hand down on nothing but air, and before he could stop, he was falling.

He tried to call out a warning to Dylan, but the words were ripped right out of his mouth, and by the yelling he heard behind him, Dylan was falling too.

Rocks and stone bit into Walt's skin and scraped his arms. He tried to grab hold of something, anything, but his hands just slid across the razor-sharp rock. The surface was like a grater, slicing into Walt's hands. With a thump, he hit something solid.

"Oof!" Van said. "Get off!"

Then Dylan crashed into them both.

"Ow!" Walt felt as if he had been tumbled in a clothes dryer—one with a jagged sharp interior. Slowly he got up and brushed himself off. His hands were bloody and his T-shirt was ripped. It was horribly hot and Walt could see why. Far below them—and it was darn lucky Van had stopped his fall—was what looked like a magma river. The fiery ribbon lit up the tight space in an orange-hued glow. Fenn stood nearby, rubbing his hip, so Walt figured he must've fallen hard too. "Where are the bazzards?" Walt asked.

Without a word, Fenn nodded up at a small hole that was several feet above the hole they'd fallen from. "They crawled in there," Fenn said. As if to prove it, a pale feather floated out of the hole.

"That there is the opening to a parasitic cone," Dylan said. "They maybe can get out that way?"

Van stared at him for a second. "That's super helpful, Dylan."

"I'm doubting your sincerity," Dylan said.

"I guess this is where they live." Walt pointed at the ground, which was covered with splotches of bird poop. "Among other things."

Dylan hopped to his feet. "Ugh! Gross!" He tried to wipe off the bird poop that was on his shirt but just managed to smear it.

"Just guano," Van said with a smirk.

Then the ground lurched and they all toppled to the ground.

"Not good," Dylan said, slowly getting to his feet after the shaking stopped. "I think that means this baby is going to blow."

"Like in a minute, or like in several days?" Van asked.

"I'm not exactly sure, but—" The ground shook again, slicing off Dylan's words. "I'm guessing less than several days."

"Let's get out of here," Fenn said.

"We still have to get the machine! It's our only way back," Walt cried.

"Okay," Dylan said. "Let's do it one step at a time. We all climb back up. Someone goes to that opening. Grabs—" The ground shook, cutting off his words. "We get out fast! That's all the steps. Come on!" His words echoed around, and then, as if it was adding an exclamation point, a fiery ball shot from the river below.

They all dashed to the wall and started the climb up, but Walt kept slipping. His hands were so scraped, it was too hard to catch hold.

"I can't do it!" he called up to Van, Dylan, and Fenn, who had already reached the hole they'd all fallen out of.

"Come *on*, Walt! You *can* do it!" Van shouted down.

The river started belching molten rock.

Walt gripped the wall again and got up only a couple feet before the pain in his hands forced him to stop. Back where he started, he wiped his hands on his shorts and looked up at his sister. He wanted to cry.

Then the earth shook so hard, Walt almost slipped off the edge and down into the lava.

Fenn started back down. Halfway, he began to fall,

and Walt caught him before he went over the side.

"What are you *doing?*" Walt asked.

"Saving you," Fenn said. He ripped off a long piece from the bottom of his tunic. "Hold out your hands!" he yelled at Walt, and Walt did what he was told. Fenn started winding material around Walt's hands, creating thick bandages.

"Hurry!" Dylan called out to them.

Walt and Fenn raced to the wall and started climbing. Walt's hands still hurt and he grimaced through each handhold, but the bandages allowed him to keep going. When he was high enough, Van grabbed his wrists and pulled him up the rest of the way, and they collapsed onto each other.

"Now what?" Walt asked.

Dylan started coughing. "We don't have much time."

Without saying a word, Fenn climbed up, but when he reached the small opening the bazzards had disappeared into, he couldn't get his shoulders through. "I can't squeeze in," he said.

"You can!" Walt shouted. "Just twist . . ." His voice trailed off. It was obvious Fenn was too big.

Fenn climbed back down. "How important is that thing?"

In answer, Van said, "I'll try."

"You can't, Van," Walt told her. "You won't fit

either." He knew what he had to do. Was there *any-thing* good about being small? He took a deep unsteady breath. "I . . . I'll do it."

Van nodded at him. "Be quick!"

Fenn gave Walt a boost, and he started to climb. The air was now so steamy and thick Walt felt like he was eating ash.

Again, Mount Yoray trembled.

"Walt!" Van screamed. "It's going to erupt! Just leave it. We'll figure something else out."

Except there isn't *something else.* Walt's hands ached and his legs did not want to cooperate and he wished he could just stop, but knew he couldn't. "Come *on!*" he whispered to himself. He made the mistake of looking below and saw the lava gurgling and sending up bubbles of liquid fire. *Okay, no more looking down.*

He reached the hole and got his head and shoulders in. Even for Walt it was tight, but somehow he managed to squash the rest of himself in. After only a foot or two, he found himself in a pitch-black tunnel. And another foot later, feathers and beaks and fingers started to poke at him. He thought he might pee himself. He swatted a hand around trying to find the machine. From what seemed like very far away, he could hear Van screaming. Was he too late?

He inched forward. The walls of the tunnel felt like

they were squeezing him, like they were *swallowing* him. Something bit him hard on the cheek. He tried to hit it, but instead his hand smacked into something soft. The traveling machine! He grabbed it and could tell a bazzard was fighting him for it, but no way was a bird going to steal his way home. Yanking as hard as he could, he tugged and tugged and finally got it free.

Now all he had to do was go out the way he came. There wasn't room enough to turn around, so he backed up, moving as fast as he could because Van's screams were getting louder. Were they being burned alive?

The walls were sharp and scratched his sides and it seemed like the hole had somehow gotten smaller, because Walt couldn't move for a second. But finally he got loose and kept crawling backward. He could make out Van's screams now, and he realized she was just screaming his name over and over.

When he emerged from the hole holding the traveling machine, Dylan hollered, "Hurry! Hurry!"

Walt was so sore. He felt like he'd been stepped on by a giant. How was he going to make it back down?

"Walter Anderson, move your butt!" Van cried.

The lava had gone from gurgling to boiling. Walt grasped the side of the wall and started down, and when his feet touched the ground he wanted to cry.

"We're not safe yet!" Fenn yelled, and they went

into the other opening.

When they got back to where they'd started, Heckett let out a relieved snort. It was so smoky, it was hard to see her except for her glowing eyes. Far below her, it was like a big bowl was being filled with magma as shoots and crevices oozed the liquid rock, and it seeped down the walls.

"I don't know if we can make it out in time," Dylan said, his voice shrill and panicked.

They started down to Heckett, but it was harder going down than it had been to climb up, especially when they were all coughing and choking. Walt's eyes burned and tears streamed down his face. He felt like he was never going to get out of this dark, hot pit. Not alive anyway.

Van and Dylan reached the small ridge first and scrambled onto the dragon's back. Heckett looked up at Fenn with a worried frown.

"I'm coming, Heck!" Fenn called down to her.

Walt's palms burned with pain and his fingertips were so sweaty. Every part of his body was tense and aching, like he'd been in a fight. Heckett was still so far down, and the bowl of lava was getting higher and higher.

Walt knew he was about to be burned alive.

Mount Yoray trembled and roared, and then it threw

Walt and Fenn right off its side. The boys plummeted down. There was nothing to grab. Smoky air whipped around them, and a huge whooshing was coming up from below.

CARE AND FEEDING
OF DRAGONS

Walt let out a terrified scream before landing right on Heckett's back.

"I got you!" Van said, wrapping her arms around her brother.

"Get us out, Heck!" Fenn cried, who was clutching Heckett's neck, his legs dangling.

Walt dug his aching hands into a ridge between Heckett's scales. She'd saved them. Flying up and giving him and Fenn a place to land, instead of falling to their death. "Good girl," he whispered, petting her like she was a dog.

Heckett exploded out of the volcano as if *she* was a

jet of lava, flying straight up as if she wanted to pierce the sky.

"Whoa, look!" Dylan cried, pointing down at the volcano. Steam flowed out like the volcano was a teapot.

Big chunks of rock flew up in the air, and Heckett kept climbing, getting them out of danger, her powerful wings swooping up and back.

Then there was a thunderous roar, and lava shot into the sky. What looked like deep orange-and-black rivers of fire ran down the sides of Mount Yoray.

Now that they weren't about to be burned by it, it actually was very cool to see. Mount Yoray belched another spray of lava before quieting back to sleep. Plumes of ash filled the air, and Heckett turned and flew high and away.

After a few minutes, Fenn soothed her to a slow glide, and they all let out a collective sigh. Even Heckett.

"That was *intense*," Dylan said.

"You can say that again," Van agreed. Then she leaned into her brother's back. "Way to go, shorty."

Maybe it was because it was the first time that being small had actually been an advantage, or maybe it was just the relief of escaping that fiery pit, but instead of getting annoyed, Walt couldn't help giggling, and then he couldn't stop. And that got Van and Dylan going. Even Fenn started to chuckle.

If it wasn't for the pain he felt pretty much all over, Walt could almost imagine that their ordeal hadn't happened. A soft breeze blew down his back, and the air around him was fresh and clear. He took a heaving breath. Heckett was gliding more than flying, reminding Walt of how he'd seen birds simply enjoying where the wind blew them. He didn't want this to end. Now that they were safe, it seemed as if the adventure was just starting.

"This is absolutely incredible," Dylan said happily.

"Yeah, it is," Van agreed.

"Those bazzards won't come after us, will they?" Walt couldn't help asking. His arm squeezed the helmets and cords protectively close to his body. If the bazzards did come, they'd have a tough time getting the machine again.

"I don't think so," Fenn said. "They're probably too busy trying to find a better roosting spot."

"Did you really have to make an active volcano, bro?" Van teased.

Without thinking, Walt said, "It was supposed to be dormant!"

"What do you mean?" Fenn asked. *"Made* it?"

"She just means . . ." Walt tried to think of something. The idea of being a mapmaker was still so new that it was hard to remember that it was bad and a secret.

"I thought you said dragons were bred for racing," Van cut in, changing the subject. "This is pretty slow."

It was an obvious challenge, and Fenn took it. "I'll show you fast," he said. Then he twisted back to look at Walt. "You may want to strap that on somehow." He nodded at the machine tucked under Walt's arm.

They were going slow enough that Walt risked letting go of Heckett to wrap the twisted cords of the machine around his waist. He pulled the cords tight and let out a deep sigh. The sun warmed his back, and the view below was better than he could've imagined. And the thought came into his head that maybe he should just stay here. Riding dragons every day and never once having to worry about football . . .

"Ready?" Fenn asked.

"Absolutely," Walt answered with a smile.

Fenn gave Heckett some type of signal, and suddenly she was rising higher in the sky, moving her wings behind her. "Bend low and hold on as best you can," Fenn called out, and then, almost before he had finished the warning, they were bulleting across the sky. The wind blew Walt's skin back like a bowstring, and his eyes poured out tears. His heart felt like it might explode from his chest. It was awesome.

Van trembled behind him. "You all right?" he yelled to her, his words whipping off into the wind.

Van gave him a squeeze for an answer and then laughed. "*So* all right!" she called out.

They jetted through the air and the ground below them flew by in a blur. Blue fields turned into copper seas, and multicolored trees gave way to barren puce desert.

Walt couldn't tear his eyes away from the constantly changing landscape. He really had done a pretty amazing job. He was glad that in all the vastness of Djaruba, the machine had taken him to this part. Flying skateboards and skyscrapers were cool, but this was where he wanted to be. Nothing beat dragons.

Right below them, a huge black triangle reflected the sun. "Zezi pyramid," he said, breathlessly. It was one thing to draw a pyramid with black crayon (to make sure it was nice and shiny—he had imagined it being made of pure obsidian), but to actually see it, pointing to the sky like the Washington Monument? Wild—in the best possible way.

In a moment, they were flying over the Yante Mountains, dipping hard into the valleys and canyons and rising up to the highest peaks, seemingly without any effort. "This is part of the course!" Fenn shouted.

Heckett had obviously flown the course many times, because she whipped through narrow openings and ducked under rocky bridge formations with no hesitation while Fenn urged her to go faster.

Some of the cols were so narrow, Walt held his breath, trying to make himself smaller, as if that would help them make it through. But no matter how many times he thought Heckett would surely clip her wings on the rocky side of a mountain, the dragon adjusted and tilted and slipped through. Ahead of them, Walt could hear the roar of a waterfall, and before he knew it, Heckett flew right through the thundering spray.

"Flipping fantastic!" Dylan cried, his soaked hair plastered to his head.

Heckett followed the path of a winding river, and the sun and air worked together to dry them.

"We're almost to the finish line," Fenn yelled. "Hold on!"

Walt could see flags waving in the distance and an enormous grandstand. His mouth started to water at the booths of food that were sure to be there. But as they got closer, he could see that the grandstand was empty, and although there were colorful kiosks, they were empty too. No fans. No vendors. It made sense, he supposed. It hadn't been an actual race, so it wasn't like fans should've been there—but still, it seemed like it wouldn't be *totally* deserted. Wasn't there like a groundskeeper or something? It suddenly occurred to him that so far Fenn had been the only person they'd seen.

Heckett landed with a whoosh. A big cloud of dust made it hard to see for a moment, and they all slid off her back, coughing and wiping their eyes.

As soon as she was free of her riders, Heckett rolled over onto her back, wiggling like a cat in the sun.

They all stomped around a bit, trying to get their legs to work properly again.

"Dragon legs," Fenn said and chuckled, but then he sighed. "That was a winning time for sure," he said wistfully. "Usually after the races are done and the celebrating has calmed down, the riders stand on the backs of their dragons and fly slow over the crowd." He crouched a little and spread his arms and rocked from side to side.

Walt figured it must be a bit like surfing. It sounded like it would be incredible to see, and even better to do. "Sounds so cool," he said.

"Yeah, too bad there's no riders here," Van said, as an obvious knock against Fenn.

Walt wished she'd quit it. The guy had saved them . . . twice! It was irritating that Van still acted like Fenn was poop she'd stepped in.

Dylan scratched his head. "Why *is* it so . . . um . . . unpopulated here?" he asked Walt.

Fenn answered as if Dylan had asked him the question. "Our town always got a bunch of dragon riders for the tournaments, and they would come into our shop for their boots and gloves and kaleids . . ." Fenn got a faraway look.

"What're kaleids?" Van asked but Fenn didn't seem to hear her.

"But now . . ." Fenn shook his head, shaking away the memory. "It's all changed. They're all gone. It shouldn't have—" He cut himself off and stared either angrily or sadly away from them—it was hard to tell which emotion was making his chin hard and his eyes sharp.

Walt worried he had done something to cause this. He had never pictured a boy living alone in this world. Well . . . that wasn't entirely true. Plenty of times he'd imagined *himself* escaping to Djaruba. Away from Dad. Or not Dad so much as the idea of not measuring up. But had he somehow made people disappear? It made his head hurt.

The idea of being in a world that was a map he'd created was already incredible. Did he create the people? Did he *uncreate* the people? Guilt crawled over Walt like hungry ants. If there used to be people and now there weren't, it *must've* been something he did. Or . . . maybe another mapmaker? He felt something. Like a small push in the air. Was that Statica? Walt shivered.

"Everyone?" Dylan asked Fenn. He looked all around, as if maybe there were some people hiding from them. "Your parents and . . ." Dylan's voice drained away, making it clear they didn't know anything about

Fenn. Whether he had a family or had just been born out of an egg like a chicken.

A baying sounded in the distance. Heckett's head perked up, and she made an answering yelp. Fenn's eyes widened. "Blam, I haven't fed them today."

"Fed what?" Van asked.

"The *dragons*," Fenn answered.

"Oh, obviously," Van said sarcastically.

Fenn started to walk away, and Heckett got up and bounded after him. "Come on," Fenn said, beckoning for them to follow.

Heckett looked back too, and her eyes seemed to say, "Let's go!"

"Unless you're leaving?" Fenn asked when they didn't follow right away.

Walt couldn't miss the worried tone in Fenn's voice, and he sure didn't want to miss seeing more dragons. "Not yet, right?" he asked Van and Dylan, and they must've felt like he did, because they both fell in line behind Fenn and Heckett.

Behind the grandstand, there was a very large, tall wooden building. And as they got closer, the baying got louder. Heckett was almost skipping with excitement.

Fenn slid the door open with a flourish, and Walt realized it was a stable. A *dragon* stable.

Huge stalls were on both sides of the room, and dragon heads poked out of some of them. The fronts of the stalls were draped with flags in various bright colors, and Walt knew each one represented a different team.

Although Walt had imagined dragon races, he hadn't thought much past the races themselves. He hadn't considered the care and *feeding* of dragons.

Heckett ran up and down the wide aisle, sticking her nose into stalls and making little yelps of pleasure. The other dragons seemed much bigger than she was, and not nearly as excited to see her as she was to see them.

"Heckett hasn't figured out the whole competition thing yet," Fenn said, and chuckled. "She wants to play, but they want to race. And they're fine in here, but out on the course? They sure will bump into other dragons hard enough to make them crash into a wall. Heckett!" he called out, snapping his fingers. She immediately stopped her eager sniffing and came over to Fenn. Her tail hung low to the floor. "Relax," he told her, and she looked at him reproachfully.

Fenn rubbed her throat as he continued explaining. "All the riders were in town getting ready for the Derby Royale, when everything . . . happened," he said. "So I feed their dragons until they get back. Heckett and I collected lots of aanarie leaves for them." He went over to a stack of leaves that were as big as elephant ears and started dragging them to the stalls. He looked over at Walt, Dylan, and Van. "You could help, you know."

They all got busy pulling the heavy leaves over to stalls, with Heckett going back and forth too, as if she was making sure they did the job correctly. After there was a sizable stack in front of each dragon, Fenn signaled that the piles were large enough. "The best way to get a dragon to trust you is to hand-feed them." He picked up one of the leaves and held it out to a gray-and-blue dragon whose head was covered with spikes. Its yellow eyes looked at Fenn for a moment, and then it opened its mouth. Walt held his breath, wondering if they were about to see Fenn get munched up.

The dragon took the leaf in one bite, swallowed, and then opened its mouth for more, which Fenn quickly offered.

Walt considered the dragon next to him. Its eyes were the same deep magenta as one of the colors in the flag on the stall door, and its scales were a mix of red and orange. It leaned forward and nudged him with a long snout, and Walt jumped and got out of prodding distance. "Okay, boy, er . . . girl? Okay, I got you." With shaking hands, he picked up a leaf and held it out to the dragon.

"You're gonna have to get closer," Fenn called out.

Walt looked down at his feet. Then he looked over at

Van, who was laughing and feeding leaves to a large red-and-green dragon. "It's a Christmas one!" she yelled. "I'm going to call it Holly." Even Dylan had found the nerve to feed a smaller brown dragon. With each bite the dragon took, its brown coloring became shinier until it looked like bronze.

Fenn had already moved on to another dragon, and Walt's dragon was looking at him impatiently. Walt took a step forward with the leaf, and the dragon happily sucked it right out of his hands like a vacuum.

Fenn came over holding something that looked like a big purple watermelon. "If you really want to make friends with a dragon, feed them one of these. It's a gropberry." He handed it to Walt and Walt almost dropped it, not expecting it to be so heavy. "This is a *berry*?" he asked. "The bush that grows them must be enormous!"

Fenn laughed. "Yep." Then he nodded at the dragon, who was staring at the berry longingly. "Go ahead."

The berry was too heavy to hand out like he had the leaf, and Walt knew he'd have to get even closer. What if the dragon bit off his hands? "Uh, it won't, um, bite me?" he asked Fenn.

"I told you, dragons don't eat people," Fenn said. "Don't they know anything where you're from?" He shook his head. "I'll figure out how to give you some exercise soon," he told the dragons.

Walt took a deep breath and then stepped close enough to the dragon's large head to hand it the gropberry. Gingerly, as if the dragon knew Walt was scared, it gently took the berry from him. As soon as the dragon crunched the berry in its mouth, a huge stink filled the air. Purple goo dribbled from the dragon's mouth.

"Ew," Walt cried. "What's that stench?"

"Is that what dragon farts smell like?" Dylan asked, holding his nose.

Fenn chuckled. "I should've warned you. Dragons love 'em, but there's no worse stink than gropberry juice. You definitely don't want to feed them too many, or it makes cleaning out their stalls really nasty." He sighed. "Speaking of which . . ."

"No way!" Van said. "You have to muck these out?"

"Well, today I think *we* have to muck them out," Fenn said with a grin. "The rakes and shovels are this way."

They followed him to a storage room that had plenty of tools and things that Walt figured must have something to do with dragon maintenance. There were also lots of posters on the walls, announcing races or advertising special dragon feed. One poster made Walt's heart thump so hard he was certain Fenn would hear.

NOT OKAY

It was like those outlaw posters they had in old West-erns.

WANTED was printed in big bold letters. And underneath, in even bigger letters, it said REWARD. And underneath *that*, there was a rough-drawn sketch. It wasn't clear if the person who had drawn it was actually trying to obscure the face, or if the artist had never seen him. But what was very clear was the word underneath the picture. *Mapmaker.*

Bad drawing or not, Walt knew he had seen that face before. In his dreams.

Van followed Walt's gaze and said, "Oh!" like she'd been poked.

"What?" Fenn said. "You know something about him?"

"Naw," Van said too quickly.

Dylan made an odd huffing sound. Like he was trying—and failing—to laugh. "Sort of wild that you could get a reward for finding someone who, uh . . ." He glanced over at Walt. "Makes maps?"

"Yeah," Fenn said. "Wild." He handed everyone tools.

Walt felt like he was under water, struggling to get back to air. "What exactly—" he started, but his voice cracked and he had to clear his throat before continuing. "*Why* is there a reward out for him?"

Fenn shrugged. "What I heard is he thought every world was his," Fenn said. "*Every* one. Whether he created them or not."

"*Created* worlds?" Dylan squeaked.

Fenn rolled his eyes. "Don't you know anything? He's a *map*maker." Fenn sucked his teeth.

"Is that . . . not . . ." Van glanced at Walt sideways. "Not okay?"

"Nope," Fenn said, in a tone that implied he was done with the topic. "Come on, let's muck out some stalls."

Walt felt like he was sinking even deeper. And like the water was thick and nasty. He stared at the poster, trying to see if he could feel Statica out there somewhere.

It was annoying that even here in this world—in *Walt's* world—he couldn't get away from hearing how awful mapmakers were. If he could only know for sure. What would Statica say if Walt could talk to him? It sure seemed like Canter was the person to watch out for. Orsten seemed okay, but what if they just wanted this big reward?

Statica? he whispered in his head. *Can you hear me?*

Fenn nudged him. "Something wrong?"

Walt tilted his head like he was trying to let water snake out of his ear. "Yeah," he said, then tilted his head the other way. "I mean, *no.* Sorry. I'm cool."

"Those stalls aren't going to clean themselves," Fenn said, making Walt smile. It was exactly something Dad would've said. But as he headed out to the dragons, he couldn't resist looking at the wanted poster.

Fenn guided them back to the stalls and explained that it was hard to clean out the stalls while there was a dragon sitting inside, so he led each dragon to an empty stall so they could clean out the used ones. Which wasn't easy at all. Even though the stalls were huge, the dragons definitely didn't want to stay in one. "They're itching to fly," he said. "Only way to get them to an empty stall is have them come after a gropberry."

"Bet I can get mine to move faster than yours," Van said, and of course after that it was a total competition of trying to maneuver the dragons from a dirty stall to an empty one and back as fast as possible.

Walt didn't even try to compete. His hands were on fire and he had to keep stopping, but Dylan moved like there might be money on the line.

"Champion!" Dylan said, throwing his hands up as he led his last dragon into a newly cleaned stall.

Van shook her head. "Nope. I already closed the gate on mine. You lose."

They argued back and forth while Fenn clipped a hose to a watering system that streamed fresh water into the stalls and Heckett, who had made herself scarce during the stall-cleaning process, reappeared and went over to Fenn, nuzzling his shoulder.

Fenn led them out of the stable, and they all stood there awkwardly for a moment as their eyes adjusted to being back in the bright sunlight.

Walt couldn't stop thinking about the poster and wondering whether being a mapmaker meant he was automatically bad. He didn't want to believe it. He remembered his idea of living someplace where mapmakers were sought out and admired. But that didn't seem to be the case after all. Maybe they should go back to the windmill. He glanced at Van. Yeah, she would totally go for *that*.

Dylan wiped sweat off his forehead. "How do you *do* all that work by yourself?" he asked Fenn.

"Seriously," Van said, leaning against the stable wall.

Walt checked his hands. Even though they were still wrapped securely, the raking and shoveling had been hard and the strips of cloth were bloody.

"Sometimes you just have to do what you have to do," Fenn said, smoothing each point of his hair.

"Uh," Van said, and then cleared her throat. Everyone turned to look at her. "Wouldn't it be better . . ." She pushed away from the stable wall and took a few steps. "I mean, I know you said they're competitive, but . . ."

"What?" Fenn demanded, his hands on his hips.

"Like, it's just you're here by yourself, and maybe . . . you should let the dragons out? They could go free?" The words came out in a rush, and Walt was reminded of when Van had thrown a huge fit the last time they had gone to the zoo. She wanted the animals to be let out of their enclosures.

"And what do I tell their riders when they come back?" Fenn asked, glaring at her.

"You mean *if*, don't you?" Van said, her voice not much higher than a whisper.

"Van!" Walt said sternly. Not that he hadn't had the same thought, but it seemed awful to say it out loud.

"You don't know anything," Fenn said, and turned away from them. Walt saw his shoulders go up and down. He hoped Fenn wasn't crying.

"I'm sorry," Van said. "I just meant—"

Fenn turned around, and his eyes were dry. "I know what you meant," he said. "Don't worry. They're coming back." He said it simply and with such certainty that Walt believed him.

Dylan nodded. "Of course they are."

Fenn nodded at the traveling machine, still wrapped around Walt's waist. "What is that, really?" He pointed at Dylan. "You called it a traveling machine. Said it would take you back? Back to where? And how does it work?"

"I said what?" Dylan asked, trying and failing to sound innocent.

Walt's face heated up. Now that they'd spent so much time together, it seemed worse not to tell Fenn the truth—but how could he? Fenn wouldn't believe him anyway.

"Our mom gave it to him," Van said, as if that explained everything.

Walt hadn't actually taken a moment to think about that since they'd gotten here. Where *had* the machine come from? Mom had said Mother Dear had given it to her, but did that mean that Mom knew magic was real? And had she given it to him so he could get away from football camp? *Football. Ugh.* "I can't believe Dad's making me go to football camp again," he groaned. "Maybe when he sees my hands I won't have to go."

Dylan looked at Walt curiously. "Can't you just tell him you don't want to play football?"

"What do you mean?" Walt asked, sounding shocked. "I *have*, a million times."

"No, he hasn't," Van told Dylan. "He says he isn't good enough to play. Or that he's too small." She faced Walt. "Or that your *hands* are hurt. A bunch of stuff that just sounds like excuses. You never just come right out and say you don't *want* to play football."

"Maybe if I was perfect like you," Walt said. "Good at *everything*."

"What?" Van cried. "Now you're just being silly."

"I'm not!" Walt said. "You do everything better than I do. Dad obviously thinks you're better than me."

"Except when it comes to football, I guess, since Dad won't even let me play," Van said.

Fenn and Dylan were looking back and forth between the twins, and it was obvious Dylan wanted to interject but didn't seem to know how.

"Poor you," Walt said. "You aren't allowed to get pounded on." Walt could hear the quiver in his voice, and his cheeks were hot with frustration.

"Dad wants to toughen you up," Van said, sounding way too bossy for Walt's liking. "That's not a *bad* thing. Maybe you should tell him about your superpowers."

"Shut *up*, Van," Walt warned.

"You talk about a lot of strange things," Fenn said.

Walt glared at Van. Why couldn't his sister keep her mouth shut?

But then Fenn just asked, "What is foot . . . balling?" and Walt relaxed. He wasn't surprised Fenn hadn't heard of it. Of course there wouldn't be football in Djaruba.

"A game. One team is trying to move the ball . . . the *foot*ball . . . down the field to score, and the other team is trying to stop them," Walt explained, his voice making it clear there was not one good thing about it.

"How?" Fenn asked. "How do they stop them?"

Van flew at Walt and knocked him down. "They tackle them!" she crowed.

"Get off!" Walt shouted at her. For a minute he'd forgotten how Van always had to prove she was bigger and stronger. He jumped to his feet and kicked her leg.

Fenn howled with laughter.

"Ow!" Van cried. "Flag on the play. That's not even cool, Walt." She got up and rubbed her leg.

Walt said, "You shouldn't have knocked me down."

Van waved off his comment and turned to Fenn. "So yeah, *anyway*. It's like that. There's lots of tackling."

"Is it fun? It sounds fun," Fenn said.

"You like being pummeled by a bunch of guys bigger than you?" Walt asked.

"Who says I would be the one getting pummeled?" Fenn squatted a little and raised his arms like he was going to tackle Van. "I think I'd like it."

"Well, my dad would love you," Walt muttered. Then he added, "It's probably fun if you're *good* at it."

"It's extremely aggravating that guys have an *issue* with girls playing," Van said, and rolled her eyes. "And obviously"—she shrugged at Walt—"my twin doesn't like the game."

"Oh, yeah, I forgot you were twins," Fenn said, looking back and forth between Van and Walt in that way Walt hated.

"What is it with you and the whole twin thing?" Walt asked her, and Van's eyes widened with confusion. "You don't have to say it all the time."

"What?" Van asked. "I don't."

The two glared at each other until Dylan said, "All this talk about football when *basketball* is the truth."

"The truth . . . ," Fenn started, and then he paused dramatically. Walt was certain Fenn was about to reveal something horrible. His face looked so solemn, but then he winked. "The truth is . . . I'm starving!"

"Son, you ain't never lied," Van said. "Where can we get something to eat?"

Walt wanted to laugh. It was the first time so far that Van had looked at Fenn in pure appreciation. Any mention of food and she was down. He thought of the empty food stalls. "I could eat," he said, rubbing his stomach. "But hopefully not gropberries."

"Not on your life. Come on!" Fenn said. He whistled to Heckett, and she settled low to the ground so they could get on easily.

Walt looked back at the stable, thinking about the wanted poster again.

"You okay?" Dylan asked.

"Yep," Walt said, shaking off his bad feeling. He wasn't about to pass up an opportunity to ride Heckett at least once more. He pulled the cords of the traveling machine tighter around his waist. He had their way back. Everything was fine.

In seconds they were in the air. Heckett flew to a thick forest, and she stayed just above the tree line. Every once in a while she'd let her feet brush against the tops of trees, scaring birds into loud, squawking flight.

Without being high up, Walt was losing his bearings. The Irstaz Forest went on for miles and miles in many directions. Which way were they going? The trees were starting to look odd. The leaves were getting deeper and deeper green until they looked black. And there were flashes of topaz and magenta. What type of trees were these?

"Okay, this part is going to seem pretty out there, but trust me," Fenn called back.

"*What* part?" Walt asked.

"The trees are too tight together for Heckett to land. We're going to jump."

"We definitely are not!" Dylan hollered.

"This is the best part," Fenn said. "You don't trust me?" He looked over his shoulder, a sneaky grin wide on his face.

"No!" Van was quick to say, but she couldn't help smiling.

"I thought you were hungry," Fenn said. Then he nudged Heckett and she slowed down. Fenn got to his feet. It seemed like a really horribly bad idea, but after only a second Van shakily stood too, crouching a bit to keep her balance on Heckett's back.

Walt shook his head. She really needed to deal with her competitiveness.

"On three," Fenn said. Then he whispered something to Heckett, and she slowed down even more.

Dylan got up and almost fell, but Van grabbed his hand. That just left Walt. "And the three travelers jumped to their death," he said under his breath as he uneasily got to his feet, amazed that he was actually standing on the back of a dragon.

"One!" Fenn cried. "Two!" As he said "Three!" he jumped. And Van, Dylan, and Walt jumped right after him. They were only in the air for a second before they hit the trees. Walt had braced himself to hit sharp pokey branches, but instead he fell into what seemed to be a blanket of the softest velvet.

It took him a second to realize that the velvet was actually enormous black butterflies. When their wings opened, brilliant splotches of color were revealed. And there were so many of them, they covered everything, the leaves, the branches, and the space between trees, so the kids landed on what felt like a big bed of welcoming feathers.

As Walt slowly drifted through the wings, he could hear the *fwoosh, fwoosh, fwoosh* of the wings beating. Or maybe it was butterfly language. Too soon, he landed on the ground with a gentle thud.

"We have *got* to do that again!" Van said as soon as her feet hit the earth.

The butterflies flew around them in a thick curtain, so thick it was *almost* creepy, but Walt decided it was so much better than being surrounded by bazzards. Several butterflies landed on his head. And then more on his shoulders. When he looked down his legs were totally covered. "Uh," he said.

Fenn started running. "This way! This way!" he shouted, and they chased after him. As they ran, the butterflies kept up with them, trying to light on their shoulders and arms, but then the air started to clear. Once the last butterfly was gone, Fenn bent over his knees and cracked up. "The looks on your faces!"

"What were they? They were too big to be butter-flies," Dylan said.

"Oh, they're butterflies, but maybe a better word is smotherflies," Fenn said. "If we had stayed back there, they would have maybe loved us too much. Hard to breathe when they light all over you like that. You saw how they completely cover the trees. Cool though, right?"

Walt felt like Fenn was asking Van specifically. And he wondered if maybe it was wearing on Fenn, just a little, how Van kept going back and forth between completely distrusting him to being ready to do whatever he said.

"Yeah, that was cool," Van admitted, and Walt could tell she was having a hard time trying to seem like it hadn't been that big of a deal. "But where's the food?"

"Right," Fenn said. For a moment he seemed unsure, and Walt wondered if he was lost. He fumbled with his tunic, and Walt held his breath waiting to see if Fenn was about to pull out a map. But then he just turned and started moving deliberately through the trees.

"Stick close to him," Van said. "We would never find our way out of here."

The trees grew tight together and there wasn't any path to follow. In some places, they had to squeeze between trunks. The air was quiet, with an occasional bird call. Walt heard water rushing in the distance. And then he thought he heard . . . whistling? What kind of beast whistled?

THE BEST BACON EVER

It wasn't an animal. It was definitely a person, and whoever it was, they were walking straight toward them. But the person was too far away to make out clearly.

"Who is that?" Walt called out.

A low branch whacked Dylan right in the face. "Who?" he asked, rubbing his forehead. "I don't see anyone."

Walt pointed. But now the person was shielded by trees.

"Who is it, Fenn?" Van asked, but Fenn didn't answer. He just kept charging ahead.

Walt was starting to get a strange feeling, and he stopped. "Wait, you guys," he begged.

"What?" Van asked. "Why?"

Walt shut his eyes for a second. He still didn't know what he was supposed to feel if there was another map-maker around, but that poster of Statica meant it was at least possible he was here in this world. *Is that you?*

"What are you doing?" Van asked Walt. "Fenn's getting too far ahead."

Walt opened his eyes and shook his head. The whistling had stopped, and there was no sign of whoever had been ahead of them.

"Come on!" Fenn hollered, and quickened his pace.

"Fenn," Walt called. "Fenn, wait up!" But Fenn didn't turn around, and then he started to run. Before Walt even realized what was happening, Fenn was out of sight.

Walt stopped again. Van and Dylan bumped right into him. "Oh, man," Walt said. "Something feels . . . off?"

"Is this another one of your Djaruba things?" Van asked.

"No!" Walt said. Why was she making it seem like there was something wrong with such an awesome place?

The silence grew around them.

"Where did he go?" Van whispered.

"I don't know," Walt whispered back.

"Why are we whispering?" Dylan asked.

A branch snapped and a chorus of frogs started humming.

"F-Fenn?" Walt called. Where was he?

"He left us?" Van asked.

"Shh!" Walt shushed her.

Fenn stepped out from behind a tree. "Sorry," he said, panting a little.

"Sorry for what?" Van demanded. "For leaving us like a jerk?"

"I said sorry," he said. His hands were full of long, thin brown bean pods. "I was just . . ." Fenn handed them each a pod. "I was in a hurry to get these. You'll see. Eat it."

Walt thought they looked like the pods that hung from the carob trees back in Los Angeles. He, Van, and kids in the neighborhood used to have carob battles, throwing the pods at each other like grenades. With a start, Walt realized it was the first time since the move that he hadn't thought *home* when he thought of Los Angeles. He took a tentative bite of the surprisingly soft pod, and his eyes widened in delight. "It takes like bacon!"

Dylan sniffed it before biting off a big chunk. As he chewed, his smile got bigger and bigger. "Bacon that's been dipped in syrup and sprinkled with pepper." He took another bite. "Oh, that's good. Correction. That's the best bacon ever."

Van shoved the entire thing in her mouth. "Gra er uh ewnurun?" she said, then swallowed in a big gulp. "Can I have another one?" Before Fenn could answer, she grabbed two more from his hands and ate them just as fast as the first.

"Whoa, slow down," Fenn said.

Walt heard something odd in Fenn's voice. Walt was about to ask him what was wrong when he realized his mouth had gone numb. At the same time, he realized that Fenn hadn't eaten any of the pods.

"Wha—" Walt started, before he stumbled back into a tree and slid to the ground. Van's mouth opened to a wide O, and then she crashed down without even trying to break her fall. "Van!" Walt cried, or rather tried to cry. The word was more of a weak whisper. Dylan groaned and clutched his stomach. Then his legs buckled.

Walt struggled to speak. "H-h-how c-could you?" he asked Fenn.

Fenn looked at him coldly. "You're a *mapmaker*!"

"Walt?" Dylan sighed. "What's—" was all he managed before passing out.

Walt's head felt like it weighed a million pounds and he couldn't keep his eyes open. He wanted to argue with Fenn, but his mouth wouldn't cooperate. "There's n-nothing . . . nothing wr—" And then everything went dark.

ONE WISH

Walt came to slowly. His mouth tasted like rancid oil. He tried to sit up, but his head seemed to be glued to the ground. He managed to open his eyes to tiny slits, but the light was too bright and it burned. He quickly closed his eyes again. He heard the murmur of voices, and he tried again to open his eyes, this time preparing himself for the shock of sunlight.

He saw a large Black man, but everything was swimming. "Dad?" he croaked. Slowly things started to come into focus. The trees around him. The dirt he was lying on. Van was so, so still. Dylan stared at him with his eyes wide open in fright.

And two people. Fenn and . . .

Walt's eyes narrowed as he strained against the fog in his head. It wasn't Dad.

Patrol Officer Canter.

And even though he was no longer in the highway patrol uniform, he was just as foreboding. Canter now wore faded jeans that had intricate drawings all over them, a button-down shirt covered by a tight leather vest, and worn, scuffed boots. A canvas knapsack was slung over one shoulder. His equipment belt had been replaced with one of those belts gunslingers wore in Westerns, and two big guns sat on either side of his hips.

But they weren't regular guns. They reminded Walt of something you'd see in a sci-fi movie. In the center of each, Walt could see glass containers filled with vividly colored swirling liquid, and he remembered the vials Canter had examined at Orsten's shop. Whatever that ammunition was, Walt didn't want to have one of those guns pointed at him.

Canter was talking to Fenn, saying something about how he must think himself a king by the way his hair was crowned.

Fenn's hand went to his hair, and Walt realized *that* was what the points were.

"No one said I was crowning!" Fenn said, his nostrils flaring.

Walt ran his tongue over his teeth. He twitched one finger.

"You're just stalling." Fenn held out his hand. "Give me my reward."

And that was when Walt saw the card in Fenn's hand. A card that looked just like the one Canter had given him. Literally a "calling" card. Walt's head felt like it was going to burst into flames.

"There's only one left," Canter said.

"I only need one!" Fenn said. "Give it. I want to get out of here before they wake—"

Walt coughed. His arms and shoulders were full of pins and needles as feeling swarmed back into his limbs.

"Looks like you won't get *that* wish," Canter told Fenn snidely.

Walt struggled to sit up. Dylan seemed to be in the same state he was, but Van was motionless. "Is sheeee . . . is she d-d-dead?" The words came out slurred and rough. He wanted to go to his sister, but his legs weren't working.

"No!" Fenn said. "She ate too many. But she'll wake up."

Walt wished Fenn sounded more certain.

"How . . ." Walt swallowed a few times and then pressed his tongue against his teeth. "How many pieces of s-silver, J-Judas?"

"Ah, not silver," Canter said. He reached into a

pocket and pulled out a golden triangular coin. It was just like the one he'd given to Orsten, except this one didn't have a jagged hole in the middle of it. Canter held it up, making it catch the light.

If only he could stand up, Walt thought, he could go over and clobber Fenn. "You sold us out for that?"

"It's going to give me my family back!" Fenn cried, snatching it from Canter.

Van moaned softly, and Walt was so relieved he almost burst into tears.

Dylan coughed, and then he spit on the ground a few times. "You . . . you *poisoned* us?" Dylan's face flamed with rage. "But we were friends!"

"Friends?" Fenn scoffed. "You all lied to me from the beginning. This whole time." Then his eyes narrowed as he looked over at Walt. *"Mapmaker."* He spat out the word like a curse.

"So what?" Walt shouted back. "I never said I wasn't. And there's nothing wrong with being one anyway. You're worse. You're a *traitor.*" Walt jiggled his legs, trying to get the feeling to hurry back. He wanted to get up and punch Fenn in the face. "Is that what you do? Hunt mapmakers? For a reward?" he shouted.

"No!" Fenn cried. "I just need to *fix* things. This was the only way."

"There's never only one way," Walt said. "And being

a dirty double-crosser is never the right way!" Walt's head buzzed while he tried to figure things out. Fenn had sold them out to Canter for some kind of magic coin? That would bring his family back? And what had Canter said? He only had one? One what? The answer came to him in a rush.

"Wishes?" Walt asked in disbelief.

"Or in this case," Canter said, "one wish." He held up a finger. "I wonder how you'll manage it, Fenn."

"I told you. I only need one!"

"Better be careful," Canter warned.

Fenn asked, "What is that supposed to mean?"

"You remember who Heckett really belongs to, don't you? You wish everything back the way it was, that goes back too."

"I'll . . . I'll say it, so that . . ." Fenn bit his lip.

If things weren't so awful, Walt would've laughed at him. Served him right that things weren't working out the way he wanted.

Van turned to her side and started coughing.

Fenn let out a huge relieved sigh, and Walt realized how worried he must've been that he really had killed her.

Canter smoothed down his unwrinkled vest. "Well, Fenn, I believe our business is concluded. Not sure if you want to stick around for this next part."

Walt felt like a bear was sitting on his chest. Whatever the next part was, it had to be awful.

"What are you going to do?" Fenn asked. "You're not going to hurt them, are you?"

"I don't think that's any of your concern," Canter said, but when Fenn didn't leave, he shrugged. "Suit yourself."

He started to reach behind him, and Walt knew exactly what was coming. He tried to scoot back, but his legs were just starting to get feeling and weren't much use. He couldn't believe this was happening. Canter was going to slap handcuffs on him and lock him up somewhere. And for what? Drawing a *fake* dinosaur?

"You . . . you can't!" Walt said, making his arms rigid as if that would help. "You don't have jurisdiction, or whatever. Not here. Not in Djaruba."

But when Walt saw what Canter had in his hand, terror ripped through him. As much as he had been terrified at the idea of getting handcuffed, what Canter was holding was much, much worse.

HOW TO STOP
A MAPMAKER

Fenn's shoulders shot up, and he stumbled back. His eyes were wide with shock.

"What are *those*?" Dylan asked.

Van looked like she wanted to scream but she was having a hard time opening her mouth.

Dangling from Canter's hand were two metal hand-shaped cages connected by a thin silver chain. The cages were like gloves made out of narrow steel straps.

Walt's stomach roiled. He understood what they were immediately. There was one clear way to stop a mapmaker: make it impossible for him to draw. Walt put his hands behind his back. "Keep away from me," he begged.

"You didn't say anything about locking his hands," Fenn said, looking like he felt sick.

"It's a little late to develop a conscience," Canter replied. "I don't recall you *asking* what would happen after you delivered a mapmaker, except for you getting what you wanted." Canter bent down and grabbed Walt's arm, giving Walt a painful reminder of the last time they had seen each other. And then, with a quick twist, Canter opened the cages, put Walt's hands inside, and snapped the cages closed. "No more mapmaking for you."

Immediately Walt felt as if his hands had just been covered in cement. The cages were so heavy, they pulled his arms down, straining his shoulders. It was like holding those twenty-pound dumbbells Dad was always telling him he needed to use for bicep curls. Scraps of the bandages made from Fenn's tunic poked through the strips of metal, and Walt wanted to yank them off. "What's *wrong* with what I am?" he yelled at Fenn. "I created *this* world! You wouldn't even exist if it weren't for me."

"Whoa," Dylan said.

Walt felt like he'd been tricked somehow. He hadn't meant to say that, exactly. As soon as the words had left his mouth, he'd wanted to take them back. He knew what he said was wrong, but . . . wasn't it true?

Van slowly sat up. "Walt," was all she said, but Walt could hear disappointment in her voice.

Fenn's whole body shook, but Walt couldn't tell if he was shocked or furious.

Walt wished he could bury his face in his hands, but he couldn't even do that. "Why is it so awful to be a mapmaker? Why do you hate us?"

Canter grabbed Walt by his collar and pulled him to his feet. There wasn't a morsel of pity in his eyes. "Because of who you hurt. Because of what you destroy."

Walt swayed on his feet, his legs threatening to give out on him. Canter pulled out one of his ray-gun things and Walt almost choked, thinking things were about to get even worse. But Canter pointed the gun away from him and shot a vertical line of glowing emerald green into the air just above the ground.

"What is that?" Van mumbled, her voice sounding like her mouth was full of marbles. "What are you going to do with my twin?"

Canter turned to look at her. "What would he do to a *world*? You're all free to go. Walter is the one I want." Then, with a yank, Canter pulled the traveling machine off Walt. He brought it up to his nose and sniffed it. "Strong magic. Old." He tossed the machine to the ground and then, in one quick motion, he pulled the glowing line like he was opening a split in curtains and forced Walt through, then followed him to the other side. As soon as they were through, the line faded away. And the way back was gone.

BLISS

Frigid air blew right through Walt's thin T-shirt, making him shiver. He couldn't even wrap his arms around himself because of the heavy hand cages. He and Canter were standing on hard, gritty sand. Ominous puce-and-rust clouds pressed down on them. It was as if a giant had gotten sick and covered the sky with vomit.

"Welcome to Bliss. My home," Canter said, expanding his arms wide.

Walt looked around in horror. Tall dead-looking reeds were behind them, and the wind was making them rustle as if things were creeping around just out of sight.

Back in the distance stood a jagged cliff with stark skeleton trees hunched over the edge. There was what looked like an expansive ocean in front of them, but instead of the scent of salt and brine, Walt got a whiff of freezer burn and mold and something worse underneath, like what a dead body might smell like. If it was an ocean, there were no waves. Actually, no movement at all. Walt turned away from the dismal sight. Across the sand, in the distance, he could make out large slow-moving shapes that were bleating as if in pain.

"Home?" Walt said, his voice trembling. He couldn't imagine anyone living in such a place. Or any place with a less apt name. There was nothing blissful here. It was *awful*. He couldn't help remembering how he'd thought Blackbird Bay was the worst place ever. What if he had to live somewhere like *this* horrific place?

"It didn't always look like this," Canter said. "Once it was beautiful."

"What . . . what happened?" Walt asked, but he suspected the answer.

"Statica is what happened." Canter hissed the name. "You asked why I hate mapmakers. This is why."

Walt wanted to argue, but it was difficult when he was looking at this monstrous evidence. Had it really been beautiful before? The distant moving shapes made sort of mooing sounds. Walt figured they were some kind of animal. But what? He strained to see them better. Large fern-looking antlers stuck out on either side of their heads, and they had broad but gaunt bodies. If an elk somehow mated with a starving elephant, these were what they might produce. "What *are* those things?"

"Glomoths. They once were majestic beasts. Now they live lives of misery. Everything here is either angry or sad."

Walt appraised Canter. He definitely fell into the angry camp. "But why? Why would he have done this to your world?"

"He wanted something, and I wouldn't give it to him. And he doesn't care who he hurts. None of you do."

"That's not fair. I haven't hurt anybody."

"Give you time and you will."

Walt stared at Canter in disbelief. Canter couldn't believe that—that Walt was guilty . . . before he'd even *done* anything? Guilty just for what he was. "It's presumed *innocent!*" he shouted at Canter.

Canter took several steps away from Walt and turned his back on him.

Walt shivered and looked around at the bleak world. "What did . . . what did it look like before?"

Canter reached into his knapsack and pulled out a loosely bound book. He flipped through the pages until he got to the one he wanted, then held it out to Walt.

"You can almost see it. Under the ruin he created."

Walt felt sick. Although he could barely make out what Bliss used to look like, he could see the green and blues and yellows of what had been there. All of it had been drawn over with the ugliness that was now all around them. Canter turned pages, revealing map after map, each damaged in some way. Torn. Covered with monsters. Scribbled over. Drawings of huge explosions. Or buried under ash. Some pages seemed burned.

It was a book of utter destruction. But underneath the horror on each page, Walt was able to see pieces of the original worlds. They all must have been full of life and beauty. He saw bits of mountains and fluffy clouds and glimpses of oceans and forests and cities buried under rubble. All of it ruined.

Walt counted as Canter turned each page. Eleven. And Walt understood immediately that these were the worlds Orsten and Canter had told him about. And Walt was disgusted with himself as he realized that when he'd heard about this, it hadn't seemed real. It hadn't seemed as if they could have possibly been talking about *actual* worlds. Worlds as real as Walt's own.

"I still don't understand why he'd do this. You and Orsten said he wanted me? But why?"

"A man like that? So full of pride and rubbish that he can't stand the idea of not having a follower? Long ago, it was said that a young mapmaker would spend time as an apprentice to the mapmaker before them. No one knows what happened to the mapmaker before Statica. Some say he killed him." Canter tossed the book onto the sand.

Walt felt the air go out of his chest like someone had punched him. Slowly he slid to the ground, the hand cages seeming to drag him down.

"Think of what he could do, raising you up as his from the very beginning of your journey," Canter said. "Filling you with all of his garbage."

Walt shuddered. "Why did he ask *you* to find me?"

"Lots of people have gifts of one kind or another. Mine seems to be a . . . a nose for magic."

Walt shook his legs to try to get some warmth. He couldn't feel his toes. "Magic has a *smell*?"

Canter nodded. "Some is crisp, almost shiny, like a sweet apple, but some is smoky and hard." He thought for a moment. "Some is fresh-cut wood. Most is bitter." He stared off into the distance for a minute, and then he snapped back and frowned at Walt. "What *you* can do? Mapmaking? It's the stink of sweat covered with cheap cologne."

"But if that's true, then why did you need me to help you find him? Why couldn't you just sniff him out?" It sounded ridiculous, and Walt got a picture in his head of Canter dressed in a bloodhound costume.

"Statica learned to mask himself somehow."

Walt was surprised that Canter was talking to him instead of doing something even worse than the cages. Like cutting off his hands. Walt bent over his knees, trying to ward off the cold. "Maybe you should've just given me to him." He couldn't help but feel that he was in some way responsible for the destruction Statica had wreaked.

Canter surprised Walt by laughing dryly. "Don't think I didn't consider it," he said. "But watch you become like him? How many worlds would the two of you destroy together?"

"Who says I would've done anything like that?" Walt wanted to cry. No, he wanted to yell. He wanted to punch something.

"With him as your guide? There wouldn't have been any other path for you to go down. Seeds planted in filth don't thrive."

"How do you know that Statica wanted to turn me into some kind of monster? Maybe he wanted help undoing the damage he'd done." Walt's voice sounded desperate, even to his ears. *Weak sauce* was what his family called unconvincing arguments, and Walt couldn't help but feel he was pouring out some *seriously* weak sauce.

"Hah!" Canter scoffed.

"What about wishes? Couldn't you have wished for . . ." Walt's voice dribbled away. He wasn't sure what kind of wish could have changed things.

"You mean like Fenn? Trying to fix his problems with a wish?"

"What's so wrong with that?" Walt argued.

"A wish is what started Fenn's trouble. Found a talisman and wished everyone away. Maybe that's not what he meant to do. But that's the trouble with wishes. They do not care what you meant. And no one is happy with one wish, or two, or three. Always more and more, trying to get things right," Canter said. "He should never have gotten his hands on a talisman. That's precisely why I take their magic."

"Why do you hate magic so much?" Walt asked. "You obviously use it."

"Hate magic?" Canter sounded shocked. "I don't hate magic. I hate people who twist it and turn it into something sick." He waved an arm in front of him. "So how do you like it? Do you find it beautiful? Would you be proud of this? Orsten showed you all those beautiful maps, but he didn't show you this."

"Okay, I get it. Statica is a monster. But he couldn't have always been that way. No one is born evil."

"Aren't they?" Canter shrugged. "When he was younger, maybe it started as experiments. Just to see what he could do. He could've drawn wonderful things. Or maybe that's just not possible." Canter scoffed. "Seems Statica started to enjoy the taste of the horror he could create."

Walt thought of the feeling he'd gotten when he'd erased the town in Djaruba. The satisfaction he had felt. And maybe a tiny bit of hunger to do something worse. But he hadn't ever wanted to destroy a whole world.

"What do you want, Walter?" Canter asked, breaking into his thoughts. "More than anything?"

Walt swallowed hard. The answer was on the tip of his tongue. For Dad to accept him for who he was. For Dad not to force football on him like it would "fix" him.

Canter held up a hand. "You can see it, can't you? Your heart's desire. And what if you could redraw the world to get it. Would you do it?"

Walt blinked fast. If there was a way? Could he? He looked around at the dead world they were sitting in. Canter's world. Statica had destroyed it to get what he wanted. Tears started running down Walt's face, and he tried to wipe them away, forgetting about the hand cages. "Take these off!" he bleated at Canter. "I don't even have a way to do any mapmaking here."

"Are you ready to tell me where to find him? I know you can."

Walt gulped. He didn't know for sure, but he needed

these things off him. The longer they stayed on his hands, the more it felt like they were tightening, and Walt thought if they stayed on much longer they would crush his hands into useless mush. "I think he's at the . . . the windmill. I maybe brought him to Djaruba?" Walt was surprised that it was a relief to say it out loud. "I didn't mean to. It was an accident. He's been . . . calling me," he admitted. "I wasn't sure if it was him at first."

Walt didn't want to say that he hadn't been ready to turn Statica over to Canter. Not before finding out if what he'd been told was true. Canter had seemed more like the bad guy than the specter in Walt's dreams.

"But I don't know. We went to the windmill when we first got here, but no one was there."

"Good thing," Canter said, but he didn't explain what he meant by that. Then he said, "Thank you, Walter." He touched his hat and got up as if he was about to leave.

"Wait! You said you'd take these off!"

Canter cocked an eyebrow. "Are you sure?" But then he knelt back down. "I may need them." He pulled out one of the ray guns. "Don't move."

Walt didn't. He could feel a tingle of warmth as Canter directed a beam of light at the clasp on each hand cage, and after a moment they clicked open and Canter pulled the cages away. The movement loosened the bandages on one hand and Walt unwrapped the strip of cloth, relieved to see that the cuts had stopped bleeding. He tore off the bandage from the other hand, not wanting to feel any type of confinement. Walt flexed his fingers in relief and then tucked his hands in his armpits to try to warm them.

"Okay, then," Canter said and frowned. He connected the cages to his belt.

Walt noticed the low set of Canter's shoulders and how grim he sounded. He sure didn't seem happy about finally getting a chance to get revenge. "What are you going to do when you find him?" Walt asked, his voice quaking.

One of Canter's hands drifted to a gun.

Even after everything, Walt was shocked. "You're going to kill him?"

Canter looked surprised. "Kill him? That would be way too kind. No. I will encase him here. In this world that is now his instead of mine. If he wanted it this way, the least he can do is stay and appreciate it. And it will keep him from doing this to anyone else."

"But what about me?" Walt asked, already fearing the worst.

Canter avoided Walt's gaze. "I'll figure that out when I come back with him."

Walt gasped in horror. "You're not serious. You're not just going to leave me here! I'm a *kid*."

"You're a mapmaker," Canter said and shrugged in that I-don't-make-the-rules way. He kicked some rocks into a pile. "Stay close to this. It'll keep you warm and keep the tulstoods away." He shot a beam of vivid orange light at the rocks, and they went from light gray to black to bright red. Heat emanated from them, but Walt still felt betrayed.

"I told you what you wanted to know," Walt wailed. "You can't just leave me."

"I repaid you for that knowledge." Canter nodded at Walt's now-free hands. Then he made another of the glowing emerald lines, and without a look back, he stepped through.

An Impossible Choice

Walt didn't know how long he stared at the space where Canter disappeared, certain the man would return for him. It felt like a very long time. Eventually he gave up.

He got up and walked to the edge of the motionless sea. He picked up a rock and threw it as far as he could. It only went a few yards before clinking down, and there was a cracking sound, almost like what had once been water was now either ice or glass. Walt wrapped his arms around himself. It was very cold this far from the heat of the rocks. The air stunk as if something was rotting close by.

He thought of Canter's plan to trap Statica here. It really was a horrible fate. And Statica totally deserved to be stuck here, after what he'd done. But Walt didn't. Canter was wrong. Being a mapmaker didn't automatically make you bad. Walt remembered the gorgeous maps Orsten had shown him. *Those* mapmakers hadn't gone on to do terrible things.

One of the large creatures he'd noticed earlier started moving in Walt's direction. It moved too slowly to be dangerous.

But then something crept out of the shadows and jumped on the large creature's back, and it moaned in pain. Was that a tulstood? Walt moved quickly back to the safety of the glowing rocks.

Canter had left the book on the ground. Looking up every few seconds to make sure nothing was creeping up on him, Walt flipped through it, trying to imagine what kind of mind would do this. It was like the worst atlas ever. The destruction of each map reminded him of how a long time ago, he and Van had gotten in big trouble with Grandma Nadine. They had gone to work with a box of crayons and one of her books. They'd just been having fun. Coloring and scribbling and making the boring pages more interesting, but Grandma Nadine had been furious at them for ruining her book. But they'd been like three years old. It was sort of what little kids did. What was Statica's excuse?

When Canter came back, Walt would convince Canter he wasn't anything like Statica.

But time ticked by and Canter didn't return. Walt's eyelids got heavier and heavier until they closed for a good five minutes or ten. Maybe it was an hour. He'd been having an awful dream. Statica was looking at him. He had one of those headlamps on his head, and the light burned Walt's eyes. And Statica's eyes were full of a look that Walt recognized. He'd seen it often enough from Dad. Disappointment. Did that mean that Statica knew that Walt had told Canter where to find him?

The rocks were no longer bright red, and they weren't giving off as much heat.

Walt wondered how much time he had left. He looked down the beach and could make out the large creatures gathered around a shape in the sand. They seemed to be rocking back and forth, and Walt was certain that thing that had crept from the darkness had killed one of the large glomoths. And this is what their mourning looked like. Walt's throat felt like he'd swallowed salt.

One of the rocks sizzled and then went dark. Walt patted his arms briskly, trying to warm up.

He wanted to go *home*.

Home. Walt straightened up. If he just hadn't fought so hard against accepting the move, he never would've gotten into this position. Mom had tried to tell him. "Home is wherever we are together," she'd said, and Walt had refused to listen. Van was right too. He had never come out and told Dad straight up that he didn't want to play football. If he ever got home, he would. No, forget that. If he got home, he'd go to football camp with a smile.

Walt sniffed and buried his head in his knees.

The wind picked up, and another rock burned out. Sand blew into Walt's ears. He raised his head and shielded his eyes. It seemed like a tornado or something.

The air swirled around him, sand biting into his skin. Then there was a loud *swoosh* and the sand calmed down and Van, Dylan, and Fenn landed on the ground in front of him.

"What?" Walt said, not able to believe it. Was he hallucinating? He must be, because what would Fenn be doing with Dylan and Van? He wiped his face and tried to look like someone who had been expecting to escape and not like someone who had given up all hope.

"Walt!" Van yanked off her helmet and ran over and hugged him.

Walt had never been so relieved to see someone in his life, and he hugged her back just as tight.

"I'm so glad the traveling machine is smart enough

to go someplace when I don't even know where to tell it!" Van said. As she talked, she grabbed Fenn's helmet and then waited for Dylan to hand his to her. She looked at the machine in appreciation. "I just said take us to Walt, and I really, *really* wanted to go there."

"What is *he* doing here?" Walt asked. He didn't even want to look at Fenn, but he couldn't help it. Fenn had a swollen bottom lip and a bruise under one eye, and his tunic was ripped at the shoulder. And he looked like he wanted to bury himself under the sand.

Van glared at Fenn. "Jury's still out." Then she shoved the machine under her arm and grabbed Walt's hands. "Where are the hand cages? He took them off? I didn't know how we were going to get you out of those things. Man, your hands are pretty wrecked. Are you okay?" Van was like a geyser that was finally able to release all the built-up pressure. She took a deep breath and looked around. "What *is* this place? It *stinks*."

"This used to be Canter's home," Walt said. The words had a chilling effect on everyone.

"This?" Dylan asked. "But it's *nasty*."

Van nodded solemnly.

Walt took a deep breath before saying, "He said . . . he said that Statica made it like this. Just because Canter wouldn't give me to him." Walt hated that a mapmaker was responsible for a world looking like this. And worse that he was at the center of it. But then he glared at

229

Fenn. "Even someone as bad as Canter didn't give me up. Not like you!"

"I—" Fenn started but then shut his mouth like a mousetrap.

Dylan thumbed over at Fenn. "Well, after being the *biggest* jerk in the world, Fenn's back on the right side," Dylan said. "Or I guess I should say, now he's on the right side after *pretending* before." He raised an eyebrow at Van. "Your sister knocked some sense into him."

Walt had seen Van fight. Fenn was lucky he wasn't in worse shape, but Walt wasn't ready to accept him back into the fold that easy. "You could have killed us if we had eaten too many of those things," he accused Fenn, glaring at him.

"I wouldn't have let you," Fenn said, and then looked at the ground. "He said he just wanted to . . ."

"What?" Walt spat. "Lock up my *hands*? And you're fine with that?"

"I didn't know about that part," Fenn claimed. "And you don't *understand*," he tried to explain. "I've heard all about how mapmakers do terrible things. Mess up worlds and even worse. And then you show up, and it was obvious what you were, even though you all tried to be so slick and everything. And the reward was . . ." Fenn clenched his hands tight. "I just want my family back."

Walt noticed the present tense. "You didn't make your wish?" He wanted to stay furious with Fenn, but he also didn't know what he would've done if he had been in Fenn's place. Wouldn't he basically have done anything to get Van and Mom and Dad back if something had happened to them?

Fenn shook his head. "Not yet."

Van explained, "He's worried that Canter is right. That he can't have both things. Get everyone back *and* keep Heckett."

"She's mine," Fenn said, and no one argued with him. They had no clue what situation Heckett had been living in before Fenn had set the things in motion that had brought her to him, but based on what Canter had said, it didn't seem like it had been great. She was now one hundred percent Fenn's, just like he was one hundred percent hers.

"So what's the plan?" Walt asked, looking around at them all hopefully.

"Plan?" Van asked. "Uh, we just wanted to *get* to you." She came closer to Walt. She whispered, "What if we distract Fenn and get a helmet on you? We'll leave Fenn here. No matter what side he's on now, he deserves it, right?"

Part of Walt felt like that was a very good plan, but no way could he leave someone here. "We can't do that," Walt said. "We need a way for us *all* to get out of here." Another rock sizzled out, reminding Walt that they didn't have a whole lot of time to figure things out. Canter hadn't come back. And Walt was beginning to think that meant he wasn't going to.

Van noticed the book on the ground and picked it up and turned a few pages, then looked at Walt in confusion. "What's this? Mapmaking for dummies?"

Walt's face heated, and he yanked the book from her. Being reminded of what he was made him feel like he was eating slugs. "If this is really Statica's work? Then he's as bad as Canter says. It's like it's a game to him. That's worse than . . . than anything. He doesn't have some *reason*. It's as if he just *likes* being foul."

Dylan threaded his invisible basketball through his legs. "But, like, what's his origin story?"

"Does it matter?" Walt asked, almost shouting. He didn't know exactly who he was angry with. "I mean, Canter said Statica had maybe just started with experiments. Like he was just . . . messing around?" Walt's voice was getting louder and louder. He couldn't help thinking about how Statica destroyed eleven worlds in order to get him. It was the grossest reason ever and it made Walt feel as if he was somehow responsible. And that wasn't fair! "So who *cares* why he became evil?" he yelled.

"*Dude,*" Dylan said, clearly shocked by Walt's outburst.

"It's cool. I'm just curious about stuff like that." He looked nervously over at Van. "But, yeah, okay. Let's just check off the villain box and move on."

Walt wished he could explain why he was upset but he didn't understand it himself. In a quieter tone, he said, "Everything Canter said about him. And what he did. Maybe Canter's right. Mapmaking should be against the law." All of Walt's anger drained away and he was left feeling incredibly sad.

"But, Walt, that's Statica, not you," Van said, reaching over and touching Walt's arm. "Just because he's a villain doesn't mean you are. Remember how that girl in fifth grade said we were sinister just because we're twins?"

Walt's eyes narrowed as he remembered Carrie Danzig. "That girl was annoying. And she'd watched *The Shining* way too many times."

"She honestly believed *all* twins were possessed or something." Van sounded as if she was still angry with Carrie. "So yeah, anyway, being a mapmaker, same thing. It's like Orsten said. It's what you have inside you that matters. And *my* twin does not have rotten disgusting stuff inside him."

Walt couldn't help asking. "Why *do* you always have to say it?"

"Say what?" Van asked.

"That we're *twins*."

Without hesitation, Van said, "Because being your twin is the best." Van's eyes were shining, but she must've seen something in Walt's face because they darkened with concern. "Don't you think so?" she asked hesitantly, like she was afraid of the answer.

Walt was stunned into silence. It had never occurred to him that Van was *bragging* when she told everyone they were twins.

When he didn't say anything right away, Van's face bent into worry. "You don't?" she asked. Her voice was a mixture of shock and concern.

Walt hated hearing her sound like that. And worse was the hurt in her eyes. He put his arm around her shoulders, even though he had to reach up to do it. "Totally the best," he said.

Van tried to smile at him, but she seemed shaky.

"Really," Walt assured her, and he was surprised to realize he meant it.

Van nodded and swiped quickly at her eyes.

Fenn said, "This is fantastic, but can we move on to whatever comes next?"

Van spun around to glare at him. "Don't think you won't catch these hands again."

"Don't think I won't fight back this time," Fenn threatened.

Something howled, and it was way too close. Walt

barely heard it. He was staring at the book in his hands.

"Snap out of it, Walt!" Van called. "We need to figure out what we're doing."

Walt didn't even look at her.

"Earth to Walter," Van said. She tried to pull the book out of his hands, but he gripped it tighter. "We don't have time for you to worry about what type of mapmaker you'll be. I told you, you're not—"

"I don't think Canter can stop Statica," Walt cut her off.

"Okay," Van said. "And that means what?"

"With the way we can change things? Mapmakers, I mean? It's a totally unfair fight. We could draw an impenetrable bubble . . . or a cannon. It must take one mapmaker to stop another one." He thought of the story Canter had told about people thinking Statica had killed the mapmaker he was apprenticed to. He turned to Fenn. "You didn't make your wish, but you still have the talisman, right?"

Fenn nodded at him suspiciously.

"I need to make a wish," Walt said, and held his breath waiting to see what Fenn would do. It was probably ridiculous, but it was all that Walt could think of.

"But it's my only way to get them back," Fenn said, his voice husky.

"Do you think there's a way you could make a wish

that would have things back the way you want them instead of the way they were?" Walt asked. What Canter had said about wishes made sense. But only because people wished for massive, almost impossible things. Keep it simple. That's what his favorite teacher, Ms. Aquilla, had always told him.

Fenn refused to answer and instead just stared stubbornly at Walt. But his eyes blinked rapidly, betraying what he thought.

"Yeah, I didn't think so." Walt knew he was asking for the world, but it was the only way. He just hoped that Fenn wouldn't ask him what he was going to wish for.

Fenn gulped. "Heckett can't go back to where she was. They were . . . they were going to kill her for being too small. I can wish for her to be okay."

"What about your family?" Dylan asked.

Fenn looked back and forth between Walt and Dylan as if they represented his impossible choice.

"Fenn, I think . . ." Walt licked his lips. "I think I can get them back *and* let you keep Heckett. Do you trust me?"

Fenn slowly came over and stood in front of Walt. "Do you swear? Do you swear on your twin that you'll get my family back?"

Walt gulped. "I swear I'll *try*. And I promise I really

think I can. I *swear* that I think I can. And if I can't, then it won't matter, because Statica will destroy it all."

Fenn considered and then must've decided that was good enough. He held the talisman out to Walt. But as Walt tried to take it, Fenn held on tight for another second. "You have to be careful what you say."

Van looked at Walt expectantly. "What are you going to wish for? A bomb to blow Statica up? A dinosaur, but a real one this time that will chomp him to bits? Oh, that you're like eighty-two feet tall and can step on him like a bug?"

Walt tried to drown her out while he thought through his plan. It was simple, all right. But was it too simple?

There was another howl. Even closer this time. Walt saw glowing eyes in the reeds behind them. And whatever it was started to growl.

"Hurry, Walt!" Dylan said.

Walt took a big breath and said, "I wish for a pencil, an eraser, and a map of Djaruba."

Walt could tell by the look on Fenn's face that Fenn was certain he had just made the worst deal of his life.

ONE WISH (AGAIN)

Even with all the magic Walt had seen in the last couple of days, he was still unprepared for the things he'd wished for to appear almost as soon as the words were out of his mouth. He picked up the pencil and eraser, pleased to see it was one of those Magic Rub ones that he preferred. He'd never thought about the name before until now.

"Do you want to share your plan?" Fenn asked, looking nervously over his shoulder.

Walt shook his head. "No time." There was only one stone left glowing, and that meant that any minute whatever was making the racket in the shadows would probably attack. But he had a map of this place, thanks to the awful book, and now he had a map of Djaruba.

"Let's get this show on the road," Van said. "Are we using this?" She held up the traveling machine, but Walt shook his head, so she tied it around her waist.

Walt took a tight swallow. This had to work. He picked up the pencil and began.

"Djaruba and Bliss had a portal that connected them. The portal in Bliss opened by the travelers gathered around the one glowing stone." Walt drew a small arch on the map of Bliss. He didn't think they'd be able to walk through a line if he tried to copy what Canter's portal had looked like. It was difficult drawing with a sore hand, but Walt ignored the pain. "Stepping through it led to . . ." He grabbed the map of Djaruba and drew a matching arch. "A portal in Djaruba. Waiting for the travelers was Fenn's trusty dragon, Heckett." As he uttered the dragon's name, the last glowing rock went out and the shadows grew toward them. Walt quickly rolled up the map and shoved it in a pocket. He folded the book in half and added that too. He really did love the huge pockets of cargo shorts.

"Come on," he said, pointing to the arch that now stood on the hard sand. They ran through it and immediately started sliding. It was like being on the longest, fastest tube slide ever made.

And it would've been fun . . . except Walt could hear something scratching and hissing behind them.

It seemed to take forever, but finally they exploded out of the tube, right through an archway that matched the one back on Bliss. And Heckett was there waiting for them.

"Heckett!" Fenn cried, running to her. But for the first time that Walt had seen her, Heckett did not seem like the fun-loving dragon that he'd come to know and love. She crouched down and her ears went back and a noise came from her throat that sounded like a mix between a hiss and a spoon caught in the garbage disposal.

Over Heckett's guttural noises, they could all hear the yowling of the beast that had followed them through the portal. Seconds later it burst through the archway. It seemed to be part eel, part sabertooth, and if it was part anything else, they didn't have time to see before Heckett blasted it with a burst of fire, then pounced on it like a cat capturing a mouse. In three bites it was gone.

"Whoa," Dylan said. "Good girl."

Fenn looked at them a bit shyly. "I said dragons don't eat people. I didn't say they don't eat . . . whatever *that* was."

Heckett burped loudly and then shook her wings like she was saying, "Let's get to business."

Even though he was feeling a little woozy and his body ached, Walt slapped open the book and map and erased the archways, to make sure no other creatures surprised them. It dawned on him that mapmaking always affected him like this—made him feel a little achy and weak. How had he never noticed before? What had Orsten said? There's always a price? This must've been what he meant.

"Well, bro, the first part of your plan was a huge success. Five stars," Van said.

"Thanks for not leaving me there," Fenn said, glancing at the travel machine. "I know you could've."

"Wouldn't have dreamed of it," Van said with a small wink at Walt.

Dylan bent low, faked left, then right, and took his favorite jump shot. Walt had to admit it was good to see Dylan in full-blown imaginary basketball mode. "What's next?" Dylan asked. "We get the bad guy, right?"

"Um, I need to talk to Fenn for a second," Walt said, stashing the book and map back in his pocket.

"Why?" Van asked, immediately suspicious. "What do you have to tell him that we can't hear?"

"It's . . ." Walt couldn't think of anything that he could say. He couldn't tell her the truth. But no way could he risk everybody's life. "It's *private.*"

Van stared at him, and when he just stared back, she threw up her hands. "Fine! Go have your 'private' chat." She added her customary air quotes around *private*.

Walt pulled Fenn far enough away to be sure Dylan and Van couldn't hear. "Look, they're not going to understand, but it's gotta be just you and me on this mission."

"What do you mean? *I* don't understand," Fenn said. He looked over at Van and Dylan, and Walt worried that Fenn was going to tell them.

"You know what mapmakers can do," Walt said, speaking fast. He didn't want to say out loud what he planned, so instead he whispered, "Like I said, it takes a mapmaker to stop another one. Canter was going to cage Statica's hands like he did mine. But Statica is too strong."

"Long 'chat' you're having!" Van hollered at them. Of course *chat* got the air quotes.

Walt adjusted his position to make sure she couldn't see his mouth and try to read his lips. "Canter never came back. I think Statica must've gotten the better of him. But I can stop him. I can *draw* it and I think this is our only hope."

"But you're sm—"

Walt appreciated that Fenn had cut himself off before saying what he was obviously thinking: *small*.

"Yeah, I know. That doesn't matter." Dad had told him, in one of those man-to-man talks he liked to have, that although Mom always said that Walt was named after the author Walter Dean Myers, Walt was *really* named after Walter Payton. Payton wasn't as big as other football players, but he was smart and fast. Dad had obviously been trying to make him feel better about being so small, but at the time, it hadn't worked. Payton might've been small for a football player, but he wasn't *scrawny*. Walt took a deep breath. He wasn't very strong, so he would have to be quick. This could work. Maybe.

"Not much of a plan. What about your promise to me? You swore on your twin!"

"That's why I'm asking you to help me. You need to keep me alive so I can keep my promise."

Fenn stared at him with the look of someone who knows they have been tricked. Like someone who suspects they are *still* being tricked. Walt didn't feel guilty. Yes, he'd made a promise, but Fenn had fed him those pods and sold him to Canter, so . . .

"You fast?" Fenn asked, and before Walt could answer, Fenn added, "You better be." Then he charged away, whistling for Heckett to follow. Walt was after Fenn like a greyhound. He heard Van yelling his name and then the pounding of footsteps. Heckett swooped above and grabbed the back of Walt's shirt with her talons. Fenn was already on her back.

Heckett started to go up, but not before Van grabbed Walt's foot. "What are you doing?" she cried.

Walt shook his leg, trying to shake her off. "Let go, Van! You have to stay here!" But she didn't let go, and worse, Heckett was getting higher. If Van didn't let go soon, they were both going to end up splatting on the ground.

"Dylan!" His friend was chasing behind Van, looking uncertain. Walt shook his leg wildly, but Van was determined to hang on. Then Dylan jumped and grabbed Van around the waist, and they both fell to the ground. Heckett must've just been waiting for Van to be safe, because as soon as Van was no longer dangling, Heckett soared high into the air. Walt could see Van wrestling with Dylan and wished he could go back and make her understand, but there wasn't time for that.

Fenn leaned down and offered Walt a hand, and Walt was able to settle onto Heckett's back.

"We gotta go to the windmill," Walt panted.

Fenn nodded and nudged Heckett to turn south.

Walt couldn't tell right away why it felt so different on Heckett from the other times. But of course. It was because he didn't have his twin or friend behind him.

As they flew in the air, Walt looked below, wondering if this was the last time he was going to have such a magnificent view of Djaruba. A world he had drawn but that was in no way his.

When the windmill came in sight, Walt was shocked to see the odd-looking rhinoceros things standing around it. Were they . . . *guarding* it?

Heckett gave an angry snort. Walt knew Heckett was tough, but he wasn't sure if she would win in a fight against that much muscle. "Land there," he told Fenn, pointing to the wide field.

As soon as they touched ground, some of the rhinos raised their heads and looked over with interest. One pawed the ground and lowered its massive head.

"Oh, great," Walt said. He jumped off Heckett and unfurled the map of Djaruba. He had no clue if this was going to work. Then the rhinos charged.

Walt dug into into his pocket, and something poked him. "Ouch!" He shook his hand, then reached back in and, this time, grabbed the eraser. As he started rubbing away the beasts he'd drawn years ago, he said frantically, "There were no . . . uh, rhinolike creatures in all of Djaruba. They had all vanished." He rubbed harder, almost not daring to hope until Fenn yelled, "Whoa! Look!"

Walt looked up. The beasts were gone. There wasn't a trace of them.

"Wow, you erased them out of existence!"

Walt felt a little funny about that, especially since it was wanting to save white rhinos that had made him draw them here in the first place. But like Van had said, his clearly weren't rhinos. They were sort of monsters. He gripped the eraser hard in his hand. Odd for such a small thing to give him so much comfort. A tiny spot of blood was on his finger. What had poked him? He reached (carefully) back into his pocket and met the usual collection of string, rocks, very mushy gum, the now-worthless talisman, and a compass. He'd forgotten all about it.

"What's that for? You going to stab him with it? I don't think it would—"

"I'm not *stabbing* him," Walt said. What had Ms. Wilhope said? "I think this is, like, a . . . uh . . . maybe a . . . cloaking device? Maybe it makes me invisible, or . . . um . . ." It was probably ridiculous to think that what Ms. Wilhope had given him could actually hide him, but he might as well try it.

Walt looked at the map of Djaruba and then looked around where he was standing. Maybe if he had some kind of reference point? The only landmark-type thing was the windmill. "Let's go," he said, and started walking over. Fenn and Heckett trailed after him, wearing matching expressions of confusion.

Walt stood right in front of the windmill. Then he

squatted down and planted the pointy tip of the compass into the map. He saw, with satisfaction, that a small divot appeared on the ground right where he was standing. That was promising. He started to draw a circle using the arm of the compass that held the graphite. "A circle of protection surrounded Walt, uh, Walter Anderson, from Statica's gaze." He hesitantly closed his eyes but didn't try to find Statica. Instead he waited to see if Statica would talk to him. There was only silence. "Too bad there's no way to know if it actually works," he muttered.

He stood up and extended his arms. He had kind of hoped he wouldn't be able to see himself. He squinted at Fenn. "Can you see me?"

"Uh, yeah," Fenn said, sounding confused. Then he cleared his throat nervously. "So new plan?"

Walt shook his head and beckoned Fenn to follow him several yards away. He hoped the circle was working, even if he was totally visible. Maybe it just shielded him from another mapmaker. Or maybe it was just hiding his thoughts. In any case, he couldn't risk anyone inside the windmill hearing the plan.

When he figured they were far enough away, he said, "Okay. I don't know what we're going to find inside, but last Canter knew, you had sold me out."

Fenn looked ready to argue, but Walt waved whatever

the excuse was away. "I know, I know, no choice, family back, yeah, yeah. That doesn't matter now. My point is, he doesn't know you're now on our side." Walt paused. "You really are, aren't you?"

Fenn nodded fast.

"Okay!" Walt clasped his hands together. "So Canter won't think you're working with me. And that means Statica won't know either." *Unless he can read my mind.* Walt hesitated. His plan didn't work at all if Statica was able to get in his head. He wasn't able to read Statica's mind. But maybe that was because he wasn't strong enough yet. There were just too many things he didn't know. "If Canter has captured Statica . . ."

Walt's voice drifted off. He didn't imagine that's what they'd find, but what if Canter *had* managed to get the best of Statica and was either inside or just gone? That meant Canter had left him on a broken planet to die. Walt knew Canter really did hate mapmakers enough to do that. But it was still hard to accept. "Statica must've gotten the upper hand over Canter. And Statica wants me. Would it really be so hard for him to believe that you would sell me out? All you have to do is tell him you'll give him what *he* wants, if he gives *you* what *you* want."

"Which is?" Fenn still looked completely baffled.

"Your *family* back, but not to lose Heckett!" Now Walt looked at Fenn like *Fenn* was a dope. Walt had to struggle not to shout. Wasn't this all obvious? "But you won't tell him where I am until after he does it."

Fenn's eyes lit with hope. "Do you think he can?"

Walt had no clue, but he nodded.

"And how do I keep him from just making me tell him where you are? Don't mapmakers have all sorts of sneaky stuff they can do?"

"Exactly what *have* you heard—" Walt started, but then waved his question away. "Doesn't matter. He'll do it because you'll be holding this." Walt held the talisman out to Fenn.

"But—"

"*I* know!" Walt said impatiently. "But *he* doesn't. You have to make him think you've got a wish left. And that you will use it to annihilate him if he tries anything."

Fenn looked completely unconvinced.

"Once he does, you know, bring people back . . ." Walt hesitated for just a second, because he had no clue whether Statica could do something like that. But all he really needed was a distraction. He hurriedly continued. "Then you just get out of here and I'll take care of the rest. And hopefully, if the circle thing works, he won't be able to see me until it's too late." Walt could see too clearly how many ways this plan could go wrong. But who better to try this with than Fenn? A guy who was *really* good at fooling people.

"Okay," Fenn said slowly. "Say he falls for it. And

he brings people back and I get to keep Heckett. What happens when I don't hand you over?"

Walt held up the Magic Rub eraser. "I'm going to erase him."

NOT A PERFECT PLAN

Thankfully Fenn didn't ask any more questions, because Walt wasn't exactly sure how he was going to erase Statica, or even if he could. But he was going to try.

Walt shoved the eraser in his pocket. "Okay, let's do this."

A trickle of fear ran down Walt's back. Someone was watching him. But was it Statica? Walt filled with dread as he worried that Ms. Wilhope's compass trick was a bust. But if she'd gotten it from Orsten's shop, that stuff was magical for sure. So why couldn't it put a protective circle around him? It just *had* to work.

Still, his breathing sounded loud and way too fast. Why was he so small? If only he was big and tough the way Dad wanted, he wouldn't need to hide in a circle. His hands trembled as he opened the door.

The inside of the windmill was still just as remarkable as before, and Walt heard Fenn take a quick breath of appreciation. The shiny gears and steel rods glistened under the string of electric lights, and the low flames of the gas lanterns shot up as if they were greeting Walt and Fenn.

Walt held up a fist, signaling Fenn to stop. He had *always* wanted to do that. It did feel a little like he was on a special ops mission. Or maybe more like he had fallen into a video game. But unlike a game, if his plan failed there wouldn't be any extra lives or do-overs.

He gulped and gave a signal to move ahead, while he scanned the room to make sure no one was lurking in a dark corner.

Only one of the ancient-looking millstones spun slowly, waiting for something to grind. And on the ground next to it was shattered glass and colorful goo. So Canter had made it there. And Statica *had* gotten the upper hand.

A small tremor fluttered across Walt's cheek as he clenched his jaw. He felt relief and disappointment in equal measure. He and Fenn stared at each other, their eyes wide with fear.

Walt's brain told him to get out of there. The evidence of Statica's superior strength over someone as tough as Canter made him feel as if there was really nothing *he* could do. A short boy with weak shoulders. He took a breath, and it was so shallow it was like taking a tiny sip of air. If this *were* a video game, he'd have a real weapon to protect himself. Not an *eraser*.

But Fenn was looking at him expectantly. Waiting for Walt to take charge. Walt slowly inhaled. Let the air fill his lungs. He pointed to the glow that came from upstairs.

Then he pointed to Fenn and mimed Fenn walking up.

But before Fenn could move toward the stairs, Walt got close to his ear. "If things go sideways, get back to Van and Dylan, and you three use the traveling machine to go back to Blackbird Bay."

Fenn shook his head. "No! That's not what you said," he whispered angrily.

"It's better than being alone!" Walt whispered back. Van could finally get Dad's attention, and Dylan would be back home and safe. And Fenn would probably be great at football. *And* no more worlds would have to be destroyed. Walt blinked back tears. It was actually a better plan than the ridiculous one he was about to launch.

Fenn looked unconvinced, but he started toward the

stairs. Then he paused and switched direction. He shot Walt an apologetic look. "Sorry," he said, and ran out the door.

Walt fell back on his heels in shock. Fenn had done it again! What kind of person was he?

For a moment Walt wanted to run. What could he do all by himself? His plan was ruined. He took a step toward the door. But then what? He clenched his teeth. He *had* to try. He looked around the floor to see if there was anything remotely like a weapon.

Something shiny near the wall caught his eye. The hand cages. They were open, and Walt imagined them getting kicked across the floor when Canter had failed to get them on Statica. Carefully, Walt picked them up. He felt like a bear that had the really *smart* idea to pick up a bear trap. If the cages clicked on his hands, there was no way he'd be able to open them back up. But what if he could figure out how to get them on Statica? He just had to get close without Statica seeing him. The cages seemed like a lot stronger solution than an eraser.

Walt wished it was as loud as it had been the last time he'd been in the windmill. But the mechanics of the gears were still. Whether Statica could see him or not, he'd probably hear Walt's panicked heartbeats. Slowly, *very* slowly, Walt crept up the stairs.

When he got to the second floor, Walt once again

felt awe at the sight of so many maps. But then something rustled above him, and Walt let out a strangled gasp. Hanging from the rafters were dozens of the horrible bazzards.

"Walter?" a low, gravelly voice asked. It was a voice that had been around the block more than a few times. Old and weathered.

Walt froze. He couldn't see the person behind the wall of bookcases, but he recognized that voice. Even though it had only spoken to him once. *Statica.* Even after his planning, he hadn't truly imagined this moment. Coming face-to-face with the evil mapmaker. His mouth dried to ash.

How did Statica know it was *him*? He should get out of there. Escape. Instead he slid the chain of the hand cages over his shoulder and looked around for a place to hide. He'd regroup. Figure out plan B. But where could he avoid being seen?

In desperation he ducked under a table. He pulled some of the maps down in order to make a small curtain and then scuttled back, pressing against the wall. Grasping his knees, he tried to make himself as small as possible. It wasn't a great hiding place. He prayed the compass circle thing worked.

There was a loud creak of a chair and then clumping footsteps. Walt squeezed his eyes closed.

"I may not be able to see you, but I can certainly smell you," Statica said. "Your fear is almost suffocating." He sounded disappointed, and his voice reminded Walt of his uncle Hunter, who smoked and had to stop to cough after every other sentence.

Walt tried to calm down. Slow his heartbeat. Make the stench of fear go away. He took small, measured, *quiet* breaths. The whole time he repeated in his head: *Don't be afraid. Don't be afraid.* But it wasn't working. He was terrified.

"There's no reason to be afraid. You can't believe all those lies you've been told. All those stories about me," Statica said. "Canter would tell you anything to try and make you ashamed of who you are." He slowly walked around the space, trying to act as if he wasn't looking for Walt, but Walt could see how he was casually smelling the air. Walt smelled himself. He *was* a bit rank. Today had been no match for his deodorant.

"Canter hates us. I'm sure you gleaned that much. He's been hunting me for a long time. Driven by vengeance for something that was a mistake. It's making him desperate and perhaps a bit . . . unbalanced."

Walt clamped both hands over his mouth to keep from speaking.

"He doesn't appreciate mapmaking. People so often want to destroy what they don't understand," Statica said, and sighed dramatically. "*I* want to work with you,

Walter. Help you become everything you can be." Statica's voice started to fill with hope. "I want to share this journey with you. I knew it couldn't be just anyone. I knew as soon as you were born what you'd become, and when I felt your skill developing, it was remarkable. I *appreciate* what you can do, Walter. Maybe I'm the only one who truly can. And it will be so wonderful for us to work together. I understand you in a way your parents would never be able to." Walt was glad his hands covered his shocked gasp. It was as if Statica could see right inside him. "Being a mapmaker is so special, so unique. And I want to share with you all of my knowledge."

Walt felt so confused. How was he supposed to know who to believe? What Statica said made more sense than anything Canter had said. But what about Bliss? Or all the other maps in the book? But what if Canter had lied? Walt wondered again if the book was some kind of trick to make Walt think Statica was evil. Canter wanted revenge. Of course he would try to get Walt to think Statica was as bad as he'd said, just so Walt would tell Canter where Statica was.

As if in answer, Statica said, "That meddlesome man, Canter, has been nothing but trouble. He doesn't understand us, Walter. Surely you must have felt that?"

You got that right, Walt thought. He was finding it very difficult to stay silent. Considering Canter was the one who had been ready to maroon Walt in Bliss,

Walt was hardly a fan. And ever since he had learned he was a mapmaker, he'd wanted to find out what it really meant. Orsten hadn't been helpful. And didn't Orsten and Canter just want to use him?

Walt still wished he could talk to another mapmaker who could explain things. And here was his chance. He braved peeking out from under the table. Statica stood near the center of the room. By the glowing crystals. He'd tied his hair back in a knot, and his eyebrows were a dark straight line above his eyes. He wore a long gown embroidered with lines, and Walt realized with shock that it was a map. Statica's shoulders were low, and he seemed more like a grandpa than an imposing evil mastermind.

"Did you hear me calling you, Walter? I didn't want your experience to be like mine. When I realized what I could do, no one came to my aid. No one explained anything. So of course I made mistakes." Statica shook his head.

Walt thought how that would have been for him. If he had just drawn things that appeared but no one explained what was happening, and everyone said he was being irrational and maybe he was . . . well, no one liked to use the word, but they would've been thinking it. And he would have felt like there had to be something wrong with him.

He remembered when he first saw the dig in Blackbird

Bay and his brain tried to convince him that he had seen it but just forgot. Imagine a whole lifetime of that. Or what if he had drawn an actual dinosaur by mistake and kids got eaten instead of them playing on the dinosaur-shaped play structure? Maybe Statica hadn't meant to mess up all those worlds. Maybe he'd only been a little kid when he did it. Walt opened his mouth to ask but then closed it quick. How could he believe anything Statica said? Hadn't he destroyed worlds just to get Walt?

"Once you know all you can do, Walter, you'll understand that being a mapmaker is a fabulous gift. No one is stronger than us. No one more powerful. Why, we are gods! Imagine that. Did you ever believe you would be stronger than everyone you know? Work with me, Walter. You can be larger than life!"

Walt felt that Statica was reaching down right into the center of him. The lumpy, hot knot of fear and frustration. Before he could think better of it, he climbed from underneath the table. "They said you destroyed worlds," he said. "Why would you do that?"

Statica's head snapped toward Walt, but just to the left, and Walt realized that miraculously, Statica couldn't seem to see him. Very slowly and carefully, Walt moved to a different spot to see if Statica tracked him, but the old man's head didn't turn.

"This is exactly the type of thing that wouldn't make

sense to anyone other than another mapmaker. Walter, the universe is overfull with worlds. What no one told you is that it is our *job* to cull the excess. There just can't be an unlimited amount of worlds! And I admit when I first learned about my gift, I created so many. Too many. It was very irresponsible. Didn't that silly ox explain?"

Walt's head spun. Obviously Orsten was the ox in question. Quietly Walt started to move to the stairs. All he had to do now was go back outside and erase the windmill. And Statica would be gone. Probably forever.

But.

A lot of what Statica was saying made sense. Shouldn't he know for sure Statica was bad before erasing him? And he had so many questions. The wind outside must be blowing hard, because the sound of the creaking sails filled the room. It made Walt wonder about something that had been bugging him almost since the beginning. And he could find out things he wanted to know while remaining invisible to Statica. While he figured out what to do.

"Did you . . . somehow get in my head to make me draw the windmill?" Walt had imagined it as his, but it was clear that this place was Statica's.

"Wasn't that a wonderful moment, my son? I knew you would need a place to escape to. Mapmakers are misunderstood and rejected by those who should love them most. I am so happy here. I was sure you would be too."

"But why a windmill?" Walt kept moving around the room so that Statica wouldn't know exactly where he was. "I mean, if you could draw any place to live, seems like it would be a palace or something." The windmill was cool, no question, but it did seem like an odd choice. And even when Walt drew it, he remembered part of his brain asking why.

"A *palace?*" Statica said, seeming to be repulsed at the suggestion. "Palaces are young and what power do they produce? But windmills? They have existed for millennia and can harness the *wind*. What place could be better?" Statica looked around the room and smiled. Walt knew it couldn't actually be true, but to him it felt as if the room was somehow smiling back. As if it were alive. The crystal nestlike thing glowed a bit brighter.

Statica looked right at Walt, and Walt quickly moved. Was there a time limit on the compass's power?

"What else do you want to know, dear boy?" Statica asked, and Walt was relieved to see that Statica remained turned to the spot he had just left.

So many questions bubbled in his head Walt couldn't sort them out. Could he risk trusting Statica? Maybe he really was the only person in the universe who could completely understand him.

"What I've done for you, Walter. Has anyone else

been willing to work so hard just to have you at their side?" Statica went back behind the wall of bookcases and Walt tiptoed after him, the chain connecting the hand cages digging painfully into his shoulder.

MAPMAKERS R US

When Walt stepped around the bookcase, he almost stumbled over the body on the floor.

Canter.

There were thick, dark red rope-things wrapped around him, squeezing him, and his eyes were wide with either fury or pain. His legs were twisting and struggling to get free, but he was completely trapped. One rope thing pressed across his mouth, silencing him. The bulging and slimy-looking things that surrounded him looked like they were full of blood, and Walt wanted to puke. Were they bloodsuckers? Canter's legs stilled and then his eyes closed.

"Don't mind him," Statica said. He was bending over a desk, busily erasing something. "He won't be bothering us anymore. Not with my syphons on him." Statica chuckled and then blew eraser dust from the desk.

Walt bit his knuckle. Statica sounded so dismissive. Like he didn't care about Canter's suffering at all. That wasn't okay. Canter was a jerk. Completely. No question. But you don't go around squeezing the living daylights out of people. Or sucking their blood out. He worried that that was what the syphons were doing. And who created such a horrible creature?

One of the bazzards circled the room and then landed on Statica's shoulder. The bat-bird thing stared at Walt with mean red eyes.

"You know, I quite like this world of yours, Walter. Pity if it was one of the ones that had to be culled."

"No!" Walt said, and Statica looked directly at him. Walt immediately jumped over Canter's body and slid across the room, hiding behind a wide filing cabinet. One syphon, which looked like a red pulsing vine of . . . goo? . . . unwrapped from Canter and grew longer and thicker and started swaying back and forth like a snake. It seemed focused on Walt, and Walt realized that it didn't matter if Statica couldn't see him if one of his monsters could.

"This will be your first lesson," Statica said. "We have to make hard decisions, Walter. Not every world can continue. But you're right. It might be too much to ask you to destroy your first world. In time, you would have cared less about it, of course. It would've bored you. You would have toyed with it as much as you could and then, *poof*." Statica blew into the air. "You wouldn't even have missed it when it was gone."

Walt wanted to argue, but that was probably what Statica wanted. And there was something wrong with what Statica had said. Well, there was a lot wrong with it. The idea that Walt would ever stop caring about Djaruba was preposterous. But it wasn't just that. It was the *way* Statica had said it. Another bazzard flew from the rafters and landed on the desk.

"You may be interested in this new project of mine," Statica said. "There's so much for us to share, dear boy."

Walt couldn't see from where he was hiding what map Statica had on the desk. What world was he creating or changing?

"Haven't you been wondering, Walter, why people try to stop mapmakers? It's jealousy, pure and simple. They are so envious of what we can do. You can't possibly believe they should be hunting us, do you?" Statica asked. "Making what we do a *crime?*" Statica gripped a pencil so tightly it snapped in two. "But witches and shape-shifters and sparks should be allowed? Does that sound right to you?"

Walt was having a hard time not speaking up. He had

no clue what a spark was, but he honestly *didn't* think it was right for there to be laws against mapmaking. He looked at the hand cages. They *were* horrible. What type of mind could come up with something like that? Walt slid the chain off his shoulder and quietly rested the hand cages on the floor. A tremor went through him, and he looked over at Canter. Walt couldn't be sure, but he thought he saw the faintest movement in Canter's arms. So he was still alive. At least for now. Walt felt an unexpected surge of relief.

"I've made them pay for what they've done to me," Statica said. "But it's been difficult at times. Have you noticed the fatigue you feel after working on a map, Walter?" Statica's voice had become soft and purring. "An ache in your fingers? Maybe you can't run as fast? Mapmaking is a bit of a tricky gift. We are given so much power, but yet it takes a lot out of us, does it not?" Statica added, "But it doesn't have to."

Walt looked down at his little hands. His skinny legs. He now understood how mapmaking affected him. How worn out it made him feel. But what if it was also keeping him small? And was there a way around it?

"I figured out the secret," Statica whispered. "Or maybe I should say, I *mapped* it out. How to be powerful *and* strong."

Walt had to know. Was there really something that

would make him stronger? Maybe even make him grow finally? "What . . . what is it?" he asked. The scary red syphon flopped to the floor with a splotch and started squirming toward him. It was like a blood-filled boa constrictor, and Walt didn't want it anywhere near him. Quickly he crawled to a new spot. Thankfully, the icky thing didn't follow. Maybe this part didn't have eyes?

"Ah," Statica said. "But we'd have to be partners for me to reveal that to you. Hardly seems fair otherwise." He grabbed a red pencil and started humming as he added some detail to what he was working on. Then he said, "What I have so enjoyed these last eleven years has been deciding which world. There's so many. Which one to choose?" He leaned back in his chair. "This year, I was tremendously excited. I knew once again the fool wouldn't give you up. I was ready with my choice. Do you want to see which world I picked?"

Walt had to know. And if he was very quiet, he could look without Statica even knowing. So without making a sound, he crept over to the desk. But what he saw shocked him so much, he forgot he was supposed to be hiding. The map was stunning. Probably the most beautiful one Walt had ever seen.

"Earth?" he croaked. "You were going to destroy *Earth*?"

Statica reached out, and before Walt could step

away, Statica had grabbed his wrist. His fingernails dug into Walt's skin. "Got you," he said.

Walt tried to pull away, but Statica was stronger than he was. "Let me go!" Walt cried. "What are you doing?"

"You're far too trusting, Walter," Statica said.

"Get off me!" Walt yelled, still struggling to get away, but it was no use.

With his free hand, Statica slid the map of Earth over, and underneath it *was* a map of Djaruba. But it wasn't exactly like Walt's. On this map of Djaruba, Walt saw bazzards flying above the bluff where Walt, Van, and Dylan had first landed. And streaks of lava coming out of Mount Yoray. And the sea creature that Walt had drawn, which had been sort of silly and wonky looking, had been altered to have big fangs and mean eyes. But maybe the worst thing was that Walt could see the very faint remains of an erased circle in front of the windmill. Whatever protection there had been, it was gone. Statica had erased it. And that meant if Walt had been shrouded before, he was now totally visible.

Statica grinned at Walt, showing wolflike teeth. "Hello there."

Walt bit back a scream. Statica's cold, dark eyes bore into him. Why hadn't he erased Statica when he'd had the chance?

"Such a silly boy. You of all people should've seen

through the impermanence of anything drawn on a map." Statica *tsk*ed at him, like Walt was such a disappointment. His grip on Walt's wrist tightened and Walt yelped in pain. Statica's eyes dropped to Walt's hands. "Silly and careless. Allowing your hands to be damaged like this? Our hands are our tools. They are our weapons. Our treasure! I should've known when I saw this ridiculous world of yours that you were quite a weak mapmaker. Re-creating it was almost too easy."

"But how can you even have a map of Djaruba? It's *mine!*"

"Is it?" Statica cocked an eyebrow. "I've been told that can be a dangerous way of thinking." He chuckled menacingly.

"That's not what I meant," Walt said, starting to sweat. "But I drew it. How could you have seen it?"

"Oh, Walter, you *dreamed* about it incessantly," Statica said. "I improved upon it, of course."

Walt looked at the map of Djaruba again. Statica had changed things. Just like Walt had changed things in Blackbird Bay. Changes that became part of the world's history. All the danger they had seen since they got here—Statica was behind almost all of it. "You could've killed us!"

"And that would've been unfortunate. Well, not the others. I have no use for them, but I would've hated to lose you, Walter. You mean so much to me," Statica said. "Who knows how long it would have been before another mapmaker was born? I simply wanted you to stay. To come to me like I asked you to. Such a shame I was indisposed when you first arrived. We could have avoided so much unpleasantness. But I was feeling a bit of a . . ." He bent his neck from side to side as if trying to get out a crick. "Strain."

Statica shook his head. "But it was so unwise to go into a volcano. Really, making it active was supposed to keep you *out*. I'm not often surprised, but that did shock me. Why would you work so hard to get back to your pathetic existence when you could simply enjoy life here?"

"It's not pathetic," Walt said, his voice small and rather, well, pathetic.

"Be that as it may, it looks like you have a choice to make, Walter. Which world will you save?" He nodded to the two maps. Djaruba and Earth.

Walt stared at Statica in disbelief. Statica's brown eyes looked like they had snakes swimming in them. "You're not serious," Walt pleaded. "You're talking about an entire planet. Earth is—"

"Rather disgusting," Statica said. "I've seen the horrors there. People talk about *my* monsters? I couldn't even dream up some of the *things* that live on that world."

"Have you seen the Grand Canyon?" Walt shouted. "Zhangjiajie National Forest? Hawaii!" Walt had a whole list in his head of stunning places around the world he wanted to visit, but he was having a hard time coming up with them. "The Barrier Reef! Mount Fuji . . . um . . ." Why couldn't he think?

"I could draw any of that," Statica said, sounding bored.

Walt didn't think that was true, or even the point. "But it's the *world*! It's full of people!" Walt felt like his throat was closing and Statica's fingernails were really digging in.

"It's *a* world, Walter." Statica waved his free hand around the room, indicating all the maps. "Just one."

Statica paused to let the weight of that sink in. All these talks of worlds and seeing Bliss and being here, and still it was hard to comprehend. Other worlds just as full and complicated as Earth.

"And you *can* save it," Statica said. "You just have to give up this one." Statica tapped the map of Djaruba and then shrugged as if he didn't care either way. Then he bent toward Walt. "Show me what you have inside you. I'm dying to see." His breath was foul, like he'd sucked on onions dipped in sour milk.

Walt's eyes watered. "But you *have* me! You were destroying worlds to get me. I get it. Game over."

271

"Yes, I did say I would destroy a world every year that Canter refused to tell me where to find you. But in point of fact . . ." Statica slid his gaze to Canter. "He never *did* tell me anything." His grip on Walt's wrist tightened. "And I never said I would stop once I had you in my grasp."

Walt's head started to spin. "I don't want to destroy worlds like you do!" he cried.

Statica cocked an eyebrow at him. "Really? Didn't you enjoy destroying that small town? Did you hear the people screaming their last breath?"

"No one was there!" Walt cried. He wanted more than anything to be certain that was true. "It was deserted."

The bazzard on the desk reached over and pinched his arm hard, and Walt yelped. Statica tutted at the foul creature. "Now, now, my pet, play nice with our guest." But then he twisted Walt's wrist painfully. "Have you made your choice?"

Walt's mouth dropped open wide. Statica was willing to do such awful things just to have Walt by his side? It was almost flattering, in a gross way. But there was something seriously wrong with someone who didn't care who they hurt just to get what they wanted.

"Okay," Walt said, sounding defeated. "I'll work with you. I'll be your apprentice." Walt felt a tiny bit of him dying. He was agreeing to never go home. To never see his family again. But maybe, over time, he could get Statica to see that if they did good things, if they created *beautiful* worlds, they would no longer be hated and hunted. No one would dream of putting something like hand cages on them.

Statica threw back his head and roared with laughter. He laughed so hard it was a moment before he could speak.

"Whatever gave you the idea I wanted you as my apprentice?" Statica kept laughing until tears rolled down his face.

"But you said . . ." Walt was confused and a bit relieved. Maybe things weren't as bad as he thought. "Didn't you say you wanted me by your side?"

"And I do!" Statica said. "I want you by my side forever and always, my boy." He smiled sinisterly at Walt. "But you misunderstood. I meant something quite a bit more literal than you had in mind."

"What . . . what do you mean?" Walt asked, a vicious itch clawing down his back. He tried to pull away, but Statica's grip was like a vise.

"I hated how weak I felt after creating my wonders. It was a completely unacceptable side effect. How could other mapmakers have simply accepted it as our fate? I supposed they satisfied themselves with making only one world. And making them *safe*." He uttered the word as if it was vile. "Not exerting themselves. I want more! Bigger. More fantastical! But the energy it takes . . ." The snakes in Statica's eyes swam faster and faster.

"I knew, I *knew*, if a mapmaker's power was draining from him, then that power could be . . . channeled. Redirected. The windmill was an inspiration, in a way. To harness something as mighty as the wind, and so simply? Oh, Walter, you won't serve as my apprentice." Statica looked at him as if he was the tastiest meal he was about to devour. "But you *will* serve me."

MAPMAKERS CAN
DRAW ANYTHING

Walt knew he was looking into the face of pure evil. If he was given another chance, he wouldn't hesitate to take Statica out.

"It's exquisitely simple, really. We really *can* draw anything." Statica rose up and started dragging Walt across the floor. Walt tried to dig in his heels, but there was no traction against the wood floor and he just slid behind Statica like a puppet.

Statica tugged him over to the shiny, shimmering nest of crystals. "Welcome to your new home, Walter. You won't be bored ever again. I'm afraid you won't be much of anything ever again except my . . . battery."

The crystals—which weren't crystals at all, Walt saw now, but more like piles of jellyfish all connected together—must've sensed that they were about to get a treat. They started squirming and glowing with what seemed like bioluminescence.

Walt didn't know how Statica's system worked, but he didn't need to. He was certain that if Statica somehow got him on that glowing pile, he was done for.

"It pleases me that with what you're giving me, I can give you something too. A gift of a world. You really can save one, Walter. And what a hero you will be. Saving an entire planet with your sacrifice." Statica said the word *planet* like it was a joke. "Too bad no one will know what a big man you were at the end."

Walt heard his dad's voice in his head. All the repetitions of drills. All the talk of being strong. How Walt needed to man up. But he couldn't make the choice Statica was asking. Saving Earth, his home, seemed like the obvious choice, but what about Fenn? And Heckett? And maybe the millions of people that lived somewhere on Djaruba that he hadn't seen yet? Their lives were important too.

Walt sniffled. "P-p-please don't," he begged, his voice trembling. Tears ran freely down his face and dripped onto his shirt. His shoulders curved forward and his head bowed. His free arm hung limply at his side. He was the smallest he'd ever been.

Statica grunted in disgust. "I knew you were small and weak, but I didn't know you were so *pathetic* as well." He spoke as if he could read Walt's mind.

"You're h-hurting me," Walt said, the tears now flowing faster than he could wipe away.

"Why I would *want* you at all," Statica said snidely. "Such a weakling."

And that was when Walt felt it. The slight lessening of pressure in Statica's grip. It was exactly what he'd been waiting for. Because he'd remembered something else Dad had said. *Looking* weak and *being* weak were two different things.

Walt yanked free from Statica while, at the same time, his other hand—which had been slowly reaching into his pocket—pulled out the compass. He jabbed the pointy end right into one of Statica's arms.

It was probably more the surprise than anything that made Statica stop reaching for him. Walt jabbed Statica again. In his other arm. And again. In his side. The compass point couldn't do much damage, but it obviously hurt a lot. Still, Walt wished he had a sword or something. Statica flailed wildly, trying to catch hold of Walt, but Walt was too quick for him. Walt aimed higher and caught Statica in the shoulder.

Dad had tried to tell him once that small guys actually had an advantage. People always underestimated them. Even while Walt stung Statica with the compass, he realized something he should've known all along: Dad really did just want the best for him. Thinking about that now made Walt go into beast mode. "I'm not going to let you destroy any more worlds!" He stuck Statica right in the neck and then ran back to the desk. He just needed to get to the map of Djaruba. He'd erase the windmill now. Even while he was inside. What did it matter? Statica had to be stopped.

A dark shape passed by the window, but Walt couldn't worry about it.

But then, before he knew what was happening, he was under attack. Bazzards surrounded him and were pinching at him and pecking at him. He hated these creatures that had no business being in his world.

"Get away!" Walt wailed at them as he pressed forward to the desk. No gross bat-birds were going to stop him.

He pulled his Magic Rub eraser from his pocket and started erasing the bazzards from the map. But before he could get them all, one snatched the eraser right out of his hand.

Walt chased after at it, but a blast outside stopped him. The window shattered and the windmill sails burst into flames. The wooden blades still turned but now were engulfed in fire.

And then the bookcases came crashing down.

Statica stood there looking like an enraged bull facing a matador. A tiny hole in his neck seeped blood, and Walt could see spots of blood staining his robe. With a shout of anger, Statica staggered toward Walt.

Walt circled away. Now that the bookcases were down, he didn't have any protection from the glowing mass in the center of the room. Whatever he did, he needed to keep away from it.

Movement out of the corner of his eye caught his attention. And, unbelievably, a mass of curls peeked through the hole in the floor. *Van?*

Sandy hair joined the curls.

Van climbed up onto the floor, with Dylan right behind her. She still had the traveling machine wrapped around her waist, and Walt couldn't understand how she and Dylan had been able to use it, but then Fenn's crowned hair poked through the opening in the floor, and a moment later he joined Van and Dylan. Walt couldn't believe it. He had been certain that Fenn was deserting him.

Fenn's eyes fell to Canter, who was almost completely covered by the crimson syphons. They pulsed and twisted around him, and Canter's eyes blazed with anger and pain. Fenn looked over at Walt, a question in his eyes, and Walt wanted to explain that he hadn't done that. He wouldn't have.

"Get away from my twin," Van said.

"You don't know what or who you're dealing with, little girl," Statica sneered.

"I'm not afraid of you," Van said, but her voice wobbled.

Walt looked over at Van and he could *feel* her fear. And it occurred to him that maybe sometimes when Van was acting brave, she was only pretending. Maybe sometimes she was just as scared of things as he was.

"Oh, but you should be," Statica said. He grabbed the maps from the desk. "Tell them, Walter, how easy it would be for me to destroy one."

Dylan's eyebrows went clear into his hairline. "Is that *Earth*?" His eyes flew to Walt. "Walt, he's not saying . . ."

Walt couldn't even answer. He just nodded.

Statica's voice suddenly became solicitous, the way it had been when he had first talked to Walt. "Fenn. I'll bring them all back." He waved the map of Djaruba. "I can do it with just a stroke of a pen. Walter could have done it for you. I wonder why he didn't."

Fenn's whole body shook. And then he took a very small step away from Van and Dylan.

Walt yelled, "He's lying. I would've done it if I could have." He made to run at Statica with the compass raised, but Statica took a step back and held both maps up. Walt stopped immediately.

Statica stared down at him. "Tut, tut, my boy. Mustn't tell lies." He started to tear the map of Earth. "A bright line appeared in the sky," Statica said, his voice honey-covered barbed wire. "And at first the silly citizens thought it was just a cloud."

"No!" Walt cried. The rip was in the top left corner, just touching the sky. If he was in Alaska right now, he was sure he'd see a small, jagged opening in the sky. And what if Statica kept tearing after that? Orsten had told him that mapmakers could destroy worlds. But he hadn't said how, and now Walt felt he knew. Destroying a map with the same intention as they created one. And he didn't doubt for a second that Statica would keep tearing if he didn't get his way.

Fenn took another step away, and it seemed to be clear which side he'd chosen. But then he dove to the floor and grabbed something shiny. The hand cages.

"Van!" he shouted, and he lobbed them to her.

"Go long, Walt!" Van shouted, and threw the cages to him. It was a terrible throw. Wobbly and off to the right, but Walt dove and managed to catch them before crashing to the floor. Fenn and Van raced toward Statica and tackled him, and Dylan shouted, "Now! Walt, now!"

Walt didn't hesitate. He snapped one hand cage on and Statica let out a roar. Before Walt could get the other cage on Statica's free hand, Statica shouldered and kicked the kids off him. And once he managed to break away from his attackers, he got up, towering over them.

He raised his caged hand in frustration, trying to shake the cage off, and Walt, without having any idea what it would do, ran at him full force and sent Statica into the shiny nest.

Statica screamed as the clear jellyfish things started to squirm around him, trapping him.

"Let's get out of here!" Van cried, and ran for the stairs. The few bazzards that were left circled and squawked about the room, and one landed in Van's hair. She waved her arms frantically, batting it away as she ran down the stairs.

Fenn and Dylan ran behind her. Walt looked at the bazzards darting around and found the one he wanted. He jumped up and latched on to the creature's sharp toes and yanked his eraser out of its mouth. "It's not even shiny, loser!" Walt grabbed the map of Earth from the floor and ran.

Right outside the windmill, Walt found his sister and friends waiting for him. Heckett was bouncing up and down on her talons like she was saying, "Look at me! Did you see what I did? Aren't I a good girl?"

Walt had to smile. "Good job on lighting up those sails, Heckett," he told her. "Very dramatic entrance." He felt great. He had done it! He'd defeated Statica.

Then Van looked at something behind him and screamed.

Dylan looked back. "What the—" he shouted.

Walt turned around with dread to see what awful thing they were looking at. He expected to see Statica, but this was almost worse. The bulbous red syphons had grown ten times bigger and were trailing out of the window, down the sides of the windmill, and one was poking its way out the door.

"What *are* those?" Dylan shrieked.

Heckett flew up and tried to peck at one, but it encircled one of her claws. She squawked loudly and flapped her wings but seemed stuck.

"Heckett!" Fenn cried.

The dragon tossed her head around as if she was trying to find a way to breathe fire at the syphon, but she was too close.

"We need to help her," Fenn said. He ran forward but the syphon coming out the door latched onto his leg like a horrible overgrown leech and Fenn hollered in pain.

Heckett stuck a sharp talon into the syphon gripping her, and dark red goo shot out. The syphon made a whistling noise, like a balloon losing air and then fell limp. But the other syphons started swinging around wildly, trying to hit Heckett. Heckett flew up in the air out of their reach and spit a fire ball at the back end of the syphon that held Fenn.

"Let's get out of here!" Fenn cried.

No one argued with him. The syphons seemed to be growing in size and were quickly making their way to the ground. Another one squeezed through the door.

"Run!" Van called out, and they all took off, with Heckett flying after them.

But they hadn't gotten far when Walt shouted, "Wait! Wait!" He bent over his knees panting.

Everyone stopped with him and Heckett landed close by. She anxiously eyed the syphons that were creeping across the ground. Coming toward them.

Walt reached into his pocket and pulled out Canter's calling card. He couldn't just leave him in there. No matter what he'd done—or wanted to do. "I just hold it and say his name?" Walt asked Fenn.

Fenn's eyes widened at the sight of the card. "I, uh . . ."

"Just tell me!" Walt demanded. "We don't have time for a guilty conscious!"

Fenn nodded but he looked uncomfortable. "Yeah. Hold it tight. And, uh, call him. I mean say his name."

Walt folded his fingers around the card. "Canter?" he said tentatively, keeping watch on the windmill and the syphons that now seemed dangerously close. "Nothing happened," he told Fenn accusingly.

"Like you *mean* it," Fenn said.

Walt gripped the card even tighter. "Canter!" he shouted.

And suddenly a faint glimmering cloud appeared next to them. Like a mass of weak fireflies. The cloud quickly solidified and became a very confused-looking Canter. He jumped to his feet and started brushing his legs and arms, but thankfully, none of the syphons had made the journey with him.

Canter stopped his frantic movements, and his hands went to where his gun belt should've been.

"Where's—" he started to say, when a shout came from inside the windmill.

Walt gasped. He wasn't surprised that Statica must've broken free somehow. And with his one uncaged hand had changed the syphons into monstrously large creatures. Any minute Statica would probably draw something even worse than blood snakes.

"Erase it, Walt!" Fenn shouted. "Remember your plan!"

"Do it!" Van said. "Erase it all!"

Walt threw the map of Djaruba on the ground and didn't waste any time. He rubbed the white eraser over and over the thin paper.

The syphons seemed to know they were in danger and raced toward them.

"Faster, Walt!" Dylan exclaimed.

Walt pressed harder with the eraser, rubbing back

and forth. The syphons grew faint and disappeared, but Walt didn't stop. He did what Dad was always telling him. He put more muscle into it, rubbing so hard he made a hole on the map.

"Walt!" Van said, pulling at his arm. "Stop!"

Walt looked over his shoulder. The syphons were completely gone but that wasn't all.

Where the windmill had been was a large sinkhole, and Walt could feel a strong pull, like the air had become a vacuum. It was as if the sinkhole was the open door of an airplane or, worse, a black hole. Even Heckett seemed worried. She tried to flap her wings, but the suction fought against her.

"Walt! It's pulling us in!" Dylan shouted.

The sucking wind got stronger and their feet slid forward. Walt looked down at his map and then over at the hole. What had he done? Statica's horrible monsters may have gotten sucked away, but now they were going to be too! A bush got swallowed. Then a tree. Walt didn't have any way to stop it. He couldn't unerase a hole.

"Do something!" Fenn said. "You're a *mapmaker*! Fix it."

There had to be a way. And suddenly Walt knew what to do.

"Walt!" Van shrieked, trying to dig her feet into the ground.

With shaking hands, Walt started to fold the map

in small accordion pleats. The ground shook and rocked beneath them. "The travelers moved across Djaruba," he said, and he could actually see the landscape whiz past them as they stood there. He pressed the last pleat, and there was a large shuddering before the ground stilled.

The sinkhole was still there on one side of them, still grabbing dirt and rocks and pulling at them, but on the other side—a big drop below them—was now desert and a large scribble. Walt recognized where he'd crossed out the oasis on his map just the other day. But the map seemed to be fighting against being folded. Maybe it was the pressure of the suction of the hole. In a second they'd be sucked into the sinkhole, and maybe the other side of Djaruba would be too.

"Jump!" Walt shouted, and they all did. As soon as they touched ground, Walt unfolded the map, sending the hole far from them.

"Okay that was . . . incredible!" Van said. "How did you even think to do that?"

Walt shrugged modestly. "I'm a mapmaker." Then he looked around at the wide expanse of desert. Wavy lines of heat filled the air. His mouth felt salty. He didn't feel the moment of victory he'd felt before. He just felt exhausted.

"We should get out of here," Canter said. "Sandstorms are pretty common in the Badlands."

Walt nodded. But then he said, "Fenn, I made you

a promise. And I swore on my twin." He laid the map of Djaruba on the ground again. The hole where the windmill had been looked awful, but he couldn't worry about that right now. He reached into his pocket for the pencil, but it was gone. Something poked his finger. "Ouch!" He pulled the compass out of his pocket.

"But you don't need a . . . cloaking device thingamajig anymore," Fenn said.

"Yeah, I'm done hiding, that's for sure," Walt said. "I'm sorry, Fenn, I . . ." Walt snapped his fingers and pulled out the small piece of graphite from the arm of the compass. He started to draw. "In a town of hundreds lived the boy Fenn with his family, and . . ." Walt looked at Heckett, who seemed to be listening with interest. "His trusty dragon, Heckett. The town bustled with people going on with the business of their lives."

As Walt drew and talked, he could swear he heard the sounds of life coming back all around them.

His arms began to tremble and his legs ached. He felt like his heart might burst out of his chest.

"Walt!" Van cried. "Stop! Stop! That's enough."

But Walt didn't stop. He drew until there was no more graphite left, and then he collapsed on the ground.

ALMOST OVER

Walt's eyes slowly opened, and he was greeted with Van's worried face.

"Are . . . are you okay?" she asked, her voice brimming with concern.

Walt tried to sit up but felt too weak. "I'm okay," he croaked. He couldn't remember ever feeling more beat-up. But behind the ache and wooziness and fatigue was a stirring of something really, really good. Map-making *didn't* have to be bad. And this pain he was in now, that Statica had been willing to destroy worlds to avoid, felt totally worth it.

With Van's help, he sat up, and then, shakily, he rubbed a hand over his head, as if he could wipe away his throbbing headache. "You can tell me if there's stuff missing," he told Fenn.

Fenn shook his head in amazement. "I can *feel* what you did. Before, everything felt empty, but now it's like . . ." He pressed a hand to his chest. "Thanks," he said, but his eyes said much more.

"MVP move, dude," Dylan said. "It was *scary* for a second there, but total MVP." He bent low, wove left and right, and then took an imaginary shot. "Game winner."

Canter took off his hat and shook it, then settled it back on his head. He held out a hand and Walt gripped it, allowing Canter to pull him to his feet. "Good work," Canter told him.

"Understatement," Van jabbed.

Walt had to smile at his sister. She was always going to be a little obnoxious, but she also was always going to have his back when it mattered. But then his smile faded, along with some of the glow of what he had just done. "So . . ." He swallowed hard, struggling to ask the question. What did it really mean to erase someone? "Did I *kill* Statica?"

"Hope so," Canter answered, too quickly for Walt's taste. Canter must've noticed the worry in Walt's face because he asked, "That bothers you?"

"What do you mean?" Walt asked. "Of course it bothers me." Killing the enemy in a video game was one thing, but actually taking someone out for real? He felt like he might throw up.

Canter shook his head. "If it makes you feel better, it wouldn't surprise me if Statica didn't have some escape clause. Mapmakers are . . ."

Walt waited for Canter to deliver his typical curses against mapmakers.

Canter's eyes narrowed and grimaced as if it pained him to say it, but he finally said, "Clever."

Walt's lips twitched, but the smile didn't reach his eyes. "That does *not* make me feel better," he said. His body tingled all over as if it was coming awake. It was better than the deep ache, but it wasn't exactly pleasant. He couldn't stop thinking about Statica. No matter how weak mapmaking made them feel, how could Statica have such disregard for *entire* worlds?

Walt picked up the maps and rolled them together. Two damaged maps, but at least the worlds hadn't been destroyed. "I'm *not* like him."

Canter settled his hand on Walt's shoulder. Walt tried not to stumble under the weight. "You're nothing like him, Walter." Then Canter dug into a pocket and pulled out a talisman with no hole. "I think you earned this. Be careful what you wish for." He tossed the coin to Walt, and Walt's hand shot out to catch it without even thinking.

Then Canter bent down and took a miniature ray

gun from his boot. "Always be prepared," Canter said.

"Maybe put it in reach next time," Van said smartly, but Canter ignored her.

"You have a way back?" Canter asked, and when Walt nodded, Canter shot a vertical line of azure blue into the air, pulled it open, and stepped through without looking back.

As soon as he was gone, Van turned to Walt. "I can't believe he gave you a wish! Lucky!" she said.

Walt didn't know how he felt, but he absolutely did not feel lucky.

Then Dylan asked, "So what's next? Back to the dragon stables? Maybe we could all take one out for a ride before the dragon racers get there?"

Walt had to grin at Dylan's enthusiasm. But then he shook his head. "We better get back." He nodded at the horizon. "Sun's down."

"Streetlights," Walt and Van said at the same time.

Fenn said, "I'm pretty anxious to go home and see my folks." Heckett fluttered her wings in agreement.

Walt nodded. He was ready to go, and yet he wasn't. He stepped closer to Fenn. Close enough to feel the heat of Heckett's breath. He tucked the maps under his arm and held out a hand. Fenn somberly shook Walt's hand and then pulled Walt into a tight bro hug.

"Come on, Walt," Van said softly. "We really do

need to go." She and Dylan both already had their helmets on.

"Okay," Walt answered. "We'll be back," he told Fenn.

"Yeah, you will," Fenn said, climbing onto Heckett. She immediately rose into the air. Fenn smiled down at them. "Next time, I'm definitely challenging Van to a dragon race."

Van laughed at that.

Walt looked up at Heckett. He took just another second to appreciate that he had drawn her really well. Fenn raised a hand, and then he and Heckett flew off, looking like they were chasing the sun.

Walt joined Van and Dylan, put on his helmet, and said, "Take us home."

MASSIVE

Walt had seen people kiss the ground when they'd returned from an awful place, but he wasn't about to kiss his fuzzy carpet. Though he did give it an affectionate pat.

"We did it." He felt like he had fought an army. And won. Like he had defeated a tyrannosaurus rex. Or jumped over the entire Grand Canyon. He felt a hundred feet tall.

"We actually made it back," Dylan said. "I sort of can't believe it."

They all took off their helmets and just lay on the floor, enjoying the safety of home.

"It's over," Van said with a happy sigh. "Did you

save one world or two, bro? I sort of lost track."

"Oh, crud," Walt said. He jumped up and, clutching the two maps, ran to his desk. First he pulled out tape and fixed the rip on the map of Earth. The Djaruba map was harder. The hole he'd made didn't seem fixable. Where his map used to hang was empty, and Walt realized with shock that when he had made his wish back on Bliss, the talisman hadn't re-created a map of Djaruba—it was his actual map. Which made the hole seem worse, somehow.

He looked around the room desperately before inspiration hit. He ripped a small piece from the corner of one of his *Phantom Tollbooth* maps—a blank corner, just in case. He turned the map of Djaruba over and taped the blank piece to the back, covering the hole. It made him happy to think that maybe he was giving just a tiny bit of Milo's magical land to Djaruba.

Then he turned the map back over and grabbed some colored pencils. "Where there used to be a sucking hole, there was a majestic redwood tree. Its branches stretched wide, and Fenn and Heckett loved to sit in the shade below it."

"Nice," Van said.

Walt sighed. "This saving-the-world business is exhausting. Someone should really warn us about that next time. And it hurts."

Dylan sat up. "Are we really saying that we're living

on a *map?*" He waved his hands around. "All this. The whole world?"

Van and Walt both nodded, looking very much like twins. "Yup," they said at the same time.

"That is so freaky," Dylan said.

Walt opened up the window and let in the cool night air and breathed deep. It was way past streetlights coming on. High above him, the sky was full of little pinpricks of light. So many stars. Maybe thousands of worlds. How many had been made by a mapmaker? After everything, Walt didn't know how he felt about what he could do.

Dylan came up behind him. "Do you think mapmaking will still be against the law?"

Walt turned to face him and shrugged. Maybe it should be. The thought made him sad. "I don't know. Maybe if word gets out about Statica being gone, people . . ." Walt paused as he thought about Orsten. "Or, you know . . . whatever type of being lives there . . . will relax. At least *Canter* won't be hunting me." He yawned so big he felt his face might break. He pulled the wish-granting talisman out of his pocket.

"I don't know how many wishes this has. Maybe just one." He thought about how upset Dylan had been earlier that day when he'd seen all the changes that had been made to Blackbird Bay. "I don't know exactly what things got changed here, but I can wish for things to go back to how they were?" Even if he only had one wish, this was something he felt he had to do. A mapmaker had messed with Blackbird Bay. So a mapmaker should try to fix it.

"What?" Van exclaimed, and Walt turned to give her a stern look.

"Naw," Dylan said. "That seems like a total waste of a wish. We'll figure out something. Besides, the purple lake is actually cool. And I think I remember swimming in it."

Walt let out a small sigh of relief.

Van joined the boys at the window. "Wishes," she said, with a sparkle in her voice.

Walt set the talisman down on his bookcase. He thought of Fenn and how a wish could go horribly wrong. "We'll think real hard before using that."

"You mean you will," Van said, smiling at him. "But *we* are going to be in so much trouble getting home this late."

"Guess we better find out how much," Walt said. He took one more breath of night air before walking over and opening his door. He could hear the sound of the television downstairs.

"Walt! Wait! Let's figure out a story or something!" Van whispered urgently.

"Nothing to do but face it," Walt said. "Dad?" he called out as he went down the stairs. But there was no answer, and when Walt got to the living room he saw why. "Dad!"

Dad was sitting on the couch, facing the television, his eyes wide open but completely blank. It was like a Dad *shell*. Walt touched him. He was warm. He was breathing.

"We need to call 911!" Walt hollered. "Dad's had a stroke or something."

Dylan pulled out his cell phone. "I can't," he said, sounding desperate. "My phone is fried from that swim in the river."

Van and Walt both raced toward the kitchen for the landline but came to a screeching halt when they swung through the door. Mom was standing at the island, setting a pizza box down.

A wave of relief washed over Walt. "Mom! Dad's not okay, he's—"

But Mom didn't turn at the sound of his voice. In fact, Mom didn't move at all.

"What's wrong with them?" Van cried.

Something very shiny came out of the shadows. "Nothing is wrong with them, dear. My goodness, you took quite a while."

"Ms. *Wilhope*?" Walt croaked. "What do you . . ."

Dylan's eyes went as wide as an owl's. "Who's *this*?"

"Our landlord?" Van answered, as if she wasn't sure.

"Yes," Ms. Wilhope said with a little chuckle. Then she explained to Walt, "Just a little spell." She spoke dismissively as if what she'd done to his parents was no big deal. "When you didn't get back, Walter, I was so worried. I thought something terrible might have happened."

Walt couldn't be sure, but Ms. Wilhope sounded a little excited. Then she said, "I didn't want you to be in trouble. Not if you were out having a wonderful adventure. So I . . . *stilled* them."

Walt was so shocked, he felt like *he* couldn't move.

Ms. Wilhope started picking at a loose thread on her top. The refrigerator quietly hummed, and somewhere outside a dog started barking. Ms. Wilhope looked up and said, "Do you have scissors handy? This thread is driving me out the door."

"You—you *what*?" Walt asked, his mouth finally unstuck. He was horrified and really, really confused. "How did you . . . what are you even saying?"

"You . . ." Van pointed at her, but then she turned to Walt. "I *told* you she's a witch!"

"But of course!" Ms. Wilhope sounded a little too jolly. "It's not like it was a secret. Although I don't go blabbing it to every, Tom, Zander, and Lo—"

"Unfreeze them!" Walt barked. "Or *unstill* them, or whatever you want to call it."

Ms. Wilhope looked at him in surprise. "Are you *angry* with me?" she asked, pressing a hand to her chest. "I was trying to *help*. I assure you they are right as soup!"

"Huh?" Dylan said.

"It's rain!" Walt said, no longer interested in sparing her feelings.

"Rain." Ms. Wilhope nodded. "I'll remember."

"Bring them back," Van pleaded.

Ms. Wilhope held up a finger. "Magic," she whispered conspiratorially, "really is everywhere, if you just look." She nodded at Van. "Why, Van, you should know this as well as your brother. Your talent hasn't quite developed yet, but in time, my dear. In time." Ms. Wilhope beamed. "Quite glorious."

"What?" Van exclaimed.

"Hah!" Dylan said, not looking a bit surprised. "I knew it."

Walt ignored him. He was too busy thinking about the compass Ms. Wilhope had given him for protection and how Statica had known Walt was using it. (And how easily Statica had simply erased the protective circle.) "Why did you give me such a useless thing as the compass? If you're a witch, shouldn't you have given me something more powerful? Something that couldn't have just been *erased*?"

"But only a—" Ms. Wilhope cut herself off and appraised Walt with concerned eyes. "So, he found you."

"You *know* about Statica?" Walt demanded.

Ms. Wilhope shuddered slightly. "Our paths have crossed." She pushed back her shoulders and pressed her palms together. "You'll need to tell me what happened. Many things could be at risk."

Before Walt could ask her what she meant, Van tugged at his arm. "Who cares about Statica now?" she wailed. "Walt, make her fix Mom and Dad!"

Walt blinked and looked at Mom, who was so, so still. Suddenly Walt was furious. Van was right. "I'm not telling you anything! Undo the spell on our parents."

"But—" Ms. Wilhope began.

"Right *now*." Walt folded his arms and glared at her the way Dad did to him all the time. The way that meant "I am waiting for you to do what you've been told."

"Of course. Of course," Ms. Wilhope twittered. "It may cause some complications, but I can see you're quite determined." She pressed her hands together and then bent her fingers in a way that looked like it might hurt. Something about the way she moved her hands seemed familiar to Walt. Very softly, she murmured a few words.

Mom blinked. And then she turned her head and looked at Walt. And *then* she screamed and dropped the pizza box.

Walt realized immediately that for Mom, they had

just materialized out of nowhere.

Ms. Wilhope looked at Walt in a way that clearly meant "I tried to warn you." Then she gave a little wave and went out the back door. "We'll have a nice chat later," she said, and Walt wasn't certain, but it seemed as if there was a tiny threat in her voice. "Mind how you go," she added just before the door closed behind her.

"What did . . . ? How did . . . ? Was that Ms. *Wilhope?*" Mom was shaking, and Walt went over and wrapped his arms around her.

He didn't know how much Mom knew about magic, but he suspected she had at least a little sense that it was real. She had given him the traveling machine, after all. "It's okay, Mom. We're safe. *You're* safe." He gripped her tight, waiting for her heart to stop racing, and when she finally stopped shuddering, he let her go.

He could see things clicking in her head. "It . . . it *worked* for you?" she asked in a whisper. But then she shook her hair back and took one more huge breath. "I don't think I want to know."

Just then the kitchen door swung open and Dad walked in, not looking at all as if he had just been still a moment ago.

Mom put a finger to her lips just for a second, as if to warn Walt not to say anything.

"Dad!" Van cried, and she and Walt ran to their father, squeezing him in a hug.

"You both are foul!" Dad complained, pushing them off him. "What is that stink?" Then he looked over at Dylan. "And who are you?"

Dylan swiped his hair out of his face and walked over to Dad with his hand outstretched. "Dylan, sir."

"Well, Dylan, you stink as bad as these two," Dad said as he shook Dylan's hand.

"Richard!" Mom said.

Dad's face lost a little tightness. "But it's nice to meet you."

"Mom, Dylan's parents left him all alone by *himself*," Van said. "For *overnight*. Can he stay over?"

Mom leaned against the island like she needed the support. "What type of—" She cut herself off. "Of course," she said instead. "No child should be staying alone. The trouble that they could get into?" She sucked her teeth. "Have some food, Dylan," she said, as if eating was the answer to any problem.

"Let me get in there before they eat it all," Dad said. He opened the pizza box, and a burst of tomato, pepperoni, and cheese hit Walt's nose.

Walt's mouth started watering. When was the last time he had eaten? Oh, yeah. Paralyzing pods.

Dad grabbed a piece of pizza, started to turn away, and then turned back, fixing Walt in an eagle eye. "You got your training in today?"

Walt thought of all the things he'd gone through.

The swimming and running and scaling volcano walls. "Sure did." He heard Van cover a laugh with a weak cough.

"Okay!" Dad nodded aggressively. "That's what I'm talking about. You're going to be so ready for camp," he said, and chomped down on his piece of pizza.

"Dad?" Walt said, trying to keep his voice from trembling.

Dad swallowed. "What's up?"

"It's just . . . that . . . I don't actually . . . wanttoplayfootballandmaybeIcoulddolikeartcamporsomething?"

Dad took another bite and then stared at Walt while he chewed. It was as if all the air had been sucked out of the kitchen. Walt could feel his heart thumping hard, and he had to fight to keep his shoulders straight and pushed back instead of slumping down like they wanted. As the moment stretched out, Walt wondered if he was going to have to repeat himself. He hoped not. Saying it once had been hard enough.

Then Dad swallowed. "You know how I feel about you playing football, right?" he asked, his voice hard and firm.

Mom started, "Richard, now we talked—"

"Let the boy speak to me, Wanda," Dad told her. "Walt?"

Walt looked Dad in the eye. "Yes, sir."

"And you're just going to stand there telling me you don't want to play?"

Van tried to cut in. "Dad, *I* think it would be fun—"

"You are not part of this conversation, Giovanni," Dad told her. "Well?" he asked Walt.

"*Yes*, sir," Walt said, not dropping his gaze.

"Hmph," Dad said, and frowned.

Walt held his breath, waiting for the lecture.

"Tell you what," Dad said. "We won't worry about football camp this year, okay?" Walt wished he didn't hear the disappointment in Dad's voice. "But how about we toss the ball around a little and I show you some moves, deal?"

Walt couldn't believe Dad was asking him instead of telling him, but maybe that was exactly why it made Walt smile. He could actually feel something loosen inside him. A dark, tangled knot that had been festering inside for too long began to unravel. "Deal," he answered.

Dad gave him a nod. "Good man," he said.

"What about me, Dad?" Van's eyes shone and her voice trembled.

"Van," Dad started with a sigh. "This is a . . ." He looked at her. Then he looked at Mom, and they had one of those moments parents have where there's a whole conversation going on in one look. "A *great* idea."

He nodded at her. "Bet you'll be pretty good."

Walt wanted to say that Van's throwing arm was lousy and Dad was going to lose that bet. But who knew? Maybe they'd *both* end up being great at football.

"And do some research on art camps, son," Dad said. "Let me know if you find anything good." He left the kitchen, whistling.

"He is full of surprises sometimes," Mom said, and gave Walt a squeeze on his arm. Then she wrinkled her nose. "And he's right, you know. You all need to throw those clothes *away*." She started to leave the kitchen but said over her shoulder, "Like outside. In someone else's garbage. And no *going* anywhere tonight except to sleep, you hear?"

All three kids nodded solemnly, and then as soon as the door swung shut, Van said, "Pizza!"

The three of them raced to the sink and washed their hands, pushing and shoving to get to the soap and water first. And then they settled at the kitchen island and started shoveling food into their mouths.

"Can't believe you called this place boring," Van said, her mouth full of food.

"It *was*," Walt said. "Until it wasn't. I still can't believe Ms. Wilhope's a *witch*."

"Tried to tell you, bro," Van said, and burped.

Which of course started a who-can-burp-the-loudest

contest. Then in between bites of another slice of pizza, Dylan said, "You know, I wouldn't mind adding football to my repertoire. You think your dad would mind if . . . I . . . joined you?"

"He totally wouldn't mind!" Walt said, grinning at his friend. Football might not even be so bad if Dylan was playing with him.

"*I'm* still playing," Van warned.

Walt nudged her with his shoulder. "Obviously. I wouldn't leave out my twin." He held out his hand and Van covered it with hers and then Dylan added his.

Dylan said, "Teamwork makes the dream work, baby."

They held their hands like that for a moment until Van pulled her hand away and wiped it on her shorts. "Grease *and* boy sweat? Gross!" she teased.

Dylan balled up a napkin and shot it at the trash, but Walt swatted it away. "Get that weak stuff out of here," he told his friend.

"Nothing weak in here," Dylan told him.

"Got that right," Van said. Then she turned to her brother. "Don't think I didn't notice that you saved our world with *tape*!" Walt thought she was making fun of him, but then she nodded in appreciation. "*Massive* move."

"Super extra-large supreme," Dylan said.

"King *Kong*," Van said.

"Blue whale."

"Sequoias."

Of course Dylan came up with, "Manute Bol!"

As their list went on and on as they thought of the biggest things, Walt couldn't help but smile. He'd learned one thing for sure. Being big wasn't everything.

"So . . . ," Dylan said, and paused dramatically. "A witch, wishes, a traveling machine, *and* mapmaking. Could be interesting. What are we going to do tomorrow?"

Not giving Walt a chance to answer, Van said, "*I* have some ideas."

Walt smirked at her. "Something that'll get us into serious trouble, I bet."

Van tried to look innocent but couldn't quite manage it. "You know me too well," she said, giggling.

"Yeah, I do," Walt said. Then he turned to Dylan. "You in?"

Without hesitating, Dylan nodded.

"All right," Walt said, smiling at his sister. He leaned back in his chair. "Let's hear 'em."

ACKNOWLEDGMENTS

Years ago, Stacey Barney was the professional assigned to my small writing circle at the Better Books Workshop. I was unagented and starting to feel I would remain that way forever and had submitted the first twenty pages of a book about a boy who loved maps in a last ditch effort to find out if I could write . . . or not. In our one-on-one, Stacey looked me in the eye and said, "You're ready. Get an agent." These words, coming from an editor I so admired and respected have made all the difference in my writing journey. I will be forever grateful for Stacey's early encouragement.

Huge thanks also to:

Jenn Kompos, who has read more versions of this

book than anyone should have had to. Best critique partner always and forever.

Stacy Stokes and Sally Engelfried for their timely beta read and their exceptionally helpful notes, and to the rest of the PM&S Club (Kath Rothschild, Rose Haynes, and Lydia Steinauer), who were always ready with encouragement.

Sabaa Tahir, who spent *hours* talking to me about fantasy and villains—who better, right?

Rebecca Stead, who tried to teach me how to plot.

Alicia D. Williams, who knew the right questions to ask and gave such sage advice and forced me to find the heart in the story (and fix a big plot hole).

Griff, who didn't even know all the story problems she helped me solve on our long walks.

Alice Petty, whose stories about artists provided a critical piece of the plot puzzle. *And* made an amazing model of a traveling machine! My favorite thing ever.

All my writer friends who have heard me talk about this idea and kept saying to just write it, and to young readers, Josh and Meagan, whose early love for the story allowed me to believe it would work one day.

Trudy Wentworth, for asking me what story did I really want to tell, and for being a constant cheerleader. And Keely Parrack, who always believes in me more than I believe in myself.

My wonderful agent, Brenda Bowen, whose excitement for this book helped me stay the course.

The incomparable and brilliant Alessandra Balzer, who absolutely would not let me turn in anything less than my best and whose editing skills made this book so much better and stronger than I could've imagined. And the whole team at Balzer + Bray/HarperCollins: Caitlin Johnson, Shona McCarthy, Anna Bernard, Emily Mannon, Robby Imfeld, Patty Rosati, Mimi Rankin, Andrea Pappenheimer, Kathy Faber, Kerry Moynagh, and Vanessa Nuttry, who do so much to support authors and their books.

Molly Fehr, who designed an amazing cover, and Michael Machira Mwangi, whose cover art blew my mind! Thank you for bringing Heckett to life. You imagined my characters so perfectly.

Francesca Baerald, map creator extraordinaire, who somehow was able to interpret my thoughts and horrible sketch into the most amazing map of Djaruba. Her talent is remarkable.

Anne Ursu, who was unbelievably gracious in the midst of her extremely busy schedule and offered such kind words.

Mamasita Baunita, who probably has a magic traveling machine she's waiting to give me. (I'm ready!) And the whole fam, who continues to be such a fantastic cheer squad. Special shout-out to James for putting up with all my questions about "boy stuff."

Jordan and Morgan, who will always tell me like it is, and also encourage me through it all. And Keith, whose love and constant support are everything.

And finally, thank you to the readers. Any world I create will always have you at its heart.